BLOOD ROOT

OTHER WORKS BY ROBERT F. JONES

Blood Sport
The Diamond Bogo
Slade's Glacier
The Man-Eaters of Zamani
Tie My Bones To Her Back
Deadville
The Run to Gitche Gumee
Gone to the Dogs: My Life With My Canine Companions
Dancers in the Sunset Sky
The Fishing Doctor: The Essential Tackle Box Companion
The Hunter in My Heart: A Sportsman's Salmagundi
African Twilight: The Story of a Hunter
Upland Passage: A Field Dog's Education
Jake: A Labrador Puppy at Work and Play

BLOOD ROOT

A NOVEL

ROBERT F. JONES

Skyhorse Publishing

Originally published in 1982 by Dell Publishing Co., Inc.

10 9 8 7 6 5 4 3 2 1

Library of Congress Cataloging-in-Publication Data is available on file.

Cover design by Owen Corrigan

Print ISBN: 978-1-63220-579-7
Ebook ISBN: 978-1-63450-018-0

Printed in the United States of America

Whose woods these are I think I know . . .

—Robert Frost

PROLOGUE

In the beginning was the Oak. Long before the first settlers came, before even the first tentative Abenaki Indian hunting parties probed that country, it dominated the mountain: awful and grim in its time-bent majesty. The weather-wounds of eons scarred its bole—ancient lightning slashes lipped over with thick, elephant-gray bark; the circular stubs of long-gone branches glaring outward like eyes beneath crusty brows; the limbs themselves—each thicker than any other tree on the mountain—moving against the sky in a cryptic, vegetable semaphore: as if the Oak were signaling to some distant star.

The Indians, watching and aware, called the tree the "Weather-Maker." Before the first hint of an approaching storm marked the horizon, the Oak seemed to stir the sky, its gnarled fingers spewing forth clouds that haled other clouds from the distance. As the wind grew in strength, the Oak began to talk. It was a language of clattering bark and pattering acorns, twigs ticking in the dry leaves below; then growing louder with creaks and groans, a dissonant howling through which ran the roar of wind in the Oak's upper branches, falling at times to a whisper, a belly-deep muttering, then rising suddenly to a strident scream. The first lightning shivered across the racing black sky; thunder rolled through the hollows. The lightning drew nearer, as if the Oak had summoned it. Flash and explosion grew synchronous: the Indians cowered and shivered as the cold rain whipped down, their eyes clenched tight against the awful glare. Trees exploded around them—boiling steam of sap, superheated on the instant by the sky's white energy, hurling great raw spears of wood in every direction; dead branches whirled through the air like Manitou's war clubs; the very mountain shook itself into a dance. And all the while the Oak roared its anger: the Oak that was father and mother both to all the trees on the mountain; the Oak, ageless and immortal, the enemy of trespassers, the master of the mountain.

The Indians collected their dead and wounded, marked the perimeter of the Oak's domain with stone cairns to warn later visitors, and fled.

The first white settlers in that region, hard-minded men and women from Connecticut who filtered north after the French and Indian Wars ended in 1763, paid no heed to the Indian legend. After all, God had created trees, even the mighty oaks, for the use of mankind: to provide the warmth of fires, to shape with their steel saws and axes, chisels and drawknives, into houses and barns and household implements. Their European minds abhorred the gloom of a forest. Let in the light! Drive away the nightmare monsters! Within the span of a generation they had denuded the valleys and hollows, laying out neat meadows scribed with stone walls, leaving a second-growth woodlot or two to fuel their fireplaces, and gradually pushing the forest higher and higher up the mountain. Trees they could not turn into sawboards they simply girdled and killed, then burned into potash, for which a ready market existed in the woolen mills of their British homeland. But they left the high forest alone, and with it the Oak. The country up there was too steep, too distant for worthwhile logging, and only a few random hunters ever passed the central grove where the Oak itself stood. Eyes skinned for deer or bear; the hunters paid the Oak no heed.

The mountain was known to the townsmen as Widdershins—a Scots word describing the anticlockwise twist the old Indian trail took up and around it (to avoid the menacing oak grove)—and the town itself as Hubleys Gore. A gore, in surveyor's parlance, is a triangular piece of land, and that was how the first settler, Josiah Hubley, had laid it out between the mismeasured boundaries of two earlier "Hampshire Grants." The region itself, in 1791, became known as Vermont—the fourteenth state of the new, young American union.

In the early years of the nineteenth century, Hubley's Gore was a bustling farm town, indistinguishable from hundreds of other villages and hamlets in that craggy, green state. The general store did a thriving business on market days; the blacksmith's shop clanged and sparked and emitted its sharp reek of burning steel; from the austere white church, Episcopal in those days, the hymns of the God-fearing rose sweetly each Sunday. The white-painted houses of the town stood trig and tight against all weathers, each with its backyard barn well stocked to meet the winter. Sheep and dairy cattle thrived on the hillside meadows; corn creaked tall in the lowland flats; maples bled their sap in season to sweeten the hard, frugal lives of the uncomplaining farmers.

Then, in the spring of 1815, two events half a world apart occurred to change Hubley's Gore forever.

The first was random: On the tropical isle of Soembawa in the Dutch East Indies, a 9,253-foot volcano named Tamboro erupted, killing twelve thousand people and sending a huge cloud of dust and smoke into the upper atmosphere. Dimming the sun to winter weakness, this vast cloud began a slow northeasterly journey toward the Americas. There was nothing especially noxious or deadly contained in the cloud; only the seeds of a year-long January.

The second event was far from random: in the spring of 1815, a wanderer with a mission arrived in Hubley's Gore. His name was Obediah Durwood Magrute, he was about thirty years of age, and he had been searching the whole world over for a god to worship. A tall, thin, silent man with the flowing beard and fiery eyes of a prophet, Magrute spoke (though rarely) in a Gaelic burr overlaid with the tones of his travels: harsh sibilants picked up in Transylvania and the Harz Mountains of Central Europe, Punjabi and Turkish gutturals from farther east, even a click or two from the rain forests of West Africa. Somewhere in his travels he had acquired a splendid walking staff that was the wonder of the Gore. Tall as a shepherd's crozier, its shaft was wound with the coiled body of a snake, each scale carved to perfection. But where the staff crooked at the top, it was surmounted with a strange device: a circular disk, like the face of the sun, from which sprouted up and backward the spread wings of an eagle.

There were some in the Gore who said the staff had magical powers; two shepherd lads claimed they had seen Magrute repel the attack of a wolf pack on their flock merely by gesturing with it toward the leader. Others said it was a sort of dowsing wand that would dip at the taste of gold beneath the ground (otherwise how would so shabby a man as the newcomer be able to pay for his supplies with gold coinage?) Others still believed that the staff was Aaron's rod, an implement involved in some way with the heretical worship of the Golden Calf, and that Magrute himself was the Devil's disciple, come to woo them away from true belief. And some, more practical, just admired it as a fine example of woodcarver's craft, a skill at which Magrute himself excelled. These last were quick to hire him to carve ax and scythe handles for them when he set himself up in business.

For the most part Magrute spent his time wandering the hills, staff in hand, as if he were searching for something. One day he must have found it, for he appeared at the door of Noah Eldridge that evening wearing the first smile anyone in the Gore had seen on his face. Noah was a prosperous sheep farmer whose land covered the upper reaches of Widdershins Mountain. Though a widower he was fat and jolly, pleased with his burgeoning flocks and especially with his large, hardworking sons who tended them, sheared them, and kept his buildings in fine repair. The only blight on Noah's life, and a worrisome one at that, was his daughter, Cassandra. A fey and woodsy girl with wild green eyes and long, wild blond hair that reached to her waist, she was at sixteen still barely able to speak. The schoolmistress had pronounced her ineducable, and Eldritch Cassie, as she was known, spent her days prowling the fields and woods of the Gore, gazing for long empty hours into trout pools or watching the dizzying, random dance of butterflies along the meadows' edge. Often she accompanied Magrute on his searches, neither of them speaking except with their eyes.

But Magrute had not come to Noah Eldridge to ask

for Cassie's hand in marriage (much as Noah would have welcomed such a request). Rather he asked to purchase from the father the wooded high reaches of the mountain.

"It's poor land at best," Noah told him honestly. "Why would you want it?"

"For my own purposes," Magrute said. He chinked a leather bag full of coins. "I'll pay you ten dollars the acre for it."

Even in the lush, lowland flats, land rarely brought that kind of money. But Noah remained reluctant. Had the stranger anything to add—say, about his daughter, the fair Cassandra? He couldn't help but notice how the dear girl followed him wherever Magrute went. Had anything transpired between them, anything of a —well—man-and-woman nature? Magrute remained silent, dour. He chinked the coins in his purse.

"If you wed her," said Noah, "the land is yours. For only five an acre, at that."

Magrute counted out the money, coin by alien coin, but when Noah tallied it, he saw that the ten-dollar rate had been paid him.

"I would not cheat you, Father," said Magrute. "Cassie and I are already wed. In my own Church, and in my own manner."

So Farmer Eldridge had it both ways: the money in one hand, his daughter off his other. He could not have been happier.

Nor could Cassie. Magrute's harsh exterior melted to sweetness whenever he entered the Oak Grove. He spoke to her in a language she had never heard before, but one it seemed she had been waiting all her lone life to hear. She understood every word, and found her own words flowing as swiftly, as supply as a trout brook over her once-wooden tongue. In this new tongue that only the two of them shared, Magrute revealed to her his true purpose and identity.

He was the Derwydd MoghRoith—the Druid Magrute—the last of a long line of Celtic priests who worshiped the way men were meant to worship: not under the spired roof of a musty church, its walls and roof built of the flesh of the forest; but rather under the living greenwood itself, before the body of God, the noblest of creation: the massive, mighty, holy Oak. For himself the Druid wanted no converts, but only to be left alone to worship as he pleased. Yet he was a man, and he needed a woman to love and love with him. Together they prayed beneath the outstretched arms of the Oak, and with Obed's tutelage she learned to understand the great tree's language.

It was frightening at first—such harsh, such heartless words! The demands for blood appalled her: at each turn of season the Oak required sacrifice. Praying in words from the dawn of mankind, Obed slit the throat of a sheep as it stood under the Oak's groping arms; the rich red blood soaked into the soil so swiftly it seemed the very roots of the tree were drinking it. Then the sheep was burned, its ashes spread in a circle around the Oak's great bole.

"In the old days," Obed told her, "the Oak God demanded human blood and flesh. The ancient Celts burned hundreds—prisoners, usually—in great wicker cages, the smoke of their searing flesh filling the Sacred Groves, their screams ascending through the smoke in an echo of the Oak's great wrathful voice. Even today, in the Punjab of India, villagers in the Kangra Mountains still offer, once a year, a girl in sacrifice to their sacred cedar. I have worshiped with them."

In return for this homage, he continued, the Oak

made the rain to fall and the crops to grow; He kept the wolves from the folds and eased the pain of women in childbirth; He caused the trees, especially the noble oaks, to grow straight and fast and flawless, thus providing his worshipers with fuel and shelter—the wherewithal for survival in a harsh world.

All through that year Obed and Cassie lived in the protective shadow of the Oak—the Bull Oak, as Obed now called Him. From deadwood Obed carved tool handles and platters, bas-reliefs and ornate mantelpieces, newel posts and intricate walking sticks, all of which found ready market in the village store. The two of them built a snug cabin under the Oak's sprawling branches and were warm with oak fires through the winter. Their love grew grand as the Oak itself, and in the spring Cassie knew she was carrying Obed's child. And she was happy.

But it was not a true spring. Unbeknownst to anyone the great cloud of dust and detritus from the Soembawa volcanic explosion had now reached the upper atmosphere of North America. People marveled at the vivid apple reds and plum purples of the dawns and dusks, but the real fruits of that year were starvation and despair. The Javanese dust worked as a thin, almost invisible filter against the warmth of the waxing sun. In the heart of the woods the snow remained four feet deep at Easter. Stock ponds in the highlands never lost their ice, nor did the black anchor ice in the brooks and rivers ever loosen its grip. Apple trees tried valiantly to bloom, only to be nipped dead in the bud by dark returning frosts. Corn would not sprout in the fields, and vegetable seeds froze hard as bird shot in the ice-fanged earth. Blizzards blew on the Fourth of July. Everywhere farms failed, triggering a flood of migration from Vermont to western New York, to Ohio and even as far west as Iowa and Wisconsin. That miserable year—1816—is still remembered by Vermonters as "Eighteen-Hundred-and-Froze-to-Death," or more simply, "The Year Without Summer."

Firewood of course was in short supply, and when available sold for the unheard of price of three dollars the cord: a month's wages for a lucky man. In Hubley's Gore covetous eyes were cast on Obed and Cassie's virgin oak grove. A group of businessmen led by Colonel Simeon Thorpe and Pastor Elihu Peggs, the two most powerful men in town, approached Obed with an offer to buy his wood. Their price was a decent one, but of course Obed refused. Threats followed, and Obed merely laughed. The stage was set for tragedy.

The raiders struck in the dead of night, masked and moccasinned for stealth. They clubbed Obed unconscious as he reared up from sleep, then dragged him outside the cabin and chained him up by his wrists from a low branch of the Bull Oak. Cassie, now in her fifth month of pregnancy, watched in horror from the cabin door. Despite their disguises she recognized Thorpe and Peggs, along with Thorpe's bullying lieutenant, Caleb Munro, who had once tried to rape her in the days of her mute childhood. Only her father's heavy fist had saved her. Now Caleb wrapped an arm around her, his big hand on her breast. "Your tiddies is bigger'n they was," he said in her ear. His breath reeked of sap beer and applejack. "That furriner must of pronged you right good, didn't he, you hoor? Soon's we get him sugared off, I'll finish up what I started long time ago." He gave her breast a vicious squeeze.

The raiders piled deadwood under Obed's dangling heels. Then Pastor Peggs, tall and rake-thin in the dark, pronounced his judgment: "You are an evil and an unbelieving man, Obed Magrute. You worship a false god, and you worship in the out-of-doors. You have committed the sin of Ahaz. That awful man, King of Judah, who brought alien and abominable rites to the Land of the Chosen. Even as you, Ahaz worshiped not in the sacred confines of the Temple, but in the wilderness. Abomination! The Lord God abjures us, Thou shalt not suffer a sinner to live. So be it."

He struck fire to the tinder and applied it to the deadwood. As smoke curled skyward and flames guttered in the dark, Cassie saw Obed's eyes flash upward to the maze of oak branches. He spoke in the language of the Bull Oak. Instantly, from the west, came the answering mutter of thunder. Sheet lightning flared over Abednego Mountain across the way. The Bull Oak began to move, to mutter, and the raiders fell back. The creaks and groans of the swaying tree continued, and Cassie understood. Obed smiled down at her, resigned, and smiled, nodding.

So he must die! The Bull Oak had said so: a sacrifice from which even greater sacrifices would be born. Tears filled her eyes as Caleb Munro grabbed her and threw her to the ground before Obed's watching gaze. She felt her nightshirt ripped from her, felt the chill touch of the clammy night and the increasing heat of the nearby fire. Caleb was on her, penetrating her, his breath sour in her face. The flames roared loud now, hotter, the smell of woodsmoke going rank with that of burning flesh. And still Obed did not cry out. She could see him still through the smoke, watching, his eyes big and brighter than the flames.

Then his voice boomed out through the woods:

"Here ye now this," he bellowed, "my curse, my blessing, my prayer! For my God has not forsaken me.

Even as I die, you shall do Him honor." His eyes blazing out of the fire held the men frozen. Pastor Peggs reeled as if struck by a heavy bullet. Cassie felt Caleb go limp within her.

"Whosoever among you or your heirs or assigns shall cut of this wood for whatever purpose, be it to build or to burn, to house your kine or kinsmen, to hew into tools or even the meanest stick—whatsoever his aim, that man shall suffer the Oak Death. Nor shall your children be spared my vengeance. Even as you have taken my dear woodwife and unborn son from me, and violated them so foully, so too shall this Wood take yours. My god shall have His disciples, and your blood shall both provide and feed them. And you, Cassandra, my dear wife and love, you shall ensure that my curse, my prophecy, is fulfilled."

His voice by now had gone hoarse with the fire and smoke that filled his lungs. He faded into the flames, until his eyes were part of them. An anvil cloud had formed over Widdershins; now thunder crashed, lightning forked downward, and Caleb Munro—running—disappeared in a sudden pink explosion of steaming meat. The raiders broke and ran, with trees hurling branches at them as they fled. The fire roared skyward to join the lightning.

The fire blazed till midnight, then slowly died to gray-shrouded embers. At first light Cassie made her numb way to the garden patch and retrieved Obed's crozier from where it lay hidden under the jungle of squash leaves. As she returned to the Bull Oak, she heard the jingle of harness and saw wagons and loggers entering the grove from the meadow. She waited, hidden in the green gloom, watching as they set about their business.

They did not fell so much as a single sapling. The first touch of the ax brought a "widow maker" tumbling from the top of a tall oak: the huge dead branch crushed two loggers and sent another reeling away with a shattered shoulder. The next axman goggled in amazement as his sharp blade bounced as if from steel when it hit the bark and buried itself in his shin. A third tree, at the very edge of the grove, its trunk straight as a die, split when the saw was a quarter of the way into it, driving a three-foot splinter into Simon Thorpe's throat. With that the loggers broke and ran, but even then the wrath of Obediah followed them: a wagon hastily loaded with deadwood unaccountably tipped as it raced down the smooth meadow slope, the far sideboard twirling like a blunt ax to smash on the backs of two men riding in the bed.

When they were gone, Cassie emerged from the wood and searched through the still-smoldering ashes until she found all that remained of Obediah: the vaulted and fire-blacked dome of his skull. When it had cooled sufficiently to handle, she carried it to the grove's edge. It was a fine summer's day, and a warm breeze ghosted up the meadow, causing the daisies and black-eyed Susans to nod and dance as lightly as the butterflies that worked amongst them.

They gazed down into the valley: Cassie's eyes were bright as flint-struck steel; Obed's stared empty, two hollow mouths that said, "Ah!"

Above them reared the sacred crozier: its blank, round face; its wings of a stooping hawk.

BOOK ONE

Spring

ONE

The current heating season was not yet over, but already Jim Boggs was splitting wood for next year. It was a raw, blustery day—better suited to work in the barn or the carpenter shop—but just like his daddy before him Boggs felt that a man couldn't start too early on his woodpile. The wood itself was fine white oak he had felled last winter, up back of the old Eldridge place when no one was looking, and he had hauled it out of the woods by tractor just as surreptitiously when the ground dried after mud season. What the hell, now that Sam was dead and his wife moved away, nobody'd miss it. Most of this wood would go to heating his own house and family, but Jim Boggs figured to split out six or eight cords to sell down in the flatlands, where townsfolk were shifting to wood heat in the wake of the sudden, OPEC-inspired rise in heating-oil costs. Ought to be able to get eighty dollars the cord for good, weather-dried oak, Jim reckoned, more if he trucked it downcountry to the Albany suburbs. The money'd come in handy for Christmas presents. He hadn't been able to afford much for Polly and the kids these past few years, what with hard times all around and his Vietnam pension spent up on the farm and the kids being borned.

That morning Polly had begged him to take the day off and come with her and the kids into town.

"You're turning into a reg'lar workaholic, Jimmy," she pleaded. "You ain't been down off the mountain since New Year's. And you know it's not safe to work the saw and the splittin' all by yourself."

"I ain't no baby, Poll," he'd gruffed at her. "You worry too much. I been doing this kind of work since I was big enough to swing an ax." But he'd hugged her to his big chest and patted her short, blond hair as he sent her on her way. She was a good woman, his Polly, though lately she'd grown very worn and wan-looking, as if maybe the loneliness of farm life was getting to her. "Tell you what," he said as she shooed the children into the truck. "First thing when I sell some of this oakwood, I'll take you and the kids up to Rutland, to the movies, and maybe a big feed at Colonel Sanders. How's that?"

The kids squealed with delight and even Polly smiled for a change. She waved at him as she bumped down the driveway at the wheel of the rusting pickup, but her eyes still wore that bruise of worry that had begun, now, to worry him as well.

Actually, Jim Boggs liked working on his woodpile. It was a form of therapy for him, in which he could take out his frustrations against a society for which he had laid his life on the line as a soldier only to be rewarded with a seemingly infinite future of grinding hard work at bare subsistence wages. Every time he split a log, he imagined it to be one bad guy or another: "Take that, you friggin' Ayatollah!" Or: "Here's one for you, Lee Iacocca, for sellin' me that worthless hunka pickup truck!" Beyond the political, he got pleasure from "reading" the sawed face of the chunk at hand, seeing where the minuscule cracks were forming as the green wood dried and split, and then laying the sharp edge of his eight-pound splitting hammer precisely on target, feeling his muscles swing full power as the maul spun overhead at full arms' reach, then the sock of the steel hitting home and the log popping open, neat and clean with the sour reek of oak sap all around him. When he got in the rhythm, his whole two hundred pounds behind it and the sweat whipping off of him even in zero weather wearing nothing warmer than a T-shirt, Jim Boggs could split nearly a cord of wood an hour. And that, by God, was fast—as fast as a hydraulic splitter, maybe even faster! He loved it.

He was in the rhythm now, his big hand snaking into the wood heap with eyes of its own, his hard fingers snagging the log, yanking it free, standing it upright against the splitting block as his other arm started the maul on its upward swing. The hands meeting on the smooth, ash haft. The maul topping out above him while his eyes read the stress crevices, then the power swing: crack! And the log laying open to either side, defeated. Grab, set, swing, crack! Again and again and again.

There was a hypnotic quality to the rhythm: his eyes began to blur out of focus as he fell deeper into it, the raw stink of split wood mixing with his own sweat, the deep grunt of his swing like some half-forgotten Montagnard war chant from his Vietnam days, the craggy bark of the oak chunks taking on the shape of leering masks, of demon faces, the howl of the wind rising in the woods at the top of the mountain. . . .

He was just into the power swing when it happened. The earth seemed to shift under his widespread, booted feet. The log teetered, fell sideways to the right. The heavy steel maul, its edge glinting fanglike in the weak spring light, swung through its arc; Jim Boggs, off balance, shifted his left foot; the first resistance the great steel tooth encountered was Jim Boggs's boot. The edge bit deep, splitting leather and sock and foot all in the same instant.

"Shee-it!"

He spun and fell backward against the log pile, his leg extended awkwardly before him. He felt nothing but a deep numbness. Then he saw the blood well up slowly through the clean-slit leather, soaking the frayed cotton of his sock as if it were a wick, spilling down over the laces into the dirty wood chips.

Who'd of thunk it? I split my gawddamn foot. After all these years a friggin' lousy flatlander trick like that! Bleedin' pretty bad, too. And here comes the pain. Get a tourniquet on that sucker, Jimmy boy. You gotta lot of juice in you, but you can't let it *all* run out. Then get down to the house and call Doc Peggs. Damn but it hurts. And Polly's got the truck.

As he shifted to reach for his bandanna, he felt the woodpile against which he was leaning begin to move. Looking up, he saw it had slid forward from the impact of his hitting it when he fell. Now it loomed over him like the lip of some great wooden avalanche about to cut loose. A heavy log teetered and then fell, knocking him sideways, dizzy, head exploding with white lights. He felt the blood start down his face, into his eyes, from his ripped scalp. Then the whole log pile tumbled, heavy still with sap, rumbled and slid, cascading down over him in a roaring cloud of dust and bark.

He was pinned.

He pushed with his right arm—the left was numb, probably broken, he thought numbly, up in the shoulder—and got his face clear. He could see his left foot sticking out from the edge of the tumbled logs. The blood continued to pump, bright arterial blood, pooling in the wood chips and dirt and stomped grass, pooling higher, then spilling downhill in a thick red rivulet. He could feel his senses thinning out into the air, like wood-smoke on the wind. The world was going pale, receding and thinning like blood in water.

He saw something standing against the light—something upright, tall. A man! But he could not focus, all he could see were the legs, the thin upper body, the dark, motionless head. The man was watching him, still and waiting.

"Help," Jim Boggs said weakly. "Bleeding. A tourniquet . . ."

The figure remained motionless. Behind it, just before he sank into unconsciousness, Jim Boggs thought he saw other figures approaching. Then it all went white.

The house had been advertised as a "handyman special," which in real-estate parlance means "total wreck." No central heating, rusty plumbing, plenty of dry rot. Still, Mark and Laura Avery didn't mind that in the least. Both of them were "handy" with tools and more than willing to give the place the abundant "T.L.C." that the chipper copywriter warned it would need. After all the house had four bedrooms, a big "country kitchen" well lighted from the south and east by authentic colonial six-over-six windows replete with wavy glass, and a cozy Dutch oven in the kitchen that needed only a little pointing up with mortar to be back in business. The floors, though creaky in spots, were of random-width white pine cut more than two hundred years ago when this hilly corner of western Vermont stood tall in climax forest. Though the roof leaked in the lightest drizzle, the walls were paneled in lustrous fine-grained hardwood that lent the low-ceilinged rooms a warm, clubby aura, and the post-and-beam frame of the house was rock solid: sturdy hand-hewn timbers of white oak and maple, wood-pegged at their joints, still bearing the bite of ancient adzes long since moldered into rust.

"Nope," said the real-estate agent, a glad-handing flatlander from New Jersey who affected a false Vermont twang, "she ain't a-goin' nowheres." He kicked one of the eight-by-eight-inch posts in the musty, cavernous attic and winced as the soft leather of his pigskin-lined L. L. Bean chukka boot buckled against the scarred hardwood. Mark Avery, who played at carpentry in his spare time, rapped a beam with his knuckles and grunted noncommittally.

"Maybe not," he said, "but it sure needs a hell of a lot of work. Who are the previous owners?"

"Old couple named Eldridge," said the agent, consulting his listing book. "Husband died last year and the widow moved downstate with her daughter's family."

"How did the poor man die?" asked Laura Avery.

"Beats me," said the agent hurriedly. "I don't live in this neck of the woods personally. Old age, prob'ly. Why don't we take a look down cellar?" He herded them toward the rickety staircase that led to the second floor. "Yaas, Mr. Avery, the old house she *do* need some work, I reckon, but a healthy young couple like you and your missus here, you should get her shaped up in jig time. . . ."

Well, Mark thought, smiling to himself, work or no work it's still a good deal. The house, a barn, a hillside root cellar and twenty acres of land for only sixty grand. Petty cash, considering today's market. The monthly payments on the house would come to less than half of what they paid in rent for their apartment in the Apthorp on Manhattan's West Side. What Mark wanted most in the world was to quit the city and his stagnating career as a commercial artist and take a crack at country living. He would keep a few of his better contracts with the magazines and concentrate most of his effort on serious painting. At the age of thirty he had already left it a bit late, but over the past year he had had two one-man shows at the Napier Gallery off Fifty-seventh Street and his notices had been enthusiastic enough to warrant the gamble. Laura's income as a television model was nearly as good as his. Their combined savings and investments were substantial, but it would take them a year or two to learn country ways and become reasonably self-sufficient, so any saving they might be able to squeeze on the house deal was welcome.

"I don't know," Mark said when they got downstairs, "your ad didn't say anything about that leaky roof and those water stains in the upstairs bedrooms. I'm just an amateur with hammer and saw, and with my wife expecting . . . I think fifty thousand would be a fairer price."

The agent's sudden smile took Mark aback. Maybe he should have started at forty. . . .

"If dat's an offer, Mistuh Avery," the agent said, reverting to pure "Joisey," "I t'ink you gotta deal."

Mark exchanged a quick glance with Laura.

"Would you mind if my wife and I talked it over in private?" he asked. "We'll just take a stroll up into the meadow, so we can get a better perspective on the house and the setting."

"Fine," said the agent. "You won't see a nicer country view this side of Norman Rockwell."

They walked up into the meadow, dead grass and winter-dried black-eyed Susans hissing against their jeans, and when they were out of the agent's earshot, Laura giggled.

"What's that about me being preggers? Do you know something I don't?"

"Hardly." Mark laughed. "But all's fair in love and real estate. I just figured it would get the price down, but the way he snapped at the offer I'm not so sure. After all, the house *will* be a lot of work and we *do* want to have a baby when and if we buy it. What do you think?"

They stopped a few hundred yards from the house and looked back down at it. From a distance the peeling paint, the loose roof slates, the crumbling mortar between the chimney bricks, were invisible. The house was indeed a Norman Rockwell dream—a snug white clean-lined block of security in the austere New England countryside. It was early spring and the big sugar maples that flanked the winding gravel road stretched their gray-barked arms crookedly at the metal-bright sky; a brook flashed and winked its way down the valley, sending bell-notes up to them as it purled over ice-polished boulders; a red-tailed hawk circled the ridge across from them, its high scream sounding faint and wild as it echoed down the hollow.

"Well," said Laura, plumping herself down in the grass, "I think it's just the place we've been looking for. That big north bedroom upstairs would make a fine studio for you, and I could use one of the others for a sewing room. There's a nice-sized room for the baby, too. Sure, it'll be hard work—but that's what we want, isn't it? To get away from that precious Bloomingdale's-Studio-54-Bloody-Mary-Brunch-at-the-Bogart-Festival bullshit, as you so daintily phrase it. And once we've got the place spiffed up, I'll have the baby and you can get cracking on your canvases."

"It is a marvelous view, isn't it?" Mark said. "Look how the light works on those far mountains, just the hint of purple in that gunmetal blue, and the flax-white of those hay fields to the north there—like hammered pewter and white gold. I could set up my easel in this meadow and paint the same scene for a year straight and still never repeat myself. And those trees up there, oaks by the look of them—you can almost see faces in that craggy bark. I could become a portraitist of trees, not to mention those great weathered human faces we saw in front of the store when we came through town."

"The town *is* terribly tiny," Laura said doubtfully. "Just the store, the sawmill, the church, and that saloon on the road coming in. But the houses are just too much—the quintessence of quaint. The place is almost a little *too* dreamy. I bet the townsfolk are mean and nasty and aloof and inbred, harboring some evil secret and only waiting the chance to work their spells on us innocent flatlanders."

"Easy." Mark laughed. "You've been reading too much Stephen King."

"Look at this!" Laura had been poking in the grass and now she came up with a tiny three-leaved plant, crinkly-edged and rust red in color. "Wild strawberry? Yes, it is—I'm sure. Oh, look! Under the grass—the whole meadow is full of them! In a couple of months we'll be up to our elbows in strawberry jam!" Her denim-clad bottom waved above the grass tops as she crawled. Unable to resist so tempting a target, Mark gave her a light swat just south of the Calvin Klein logo.

"Come on, you budding horticulturist." He laughed. "I happen to be allergic to strawberries as you well know. But if you keep waving that delightful derriere at me I'll be right down there in the weeds with you. And we won't be studying botany. Let's go down and buy ourselves a farm."

Driving back through town later that afternoon, having given the agent a binder on the property, Mark and Laura again commented on the old-timey quality of Hubley's Gore (population 608 at the 1980 census). Apart from the sight of a few cars and pickup trucks parked in driveways and the two shiny Mobil pumps in front of Minter's General Store, the town might have been bypassed by the twentieth century. There was none of the sullen seediness common to so many poverty-wracked and dying American small towns, no peeling paint and junked cars growing rust in muddy backyards, no tawdry shopping centers on the edge of town with their ubiquitous Radio Shacks and pizza/submarine parlors, no scruffy sporting-goods store with the ominous word GUNS tolling in faded capitals above a window glittering with Saturday-night specials.

No, the Gore was different. The houses were neatly painted, the lawns carefully raked of the winter's leaf and branch litter. Covered tin sap buckets hung from the thick-trunked maples that lined the streets at this, the end of the sugaring season. Broad-beamed housewives in worn denims and rubber knee boots worked busily in their garden plots, turning the soil and planting early crops: peas and spinach and radishes most likely. Laura's own latent gardening instincts stirred: she longed to feel black dirt under her carefully manicured nails. Far back behind the store, where the rarely used railroad track skirted the town, smoke rose from the chimney of the Widdershins Sawmill & Lumberyard, apparently the only industry in the Gore. The high ripping whine of a buzz saw echoed faintly through the chill spring air.

"Something's up at the cemetery," said Mark as they passed the churchyard. Laura looked and saw a funeral in progress. A simple coffin of raw yellow pine stood on sawhorses beside the wet brown maw of a newly dug grave. A knot of mourners in drab but tidy suits and dresses stood hatless at the graveside. As Mark drove past, Laura noticed a young woman of about her own age, blond and hollow-eyed under a veil, standing with one hand on the coffin lid. Four children, ranging in size from toddler to gawky preteen stood stiffly beside her, the older boy uneasy and solemn in a sport shirt buttoned at the throat. The woman held a pink-blanketed bundle in one arm: a baby. Laura felt a stab of anguish at the sight of the obvious widow and her young brood. She wanted to look away, but the horrid pathos of the sight held her gaze for a long, aching moment. Next to the widow stood a very tall, distinguished-looking older man—the woman's father?—with iron-gray hair bared to the April wind. He looked up at that instant and his gaze caught hers across the weatherworn and canted headstones. His eyes were deep-set and glacial blue, penetrating and hawklike. He nodded to her as Mark pressed down on the accelerator and they sped out of town, back to New York. The eyes stayed with Laura for days afterward.

Somehow the memory of the old man's glance came back to her most strongly the night, a month later, when they said good-bye to Bill McGregor. The best of their many friends in New York, Bill had courted Laura before she met Mark. It hadn't worked out: Bill was by his own admission a perpetual bachelor, the result, he said, of having studied for the priesthood in his youth. The "crisis of faith" that dropped him from the ranks of the nascent Jesuits had left him agnostic, but still saddled with many of the psychic side effects of the priestly life. He was a tall, slim, sandy-haired man of forty, wry and bespectacled, and he taught history at New York University, specializing in pre-Civil War Americana. One night in bed Laura had asked him what constituted his "crisis of faith."

"I could give you a whole night's worth of metaphysical mumbo-jumbo replete with Thomistic proofs and Kantian refutations," he said. "But what it really came down to was that my balls were more influential than my intellect. Or to couch it in sporting terms, it's groin over grace in the human race. And yet, that dry priestly voice still mutters to me at night behind the confessional screen. I'd make a lousy husband—at least right now I would. Perhaps in a few years . . . say ten or twenty . . ."

Then Mark came along, ardent, creative, perhaps not as "deep" as Bill nor as witty, but blessed with a paucity of hang-ups. Bill had taken Laura's change of allegiance with good grace, and indeed he and Mark soon became the closest of friends, arch-rivals at racquetball and football betting and her favorite sport of all, Being-Nice-to-Laura. Indeed it was Bill who indirectly steered them to Hubley's Gore. For the better part of a year their house-hunting had proved disappointing. They had written off the Hamptons at the outset as too expensive and far too Manhattan Inbred. Starting on the western slopes of the Catskills, they had found incredible land values—one place in Chenango County, a well-built house, three cathedrallike barns, two ponds, a trout stream, and a hundred prime acres, was priced at sixty nine thousand dollars: cheap dirt indeed—but a cultural wasteland. The closest big town had only one bookstore, and that of the "adult" persuasion. The Adirondacks, though wild and scenic enough, were scuzzy and teeming with ticky-tack in the areas where land was available. The ski zones of Vermont and New Hampshire were high-priced, studded with mock-Nordic and Alpine architectural abortions, and aswarm with screwed-up, displaced New Yorkers—the last people they wanted for neighbors: losers to a man (or bull dyke).

"When I was a kid," Bill told them one night when they had about given up hope of ever finding the Right Place, "my folks had a summer home—a 'camp,' they called it— in a township called Hubley's Gore. It's one of those out-of-the-way Vermont valley towns in the Taconic Mountains that you'd never find unless you were looking for it. My mother's people—the Cowpers—came from that country. I was through there a few years ago, coming home from skiing at Stowe, and the place hadn't changed a hinge or a doorknob's worth since I saw it last in the early 1950s. You might take a look."

So they did; and they found it.

On this evening Bill, who hated dining out, had prepared them a splendid Last Supper: spicy gazpacho, fresh young asparagus from Balducci's, a crisp-skinned yet rare rack of lamb studded with garlic, boiled new potatoes, a tender salad from a neighbor's mini-greenhouse, and his own crusty, inimitable French bread, all counterpointed with fine vintages from his well-stocked cellar (double-locked in the apartment-house basement, far from the laundry room and prying tire irons).

"So you're going to become a pair of shitkickers," Bill said over the cheese and fruit.

"Or die trying," laughed Mark. "I'm really fed up with this pop stand. Not long ago I'd have laughed at the notion: Back to Nature, my patoot. Romantic self-delusion. But now I feel different, and Laura does too. Maybe it was when that freak plugged John Lennon, maybe it's just too many years of dirt and doggy-doo and ducking reflexively every time a door slams. Maybe it's just too many nameless faces, too many wild glares in the crowd, too many people walking up Fifth Avenue cursing out loud to everyone and no one. Up there at least we'll have silence. Blessed silence."

"Except for the chainsaws, the deer rifles, the snowmobiles, and the gentle purr of unmuffled tractor engines. The patter of acid rain on the roof."

"By God I'm going to learn how to do all of that country stuff too," Mark said. "Hunt, fish, cut firewood, work a garden patch—all those good things. No more city softie, me. If I'm going to paint these people and their country, I'm going to have to learn how they function and how they feel."

"And what about fair Laura? What's she going to be doing while you run around in your macho man suit?"

"I'll be growing a baby," said Laura.

"Hey, really?" Bill jumped to his feet and leaned forward. "That's terrific, just terrific." Then, shifting gears: "Hey, can I boil up some water, shred a few clean sheets? Bring you some pickles and ice cream?" But his eyes were kindly even as he joshed her.

"There's nothing 'in the oven' just yet, Willie." She laughed. "What I mean is, now that we have a house and all, we want a baby to go with it. As soon as we get the place fixed up the way we want it." She spread some runny brie on a water biscuit and chased it with a swallow of Margaux. "But even at that, I'm eager to get 'countrified' myself. Just the other day, after we'd made the deal on the house, I saw some women in town working in their vegetable gardens. I used to help my mom and dad when I was little, pottering in the big kitchen garden we had, and it all came back to me: the warm smell of the earth and that wonderful feeling, like found money, when something you've planted actually comes up—so big and beautiful that you feel guilty and happy at the same time when you cut it to eat. There's nothing like your own sun-warmed tomato, fat and dusty from the vine."

"Well, I'm sure you'll be happy in the Gore. The people are a mite-bit strange, of course. After all, for the better part of two hundred years they've been living in that little pocket of a valley, cut off most of the year by snow from the rest of the world. All America was like that not long ago. That's how we came to be so diverse a people, even when the ethnic stock was the same to begin with: Scots-Irish yeomanry. Each tiny hill town developed its own peculiar kink in the national fiber, particularly in my period of interest, the early nineteenth century, before the railroad and the telegraph came along to shape a broadly American style. Every little dorp and hamlet had its own signature tune, so to speak. Especially when it came to religion. Mormons, Shakers, Holy Rollers, snake cults—you saw them all popping up in that era. Hell, even the Gore, as I recall from the old-timers, had its own little cult."

"What was that?" asked Laura.

Bill laugh a bit sheepishly. "It sounds kind of silly," he said, "but they were tree worshipers. Latter-day Druids of a sort. Still are to this day. You see, that particular section of Vermont contains one of the finest stands of virgin white oak left in the country, truly colossal trees, some of them. One of the early townspeople, a woman named Cassandra Eldridge, saw the economic promise of that oak stand back in the days when trees were disappearing all over the Northeast—into railway ties and new homes, courthouses and the like. She established the sawmill that became, and still remains, the town's bread and butter. It's a communally owned business, as is most of the oak woods itself, and the Gore folk make sure they never overcut it. Then Cassie's son, Ahaz, established the Church in the Wildwood there in the mid-1800s. Four times a year, at the change of the seasons, the townsfolk, or those who belong to the Church anyway, traipse up into the oak grove and pray for good wood for the future. So far they've gotten it: the Gore is able to support itself from the mill's profits without having to take 'charity' in the form of state or federal aid of any sort, a rare thing in Vermont these days. The people maintain their independence at the price of a little harmless superstition."

"What happens to people who move to town and *don't* join the Church?" Laura asked.

"Beats me," Bill said. "We only summered there when I was a kid. My mother worshiped in the Wildwood when she was a girl, but she converted to Catholicism when she and Dad got married. She never talked about her girlhood religious experiences. But I wouldn't worry, Laura. I doubt that the good people of Hubley's Gore will sacrifice you and Mark to their Oak God if you don't join the Church. The taxes you pay on your property will more than make up for any failure to keep the faith. . . ."

It was then that Laura remembered the tall old man in the graveyard. She shivered slightly and cuddled closer to Mark on the couch.

TWO

That first month in Vermont the Averys worked harder and longer than they had in all their lives. They ripped off rotten clapboards and replaced them with fresh cured spruce from the Hubley's Gore sawmill. They tightened down the loose slates on the roof and reglazed broken windows. While Laura mixed "mud" in a cement trough, Mark pointed up the decaying joints of the masonry, leveling as best he could the old ballast bricks that had been used to build it and tidying up the seams with his trowel. They both loved the sharp reek of lime and mortar and even the crisp burn of the cement on their hands—"Like playing with mud pies again." Laura laughed. They painted and stained and sanded and sawed. They even replaced the house's leaky, rusted-out plumbing with new plastic PVC pipe.

And at night they slept the good sleep of physical exhaustion.

But country living had its price. During the first month Mark managed to "prang" the muffler of their silver Porsche Targa twice on potholes in the gravel road. Reluctantly, and with a true ping in his motoring heart, he traded the sports car in on a new roadmuck-gray Chevy Luv 4x4 pickup. He had bought the Targa ten years earlier, when he and Laura started dating (part of his woo-her-with-worldly-sophistication campaign), and they both were sorry to see "Helmut" go. But the truck was just the ticket, as the salesman had said, for the alternately gumbo and granite back roads of the region, and they had enough left over in their "car budget" after the transaction to buy a used year-old Troy-Bilt rototiller as well.

By early May the soil had drained and warmed enough for Mark to risk turning over the old Eldridge garden plot on the south side of the house, near the brook, for Laura's new adventure in organic fingernail-breaking (as Mark liked to call it). Laura watched happily in the warm May sun as he cut the first few rows, the crooked steel tines of the tiller churning through weather-hardened soil like so many tireless robot fingers. But soon the engine roar, the dust, and exhaust fumes, not to mention the rocks and clods of dirt thrown viciously and randomly by the whirling teeth, proved too much for her. She went back in the house, looking for something equally grubby to do.

For weeks now she had put off cleaning the attic. The big, echoing room with its masses of ancient cobweb and the sharp smell of dust underlaid by the dank one of mildew was just too formidable an adversary. Actually, she admitted to herself, it wasn't the work she was avoiding: she was deathly afraid of mice and bats. At night, from the ceiling over their big brass bedstead, she had heard the swift, erratic scritching of many little feet, and at times a high, panic-inspiring chitter as tiny, energetic rodents did battle (or whatever: maybe they were mating?) within the walls. But now it was time. After all Mark was out there doing battle himself—with that big, smelly, loud machine and that obdurate soil. The least she could do was sweep up a few inches of dust and cobwebs.

But she dawdled in the bedroom as she changed into her work clothes. She decided finally to put on the designer bib overalls (by Gloria Vanderbilt, yet) she had been given as a going-away present by some of her modeling pals. Freddie Overstreet, a lissome redhead, and Midge Bunyan, blond and pert, had gotten quite a giggle over the gift when she opened it at La-Petite Marmite that afternoon. Judy Monkhouse, her best friend and another redhead, had placed her own offering inside the box: a tiny chromed claw hammer with brass handle and head from Hammacher Schlemmer. Inside its handle nestled a set of screwdrivers, each tinier than the last. It had been a fun lunch, and a sad one, too. She wished her wise-ass pals were with her now, to help her confront the Awful Attic.

Actually, she realized, once she'd opened the windows at either end of the place, it wasn't too bad up there. There was plenty of light, and the smell of age and disuse disappeared almost at once. She had developed quite an eye for good lumber by now, and once she had swept the floor clear of dust she realized that the attic floorboards were of even better quality than those downstairs: some were fully three feet wide, finely grained virgin white pine of a size that will probably never again grow on the North American continent. She paused to count annular growth rings in one board and reached one hundred before she was halfway across. Because of the short growing season in this latitude, it took damn near forever for a pine to reach that size. For a moment she could see that long-dead forest as it must have looked: great sighing pines shooting two hundred feet into the sky, the floor beneath their feathery distant tops a deep, springy cushion of long-since-fallen needles now rotted to rich loam. A breeze had sprung up outside, and the house itself was swaying ever so gently to the push of the wind. The old oaken posts and beams of the attic seemed to murmur and groan like the voices of old men, long dead, long gone. What a time that must have been!

Well, she thought, enough daydreaming. Back to work! At the far end of the attic stood the usual array of boxes, trunks, and broken or discarded furniture: the accumulated debris of how many forgotten lifetimes? As she sorted through them, steeling herself against the fear of furry things, Laura found boxes of nails, screws, and bolts congealed by rust into abstract junk sculptures; old rain slickers so hardened by time that they crackled when she lifted them; worn-out boots and high-button shoes; musty dresses turned to cheesecloth by moths; a pair of long, heavy wooden skis of the sort used by American alpine troops in World War II (she noticed with a shudder that the leather bindings had been reduced to shreds by hungry mice); a marvelous old hobbyhorse that, cleaned and painted, would be perfect for the baby; three-legged coffee tables, cracked kerosene lamps, a rocker with a broken arm, stacks of old *National Geographics*, the headlamps of a long-defunct automobile. Behind all this stood an ornate, dark, and heavy breakfront. Laura opened the biggest drawer.

The face of a woman stared up at her. Laura stood transfixed in the gloom. The oval portrait, though crudely wrought, held a strong, almost hypnotic quality for her: the eerie anomie of a Bosch or a Holbein. The woman's high forehead had a mushroom-like tone to it, accentuated by white hair pulled severely back into a bun. The eyes were deep, unfocused, dreamy—and yet freighted with a sense of tragedy and vengefulness; the mouth hard, severe, beneath a baby's tiny snub nose. Behind the woman stood the most fearsome-looking tree Laura had ever seen: craggy, crook-armed, the sort of tree from whose limbs one expected to see corpses swinging. Superimposed on its trunk was a strange symbol:

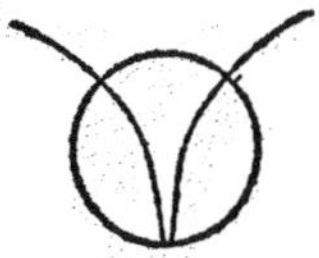

Laura stood for a long time studying the portrait. The attic seemed to grow cold; the smell of the dust turned bitter, acrid. A cloud covered the sun and the light level in the attic fell swiftly from yellow to cold blue. The woman's eyes seemed to grow deeper, almost luminous in the midday dusk; her bulging forehead glowed with a vegetable phosphorescence. . . .

Then something moved in the drawer. A leathery wing unfolded and a fanged, furry, big-eared head gazed up at Laura. The bat exploded from the drawer with a rattle of wing on wood, flapping up at her face and then crazily out into the open air, swooping and twisting with the frantic fury of a trapped animal. Laura screamed, ran, stumbled over the boxes, smashed into the hobbyhorse, tumbled down the attic stairs, and screamed again, unaware of her scraped and bloody elbows.

It was not until she reached the yard and Mark ran to her from the rototiller with worry dark on his sweaty face that she realized she was still clutching the portrait.

"Easy, hon," Mark said. "Just relax and take it easy." They were in the kitchen now and Mark brought her a steaming cup of tea. "Drink this chamomile, it'll calm you down. After all, as they say on TV, bats are people, too. They're part of the ecology, and you love the ecology, don't you, honey?"

"Oh, stop treating me like a baby," Laura snapped. She dabbed at her skinned elbows with a cotton wad soaked in hydrogen peroxide, then winced as she applied iodine. Mark taped on the big Band-Aids. "I know it's silly to be afraid of creatures that mean no harm, but I just can't help it," she said.

"You know," Mark changed the subject, picking up the portrait, "this is a damned fine primitive. Well worth a tumble down the stairs, so long as there were no bones broken. I guess the Eldridges just didn't realize its worth."

"She gives me the creeps," said Laura. "I'm never going up in that attic again, I don't care what happens."

"Easy, babe, easy. I wonder who this old gal is—or was. That symbol on the tree, didn't Bill say something about it at dinner that night when he was telling us about the religious cults? A winged disk—that's what it is, sure enough. This bimbo must have been involved in the cult, maybe a high priestess or something."

"She looks like something that grew on a rotten tree stump," Laura said.

"I don't know, I kind of like her. Eyes like a wounded doe and a mouth like a hungry shark. We'll have to ask around town about her—maybe they have a historical society or something. Now, about these mice and things that send you up the walls and down the staircase. I think we ought to get a cat. A good, tough barn cat that'll keep the critters down."

"Oh, honey, could we?" Laura jumped up and hugged him. "I always wanted a kitten when we lived in the city, but it would have been cruel to keep it locked up all the time in the apartment. You're not allergic, are you? I know I'm not, we had cats all over the place when I was a kid in Winnetka."

"Okay, okay." He laughed. "No, all I'm allergic to is strawberries, far as I know. We'll stop by one of the farms on our way to town next time. I've never been in a barn that didn't have more cats than cows. We'll make some farm lady happy by taking a big, mean, rugged old killer barn cat off her hands. The very next time we go to town."

But they didn't have to wait even that long.

Laura's first visitor arrived the very next morning, a sturdy old lady who whizzed into the gravel-topped barnyard in a rusty red Ford pickup, vintage 1952. She bent within the cab for a long grope before emerging with a linen-covered wicker basket in one hand and a brown paper supermarket bag in the other. The paper bag, crimped tight at the top where it was firmly clutched in her bony old hand, bulged and writhed as she walked to the door. She was short, plump, clad in a weathered Navy pea coat despite the seventy-degree temperature, and a pair of patched rubber knee boots peeked from beneath her faded dungarees. Her face was pale, unseamed, highlighted with the apple-pink glow one associates more with Sweet Sixteens than septuagenariennes. She was, Laura thought, just plain beautiful—even when she smiled and showed only two opposing teeth in the front of her otherwise pretty mouth.

"Hi-dee," said the old lady. "I'm Mrs. *Mun*-ro from down the holler. Huldy Munro. Glad to see you in the neighborhoo-ud." She stumped her way to the door and handed Laura the basket. "Thought you might want some greens and radishes, seein's your garden patch ain't up yet." Then she gestured with the paper bag, from which sounded a plaintive, puzzled meow. "This here's only if you need it. But I reckon you do, since the house's been empty for so long."

She opened the bag and unceremoniously tumbled its contents onto the grass: a husky black and white kitten that stood up, bowlegged, and promptly began grooming itself.

"Oh, how darling!" Laura blurted. "You've read our minds! Mark, Mark—take a look at this!"

Mark's head appeared at the edge of the roof and he peered over, hammer in hand.

"I'm sorry," Laura said, flustered now at having forgotten her manners. "I'm Laura Avery, as I guess you know, and that is my husband, Mark. Mark, meet Mrs. Munro."

"Just call me Huldy," the old lady said.

"Pleased to meet you, Huldy," said Mark. "And thanks for the pussycat. We'd just decided on our own to enlist one in the campaign against the rodent population, so you've saved us a cat hunt. Now if I could teach him how to swing a hammer I could come down and join you, but unfortunately . . ." He disappeared with a wave back up the roof.

In the basket with the vegetables lay half a dozen doughnuts, homemade by the look of them. Laura put water on the stove to boil for tea, then poured a saucer of milk for the kitten, who promptly fell to with a lapping pink tongue.

"Is it male or female?" Laura asked. "Does it have a name?"

"Tomcat right enough," said Huldy. "If you look real close, you can see his little ballocks asproutin'. Ten weeks old he is. The young-uns down to Markham's, where I fetched him, call him Bone, though I don't rightly know why. Mebbe he was just skin and bone afore they started feedin' him up."

"Well, he won't be hungry for long around here," Laura said. "The house is crawling with mice and I don't know what-all."

"He'll eat flies for you, too," said Huldy. "Grass-hoppers, crickets, butterflies, leftover mashed potatoes —he battens on 'em all. Fuzzy little garbage can is young Master Bone." She turned and gazed around the kitchen. Laura had painted the walls a pale daffodil yellow, feeling that the original oak paneling made the room too gloomy. Pots, pans, and serving forks hung from the ceiling beams. An old Waterbury school clock, its face yellowed with age and mottled with stains, ticked cozily on the wall beside the oven. Laura had paid too much for it at a nearby flea market, but the sound was well worth the extravagance: the steady tick-tock ordering each day and night into tidy, coherent chunks. It reassured her somehow.

"Ah, me," said Huldy, "the old Eldritch place. You've done it up right perky."

"Thank you," Laura answered, busying herself with cups and saucers. "We never met Mrs. Eldridge—she must have moved before we saw the house—but the real-estate agent told us about her husband."

"Ayup," said Huldy. "Bad luck on him it was indeed. Oh, the Eldritches was an old, old fambly here in Magrute Hollow. Been here for longer'n most, I reckon, an honored name in the Gore for many a decade. We uz all right sorry to see Ellen move south after Sam'l died."

"What happened to him?"

"Real-estate dude didn't tell you, eh? Well, Sam got greedy, is the long and short of it. Decided to turn a few extry dollars last winter by selling firewood. What with oil prices so durn high thanks to them uppity Ay-rabs, most folks hereabouts has gone back to heating with wood of a winter. Sam'l decided to cut up in

Drooker's there." She gestured out the window, up toward the oak grove—just coming into leaf—that glowered into the hollow from the ridge to the east. "Should've knowed he was too old for that kind of work. Hey-ull, he uz near as old as me, and I'm eighty-four. Anyways, a tree fell on him. He should've knowed it would."

"How dreadful!" Laura said. "But how could he have known it would happen?"

"Becuz it always does up there in Drooker's. There's some who say that oak grove is cursed. Folks hereabouts have always shied away from it, since olden times. When people go in there to cut, strange things happen—branches fall on windless days, trees split in midsummer, axes slip, and chainsaws explode. I don't know the right of it myself, but the Drooker's Woods makes trouble for loggers. That's why it was always a fambly tradition with the Eldritches never to cut in them oaks, though they had plenty of offers over the years from the lumber companies to sell it for a right pretty penny. Hardwood like that you don't find nowheres nowadays."

"How awful, all those accidents." Laura shuddered, thinking of a chainsaw—ugly instrument just by itself—suddenly erupting into an orange fireball with a man at its heart.

"Yaas," said Mrs. Munro softly. "Pretty awful. But those things happen in these parts of the kentry, always have and always will. It looks like a peaceful, well-tamed landscape, but it ain't. It's hard, as you'll only too soon find out. Look at poor Jim Boggs there a few weeks ago. End of March, it was. Splittin' wood up by the edge of his medder, simplest job in the world, you'd think. Then, in a wink, his hammer slips and he splits his foo-ut. Bleeds to death afore he can get help."

"My God," said Laura. "That must have been . . .

Does he have a young wife, blond, and four—no, five children? One of them an infant?"

"Ayup, that's the Boggses."

"We saw the funeral going on the day we decided to buy this house. That poor woman! What's become of her and her children?"

"Kids took it hard at first, but they're come round all right," said Huldy. "Young Polly, though." She shook her head. "Hasn't really come out of it yet. Still mopin' and not lookin' after herself, like. It's tough to lose a man, all right, that I know—widdered myself many a long cold winter ago. But it's like I say-ud, this here's a mean kentry, a poor kentry, no one never said it wasn't. And the woo-uds, they will have their revenge."

She finished her tea, picked up her now-empty wicker basket, and made her good-byes. Laura stood at the window as the red truck wheeled away, tires spinning like a teen-ager's. She picked up the kitten and held it close, feeling the rough-throated purr vibrating against her chest. The cat stared up at her with wide, grave eyes.

He sat on a simple stone bench under a shade tree in the Hubley's Gore cemetery, whittling on a piece of basswood. The bench was made of marble, a common rock in that country, and its surface had been polished smooth with use. Families still made it a practice to come to the cemetery at least once a month and tend the graves of their dead: digging weeds, planting and pruning flowers, straightening the simple headstones of marble that had been shifted and canted by the frost. Some of the headstones dated back as far as 1765, and on these older monuments the carved dates and names and epitaphs had eroded to near illegibility. At one corner of the cemetery, not far from the marble bench, lay a special plot segregated from the rest of the graves by a paled, wrought-iron fence. It was there that Jim Boggs lay buried.

The epitaphs on these stones were all sylvan in nature. "She walks now in God's forest," read one. "Taken in the Fourth Year of His Age by the Woods," said another. "Felled by the Heavenly Sawyer," stated a third. A lumberjack's corner of the graveyard, one might have thought. But why then the children, the women?

He put down the basswood and folded the blade of his pocketknife, then walked to the wrought-iron fence. Near Jim Boggs's grave lay half a dozen others, close together as those of a family, all dating from the late 1960s and early seventies. Yet the surnames on the stones were different. He remembered them well. Longhairs they were, hippies, flower children—gentle and wide-eyed, with sweet smiles and simple ways. They had come to the Gore because they had heard of the Church in the Wildwood. They too loved trees and nature, and here they thought they would find the real thing: native American Druidism. Now they all lay dead beyond the iron paling. It was a shame, he thought. And chuckled.

But now we have newcomers in town. It will only be a matter of time before I meet them.

He couldn't remember how the first members of the hippie family had died. That was one of the worst things of aging—toward the end even the warmest, loveliest memories fade, so that at the finish you were living, like a baby, moment for moment. But the last three hippies, ah, there was a fine offering! Like a bolt from the blue, as they say. He chuckled again. Two young men and a beautiful girl, her red hair flowing loose to her waist. What were their names? Yes: "Root" and "Branch," the men. And the woman, "Lovemoss." Absurd! They had hiked that day up to the Oak Grove to celebrate the autumnal equinox. All well and good. But with them they brought their abominable chemicals. Noxious weeds; alien mushrooms. They had been warned time and again that these lesser forms were unsuitable, obnoxious to Him they claimed to honor.

It had been a gorgeous fall day, the air crisp as apple wine, the sky that electric blue that sets the heart to racing and the blood to bubbling, and the leaf colors glowed like rare gems on the hillsides. Stoned, they reveled in the day, the sylvan palette, praying to the Bull Oak and making love in turn against His mossy roots. They should have noted the rage trembling in His upper branches, the rising sough of wind from the west, the small dark cloud that suddenly appeared in the virgin blue vault and swept toward them as they rutted, growing and blackening, lending a hard green tone to the light.

The girl saw it first: a splendid oak branch, ruby red in this strange light, swaying just within reach beyond the umbrella of the Bull Oak's crown.

"Ooooooh!" She rose and stumbled toward it, naked, her nacreous curple swaying Eve-like, seductive, as she walked. "The colors! How they change with the light!"

The men followed her, entranced, still lecherous for all their sinful poking.

They stood beside her as she reached for the dancing red leaves.

The black cloud stooped on them like a hungry harrier.

As her fingers touched the bough, the bolt snapped down: God's heavenly spear, blinding white in its swift power.

The girl's body jerked and swelled instantly, lobster red. Her hair disappeared in a puff of rank smoke. Her eyes boiled and blackened as she fell. Beside her the men exploded. Just . . . Like . . . That . . .

That night, with proper ceremony, their ashes enriched the roots of their angry God.

What was Carl Sandburg's fine line?

"Always the Young Strangers."

He laughed aloud this time. So it was, so would it always be.

And now we have the newcomers. Only a matter of time before I meet them.

THREE

May is a month of marvels in those hills. Winter's reluctant grip is suddenly broken: the meadows shade up from dun to pale green, the woods go pink with fattening buds, then open out into leaf. The blackflies have yet to hatch from the swift-running brooks, yet trout are moving up through the riffles and hanging on quivering pectoral fins in every pellucid hole. The song of returning spring migrants turns dawn to din: armed with her newly purchased Peterson field guide, Laura learned to identify the gaudier returnees—rose-breasted grosbeak and rufous-sided towhee, bluebird and barn swallow, the swift glitter of the goldfinch and the rare, jewel-like gleam of a blue grosbeak, a rusty sapphire lodged high in a bank-side willow.

With worms turned up as he spaded the garden, Mark took to fishing the deep holes of Cauldron Brook, returning each morning wet to the knees, briar-scratched of hand and cheek, but grinning broadly as he held up their "breakfast trout"—three or four of them, usually, bright and pink-fleshed "natives" that Laura fried with scrambled eggs and onion. Though small (rarely more than eight or ten inches long), they tasted better to Laura than any *truite meunière* she had eaten at the French Shack or The Four Seasons. Mark insisted that since the fish were so small, she cook them "in the round," i.e., with the head attached. That was the way his father, a great hunter and angler, had liked them. Mark had hunted and fished a lot as a boy, then lost interest when he left home. Now he wanted to get back to it, completely. Laura was squeamish at first, particularly as the eyes, in cooking, turned white and opaque, staring up accusingly at her from the sizzling pan. And though Mark sucked the meat off his trout heads, she fed hers to Bone, the cat, and his enjoyment of them soon ended her reluctance.

The cat had proved his worth that very first night. Laura was awakened by the thump of his pounce and the suddenly silenced squeak of terror from Bone's first mouse. She flicked on the bedroom light only long enough to see him crunch down on the bright-eyed head of the victim—he had leaped from the foot of the bed, now his customary nighttime lookout, to seize the interloper on his mistress's slumber—then turned it out and hid her head under the pillow. Even at that she could hear the kitten's tiny teeth snickering through fur, flesh, and bone. Fortunately he was a quick eater: three crunches and he was back on the bed, warm against her feet. In the morning she looked cautiously for "leftovers." There were none. He had eaten the mouse to the last whisker. She loved him dearly.

Huldy dropped in every now and then with more garden goodies and just to sit and gossip. Occasionally her grandson, Billy, came with her: a skinny, surly man of about thirty-five with bad teeth and a two-word vocabulary ("Ayup" and "Noo-up"). On his first visit Billy studied her garden, then showed up the next day with a truckload of manure which he spaded in for her uncomplainingly, refusing Laura's offer of five dollars for the work. Instead he took his pay in the form of "dinner"—four cheeseburgers, a heaping plate of coleslaw, two huge dill pickles, and a king-sized bottle of Dr Pepper, the last of a six-pack he'd brought with him in the truck. Then he stuffed a quid of Red Man in his cheek, pulled his greasy Boston Red Sox cap down tight over his protuberant ears, nodded gravely, and drove away.

One morning when Huldy came over by herself—Mark was fishing and sketching up the brook—Laura took the old woman on a tour of the house. In the living room Huldy's eyes immediately riveted on the strange portrait Laura had found in the attic. It hung in a far, dark corner of the paneled room, glowing as always with its odd effulgence.

"Be damn," said the old lady as if to herself.

"Do you recognize that painting?"

"Oh, no, no," Huldy said hurriedly, coming back to herself. "It's a nice un though, ain't it? You find that down in New York City?"

"No. Right here. In the attic."

"Some Eldridge or t'other must've picked it up at an auction or flea market, I reckon," Huldy said finally. "Now *say*, you *do* have a right many boo-uks on your shelves, don't you? Don't tell me you've read all of 'em?"

Laura did not press her further.

But Mark and Laura met other interesting neighbors as well.

"Being a drunk is damned hard work," said Dolph Rooney. He skittered like a long-legged bug around the kitchen of his tiny cottage just down the road from the Eldridge place, fetching cups and pouring coffee. "You're always tired. Just waking up in the morning can wipe you out. You gotta be a regular weightlifter to open your eyes. Climbin' outta bed, if you managed to git that far the night before, takes every bit of strength you got. Walk to the mailbox—and mine's ony twenny feet from the door—forget it! You might as well ast a drunk to walk to Noo Yawk." He smiled, and his wizened monkey face grew even more wrinkled, if that was possible. He offered Mark and Laura steaming (if lip-cracked mugs of rich-smelling coffee. "Anyways, that's why I quit a promising career as the A-number-one lush in Hubley's Gore."

Mark and Laura had passed Rooney's little cottage frequently on their walks down the winding dirt road that threaded the hollow. It reminded Laura of the wicked witch's cottage in *Hansel and Gretel,* though built of curlicued wood rather than gingerbread: every eave and windowsill erupted in whirling, twisting, intricately fretted band-saw work. An old-fashioned wooden waterwheel turned in the splash of a waterfall along the brook, and a sign on a nearby tree cautioned: DANGER, LOW VOLTAGE. Another sign, beside the road, said: SLOW. CHIPMUNK CROSSING. Until this morning, however, they had never seen the occupant, though often when they passed the place they heard the whine of a table-saw from the shop attached to the cottage and saw signs of movement within. This morning, though, the master of Chipmunk Manor had been taking the sun on a rough-hewn bench beneath the LOW VOLTAGE sign. They had accepted his invitation to coffee.

Dolph Rooney had arrived in the Gore, he told them, shortly after World War II. He had five thousand dollars in his kick—money he'd won in the V-J Day pool at the Brooklyn Navy Yard where he worked as a shipfitter—and with it he bought the dilapidated shack on Cauldron Brook just down the road from the Eldridges. That had taken three grand. With the rest he proceeded to get and stay drunk for a year straight. "Woke up one afternoon in the fall of '46 with my pockets empty and my brain fulla holes," he said. "Couldn't remember a thing since I left Brooklyn. My mouth tasted like I'd sent my tongue to summer camp at the town dump. I walked with a heavy list to starboard—my liver was big enough to fill a wash tub. So weak I could hardly stand up. You coulda played 'Mairzy Doats' on my ribs. Anyways, I'm rummaging around this grubby shack for a something to drink—all the dishes had grown green fur and the toilet was a fungus farm—when I come on this box of brand-new wood-carving gear. Drawknife, checkering tools, etchers, and edgers—the works. Couldn't drink that, hell, there wasn't even a can of Sterno in the joint, so I started carving wood. Nothing better to do." He gestured around the cluttered interior of the cabin. "This is the result."

The cottage was chockablock with Dolph's handiwork. The wood-paneled walls gazed inward with the strange eyes and stranger faces of what might have been fanciful animals—monsters, some of them, Laura thought—but were in actuality odd-shaped knots and whorls of pine he had cut himself up on Widdershins. From the walls projected what looked like an animal farm of horns—coat racks and gun racks, pegs and prongs hand-carved from weirdly crooked branches Dolph had found in the wrack and litter of the ever-dying, ever born-again forest.

Yet the real hallmark of his skill, Laura saw, lay on the four-inch-thick oak mantelpiece over Dolph's fireplace, the mantel itself grained in such a way that when you looked at it edgewise it resembled the waves of a sea in the first writhings of tempest. On the mantel stood an eerie collection of gnomes and trolls, owls and toads, cretinous heads with leering jaws, a creature that resembled a python with the head of a stag—all carved by Dolph from the bulbous burls of trees he had scavenged from the woods. "Crazy wood," he called it. The carvings had a grotesque inchoate power to them, as if some vast and monstrous Unconscious (or perhaps just the twitchings of Dolph's half-petrified liver) had sought expression through weird twists of wood fiber. American gargoyles, Laura thought with a slight, delicious shiver. And Dolph himself is a kind of Grandpa Moses with nightmares.

"Have you ever thought of showing these in an art gallery?" Mark asked as he studied the carvings.

"Naw," said the author of the artifacts. Grinning and leathery, with a fist-bent nose and deep-set, burning eyes, his hair at the age of at least seventy-five was still jet-black and shaggy as a rock singer's. His hands were out of proportion to his jockey's body, Laura noticed—huge, horny, big-knuckled, and scarred on palm and digit with white hash marks where his knife had slipped. The nails gleamed thick and yellow, like those of some nocturnal predator. "Shucks, Mr. Avery, this is just my hobby. It ain't art, or at least I don't think of it that way. I just loved wood—the way I use to love the booze. I love to see what it's trying to say, with its twists and turns and bulges and warps. Then I take my tools to it and help it out."

"It doesn't seem to be whispering sweet nothings," said Mark. He held one of the carvings in his hand: a flat and mutant skull-like object whose fanged jaws seemed locked in a silent scream. "You can almost feel the rage and hate pouring out of this one."

"Right!" said Dolph, jumping excitedly to his feet. "You're dead right, Mr. Avery! The woods is not a gentle, jolly place. It's mean and fierce and full of evil, crueler than the worst slums of the worst city in the world. The forest hates us because we cut it down and turn it into houses and toothpicks and Popsicle sticks and firewood. I've always felt that, known it, ever since I been up here. I remember one day back when I was drinking, I went into that oak grove back of your place, just wandering and reeling and belching with a bottle of Seagram's Seven in my mitt, and I must've gone to sleep up there. I woke up in the dark and I could hear the trees talking to each other. Deep voices they had, guttural-like, frogs in their throats, talking in some strange language that I couldn't make out a word of it, like listening to Mafia hitmen behind a curtain in some dago joint down in Little Italy, not knowng the words but knowing damn well that it meant somethin' rotten goin' down. Like death." He sat back in his hand-carved chair, exhausted and proud of his outpouring, grinning his gargoyle's grin, and Laura saw that he resembled his own carvings.

"Well," she said a bit uneasily, "I happen to think it's beautiful work, strong and individualistic, and I think that if you ever wanted to try, Mr. Rooney, you could sell it in the best galleries in New York. So there! And even if you don't, I'd like to buy a piece from you for our mantelpiece."

"Oh, I couldn't sell nothin' to a neighbor," Rooney said. "That wouldn't sit right with me. But I'll carve you somethin, Miz Avery, you wait and see. Somethin' real strong and injividdulistick." He whipped a thin-bladed knife from the rude sheath at his hip and made carvng motions in the air, grinning all the while. "You wait and see!"

"Just so you don't go looking for wood in that oak

grove." Laura laughed. "Huldy Munro tells me it's cursed, that anyone who goes in there to cut wood is going to end up in the hospital."

Dolph grew suddenly somber. "She's right," he said. "I stay clear of that place, good as the wood may look. For a long while after that night when I fell asleep up there I hung clear of the grove, remembering. Then one day I says to myself, I says, Dolph, you just had the ol DTs, there ain't nothin' up there gonna grab you. So up I went, huntin' for crazy wood, and you know how it is when you're lookin' for something, you don't pay much heed to other things around you. All of a sudden, though, I got this creepy feeling up my back and I looked around. Then up in the sky. My golly, there was a big dead limb hangin' there in the tree right over my head, and it was teeterin' as if to fall. I jumped the hell out of the way and just then, *whoosh,* down she come. And *whap!* Stuck there in the ground, raggedy edge foremost, right where I'd been standing. No, don't you worry none about me trespassin' on your woodlot. I been around here too long, heard too many stories. I don't want to end up in no early grave."

Later as they walked up the road toward home, Mark laughed and shook his head. "Poor old gink," he said. "Did you ever hear such hogwash? H'anted oak trees, no less. Just goes to show what boozing can do to the brain."

"Don't be so sure, Mr. Know-It-All," Laura answered. "Huldy says so too. And after all, old Mr. Eldridge got killed up there, didn't he?"

"Doesn't prove a thing. Logging is dangerous, that's all. Everything I've read about the care and feeding of chainsaws, axes, splitters, the works, says you can't be too careful. But nowhere does it say anything about accursed oak trees. When I start cutting up there, I'll keep my eyes peeled for wood sprites and dryads, don't worry, and if I see one I'll eat your . . . pancakes."

"Yeah." She punched him on the arm. "You eat them anyway, you glutton, three stacks a day."

FOUR

When Mark and Laura lived in the city, shopping came as naturally and nearly unconsciously to them as breathing. If they were running short of spread for their customary breakfast bagel, say, one or the other simply popped into Zabar's on the way home from work—and generally emerged not only with half a pound of fresh, bulk cream cheese, but a few slices of lox or whitefish, a can of macadamia nuts, a gleaming round rye bread or something equally "impulsive" to surprise the other. Now that they lived in the country, however, each shopping trip became a conscious foray into town, an expedition that required close planning and a certain degree of anticipation—almost an adventure.

Minter's General Store was as general as they come. Laura never knew what she might find next on the dark, crammed, utterly disorganized shelves. She tingled with the same sense of serendipity she had felt as a little girl when she first discovered public libraries, and which had only been matched in later years by her virgin visit to Bloomingdale's. In Ike Minter's cozy maze of a store, half an aisle of fishing tackle might be succeeded by a sagging shelfload of intermixed kerosene lamps and flour sifters. Barrels of nails stood stave by bellyband with pungent vats of pickles. Huge waxy-skinned wheels of cheese—tangy Vermont cheddar, mainly, though Swiss and jack were also well represented—added their rich aroma to that of the hard, spicy sausages that festooned the beams over the worn plank counter. Fanbelts and fireplace tools, braids of red onions and boxes of shotgun shells, house paint and baby bibs, earmuffs and waffle irons: you name it and Ike Minter carried it.

Once, when a movie company was shooting a film in a town across the mountain from the Gore, a harried young prop assistant came into the store looking for "old-timey" items with which to authenticate the set.

"Would you have anything in stock from the 1920s?" he asked Ike. "Gangster-era stuff. Price is no object."

Ike fingered his stubbly gray jaw and sucked thoughtfully on a bad molar. His sunken eyes flickered momentarily in the leathery mask of his countryman's countenance.

"Ayup," he said at last, then disappeared into the gloomy catacomb of shelves at the back of the store. While the prop man poured himself a cup of "home-ground mocha java" from the crusted pot that bubbled, summer and winter, atop Ike's ancient wood stove, he heard clanking and shuffling from the abyss. Ike emerged finally with a cardboard carton in his wiry arms. From it he produced can after rusty can of dehydrated potatoes.

"Put up by the guv'mint for our doughboys in World War One," he announced proudly. "My pap bought 'em as surplus right after Armistice Day in '18. Let you have 'em for a dollar a can, twenty for the carton. You don't have to bring 'em back, neither. *We* sure don't eat 'em."

"That's not quite what we had in mind," said the movie mogul. "Do you have anything more . . . er . . . *visual*?"

"Like this?" asked Ike. From under the counter he produced a well-oiled, drum-fed Thompson submachine gun with Cutt's compensator and wooden fore-end pistol grip. The prop man's eyes lit up.

" 'Tain't for sale," said Ike. "Sorry. Count on it for perteckshun in case we ever have a urban riot here in the Gore."

An hour of heavy haggling ensued, culminating only when the prop man signed over five hundred dollars in traveler's checks. He left the store beaming broadly. After his rent-a-heap roared away, Ike went again to the back of the store. He returned with another, newly uncrated tommy gun, loaded the drum with .45-caliber rounds from his endless supply of ammo, and placed the weapon tenderly back on its hooks under the counter. Laura and Mark, who had witnessed the conclusion of the deal, laughed aloud. Ike winked at them and ventured a brown grin.

"I 'spect that fifty years down the pike, my grandkid will be skinning the flatlanders with take-down A-bombs out of war surplus," he said. " 'Ain't Nothin' So Rare But at Minter's It's There.' That's our motto."

Later, while Laura was poking around in the back of the store, Mark took Minter aside. "I might be interested in one of those guns," he said guardedly. "If you could put a reasonable price tag on it."

"What'd you need such a weapon for, Mr. Avery?"

"Well, you know, up there on the mountain," Mark said, flustered. "All by our lonesome. Bears maybe. I was reading in the *Rutland Herald* the other day about the sharp increase in burglaries by those snowmobile gangs. Like that."

"Buy yourself a shotgun," Ike said. "Cheaper and surer by far, plus you can use it for partridge, wild turkey, and even deer. Anyways I couldn't sell you a tommy gun if I wanted to, not even if you was bein' invaded by booby-snatchers or whatever they call 'em on the TV. That gun I sold the flatlander had no firing pin and a plugged barrel to make it both unshootable and legal under the federal gun-dealer licensing law. I'd heard tell of that Hollywood outfit makin' the rounds of the general stores hereabouts and slipped a ringer in on him. My old pap, he told me, Ike, he said, you don't want to let no real firepower loose in this town. If there's to be real firepower, you want to own it personal."

Mark ended up buying a twelve-gauge Remington Model 1100 semi-automatic shotgun from Ike, along with four boxes of bird shot and buckshot.

But Minter's was more than an emporium purveying the practical, the necessary, and the exotic to the people of the Gore: it was the town nerve center as well. At the caged-off far end of the counter resided the Hubley's Gore Post Office, Isaachar Minter, Postmaster. In a cubicle to one side stood a Telex machine wearing the Western Union colors, with I. P. Minter, Telegrapher, ready and waiting. Outside the store reared the two Mobil pumps, I. Petrarch Minter serving as elderly pump boy if you didn't want to pump your own. Newsbutcher Minter sold *The New York Times,* the *Rutland Herald,* and nearly every magazine that didn't have a naked lady in it. The store was open from seven in the morning to seven at night, and at any given hour a small clot of townsfolk could be found foregathered near the stove or the coffee counter, discussing everything from chilblains and church socials to the latest episode of *That's Incredible*. Mark and Laura loved the place, and whenever their work load permitted, made the weekly store-run together.

On this bright May afternoon, however, Mark had taken sketch pad and pastels up into the Cauldron to do some spring color studies and Laura made the run alone. Below Dolph Rooney's and the rather seedy Munro farm, the road wound along the widening brook, overarched by big sugar maples now in full leaf. As she rounded a curve, Laura saw a figure walking toward town at the far end of the leafy tunnel formed by the trees. A woman. With a baby held on her back in one of those papoosey backpack things now favored by young mothers. A blond young woman: Polly Boggs! Laura's heart sank. For weeks she had kept her fingers figuratively crossed in hopes that she would not meet the young widow, and now for a moment she actually considered driving right past with perhaps only a cheery wave, pretending that Polly and her baby were just out for a stroll. Then she blushed at her cowardice: Look here, Laura Pierce Avery, some people die and other people live. It's up to the living to be kind to the living.

She stopped the truck and opened the passenger side door.

"Hi—need a lift into town? I'm Laura Avery from up at the old Eldridge place. I'm heading in to Minter's."

Polly Boggs smiled shyly and gratefully as she climbed into the cab and settled the baby on her lap. Her hair, on close inspector, was a bit rat-nesty and needed a shampoo, and she wore no makeup, but she was really quite pretty, and, unlike so many people in town, young and old both, had a full set of clean white teeth.

"Boy, do I," she said. "This little filly of mine is getting to weigh a ton!" She bounced the infant on her bedenimed lap and the little girl burped, then cooed.

"She's darling!" Laura said sincerely. "What's her name?"

"Jamie Lynnette Boggs," the girl smiled proudly, "but I call her Jamie Lynn." Then she paused. "The Jamie's for her father," she said with a fall.

"Yes," Laura said after a pause of her own. "Mrs. Munro—Huldy?—told me about the . . . accident. I'm so awfully sorry for you. I . . ."

"Damn durn old woods," Polly Boggs said. She looked out the side window.

"Well, she's just a lovely baby—pretty as her mommy," Laura quickly continued.

"Do you think so?" said Polly, brightening again. Then she blushed. "I don't mean to say that I'm pretty or nothin', but do you really think she looks like me? I thought she favored Jim—but you never knew him."

Polly too was heading for the store, and the young women did their shopping together, with Polly blithely packing her bags full of junk foods: Twinkies, Chee-tos, Count Chocula cereal, Doritos, and a crinkly package of Mallomars. "It fills up their little bellies," she said. "when I can't afford much real meat." Polly had planned to wait for a ride back up the mountain—her truck, she said, was "on the fritz"—when Pastor Thorpe brought her older children home from the church-sponsored after-school play group, but Laura offered to take her right to her door.

"Much obliged," Polly said. "But only if you promise to come in for a cup of coffee."

The Boggs driveway was steep and potholed, winding

up through a scruff of second-growth birch and aspen, many of them wind-uprooted and tilted crazily one against the other. The old house loomed above them as the woods thinned, a drowsing wooden idol, its windows blank with drawn, water-stained shades. The house looked as if it had not been painted since Calvin Coolidge chose not to run. Gray wood showed under long yellowing curls of peeling paint. Farm folk, Laura thought, don't really care what a farmhouse looks like. It's the land that counts.

A few black and red chickens scattered gawking at their approach and a big yellow dog—part husky by the evil slant of his eyes—bellowed hoarsely as he strained the rusty chain that bound him to the sag-roofed cow barn. Two elderly vehicles—an International pickup and a motorless Plymouth sedan up on blocks—stood beside the barn, flaking their paint jobs into the dirt. A column of sour-smelling woodsmoke curled weakly out of the brick chimney of the house.

"You keep a fire going even in the summer?" Laura asked as they carried the shopping bags inside.

"It's always chilly in the house," Polly said. "Got a wet cellar hole."

"Maybe if you left the shades up, the sunlight would warm it and save you on firewood."

"Then I'd have to look at the woo-uds," Polly said plaintively. "I can't stand seeing the woo-uds."

The kitchen was dimly lit and airless, acrid with the smell of woodash and unwashed diapers. No sooner had Polly placed her bags on the cluttered counter than she switched on a portable black-and-white television set in the far corner. Then she squatted in front of the wood stove and opened the door. A puff of smoke ghosted into the room. With a sawed-off garden hoe she raked smoldering coals forward in the box and pitched in a few finely split sticks from the woodbin.

The door of the black, sheet-metal stove had a wheel-shaped damper on it marked with numbers from one to ten. She turned the wheel to ten—wide open—and closed the door. In a moment the stove was roaring with a guttural, hungry sound that competed ominously with the tinny laughter of a game show on the TV set. Polly filled a chipped coffeepot from the sink and placed it on the stove.

"Won't take a minute," Polly said with her shy smile. "You don't mind instant Nescafé, do you? Hey, I got to go to the toidy and then put Jamie Lynn down. Be right back." She disappeared with the baby into a dark corridor that led from the kitchen toward the front of the house. Laura surreptitiously turned down the volume on the television set and then peeked into the corridor. The wall board bulged in spots and the ugly, flower-patterned wall paper was marred with water stains. Halfway down the corridor hung something rectangular and faintly glowing. Another portrait of the Lady in Weird? she wondered. That was Mark's wry nickname for the painting she'd found in the attic. If so . . . She walked down to look at it, but found instead a paint-by-the-numbers study, in Day-Glo colors, of John and Robert Kennedy, with the late John Lennon peering insanely over their touching shoulders as if he were an afterthought. Lennon's eyes were slightly crossed and Jack Kennedy's jaw hung lopsided. She heard the toilet flush and ducked back into the kitchen to avoid appearing snoopy. When Polly reentered the room, Laura was studying a framed photograph that stood on the kitchen counter. It showed a husky young man, almost brutally handsome, looking serious in army dress greens with the crossed rifles of the infantry on his lapels.

"That's Jim," said Polly. "He was in *Veet*-nam. Dropped out of high school to fight for his country."

She gulped on the last, turned quickly to the stove where the water was boiling, and carried the pot to the counter. Her shoulders shook once or twice and Laura looked desperately at her watch. Perhaps she could plead a roast in the oven. . . . But that would be cowardly.

"Did you both grow up here in the Gore?" she asked instead.

"No," Polly said, under control again. She spooned freeze-dried coffee into two hastily rinsed cups from the sink. "In Shrewsbury over to Rutland. We went together from the ninth grade on and I wrote to him every day while he was overseas. We got married right after he got out in '68, but we couldn't find no land up to home. None we could afford, anyways. Lived in a trailer for two years on his folks' place there, while Jimmy worked construction in Rutland and I had the babies. But the best we could've hoped for was to move up from the trailer to a double-wide, or else rent something in town." She grimaced at the idea. "Both of us growed up on the land. So then Jimmy heard about this place here, and it was better than any double-wide even with the wet cellar and the holes in the roof, and it had twenty acres of land with it—enough for some chickens and a couple of cows, plenty of firewood up the hill, and best of all a job opening down to Ashburn's mill. Who'd've thunk . . ."

They sat at the kitchen table, sipping their bitter coffee and discussing the town. Polly seemed far more cheerful with each passing minute, as if she'd had no one to talk to but children for far too long. Laura asked if she couldn't raise the shade just to see if it would warm the kitchen, and Polly reluctantly agreed. The moment light flooded into the kitchen, however, she grew sullen again.

"I hate this town," she said flatly.

"Well, I don't know, the people certainly seem friendly. . . ."

"It's not the people. No, I take it back, it *is* the people. But they can talk to it." She was staring out, across the meadow, up to the wooded mountaintop.

"Talk to what, Polly?"

"Oh . . . nothing," Polly began, blushing and averting her eyes. Then she seemed to stiffen and looked Laura straight on. "Yes. The woods. They can talk to the woo-uds! It's the woo-uds that runs this town, and everyone in it, the awful dark twisty cold ugly old durn *damn* old *woo-uds*!" She bowed her frowsy hair over the table and began to weep. "And then Jimmy goes up to cut firewood, for to sell it and make us a little extra money for the baby, and then I go out with the kids and when we come back I don't hear his saw goin' no more, nor his hammer hittin', and then Doc Peggs, he's standin' here and he tells me Jimmy's . . . Jimmy's . . ."

Laura got up quickly and put her arm around Polly's quaking shoulders. Her own stomach felt twisted and cold, sick with the violence of the other woman's anger and anguish. At that moment a van pulled into the barnyard and disgorged a babble of sunburnt, raucous children. They pelted through the kitchen door and scattered like flushed quail through the room. One, a gangling girl Laura recognized from the funeral, dove at the television set and switched channels until she found an obviously addictive soap opera. A boy, the eldest, looked disinterestedly at Polly as he rifled through the shopping bags.

"Shoot," he said with a twang of contempt, "Maw's cryin' again. Hey, there's Twinkies!" He ripped at the cellophane and stuffed a gooey tube of dough into his mouth. "Gimme, gimme!" yelled the little ones.

A dapper young man in a seersucker sport coat and clerical collar dismounted from the van and came smiling into the house.

"Hi," he exclaimed cheerfully, hand extended, "I'm Ben Thorpe, from down to the church. You must be Mrs. Avery." Then he noticed the red-eyed Polly. "Aw, Polly," he chided automatically. "You been cryin' again? There, there, there. Did you take one of those pills Doc gave you? You didn't? Here, let me get you a pill, Polly." He found the bottle quickly on a kitchen shelf, drew a glass of water from the tap, and tipped it as Polly swallowed what Laura recognized as a Qāālude. No wonder the poor thing's so freaky, she thought. They've got her zonked to the eyeballs. Well, maybe if I'd just lost my husband . . . She didn't dare think about it.

"Now Miz Avery," said the pastor cheerily. "Haven't seen you or your husband down to church yet. You look like clean-cut, God-fearing folks. We've got us the nicest little nondenominational congregation you could hope to find down at the Church in the Wildwood. I do hope you'll come and worship with us some Sunday soon. Help you to meet with the fine folks in town—why, we're more a social club than one of your hard-rock prayin' outfits, isn't that so, Polly?" Polly nodded blankly, her red-rimmed eyes now dry but sliding into wide focus. "Everyone's eager to meet you, too. This is a friendly, a right neighborly town, Miz Avery, with folks only too glad to help out a newcomer. We've got a gardening club, and a men's choir that sings country-and-western as well as the usual hymns, we've got a sewing circle and our orphan's relief, and, oh, my, just about everything you could want. And of course our youth group." He smiled benignly at the Boggs children, now all squatting and gobbling in front of the television set, paying no heed to the grown-up talk. Kermit the Frog was saying something profound.

"Well, that's very kind of you, Pastor Thorpe," Laura said as diplomatically as she could, "but Mark and I are neither what you might call practicing Christians and—"

"Oh, that's all right, Miz Avery. We take all kinds. Why we even had a family of the Hebrew persuasion in the Wildwood not long ago. Now I don't want to pressure you like some of these fellers do nowadays that've watched too much Sunday-mornin' TV. You just take your time and think it over."

"I will indeed," said Laura, mustering a toothpaste-commercial smile. "Well, I've got to be going. I've got a roast in the oven and I've stayed too long as it is." She put an arm on Polly's sagging shoulder and then, on impulse, bent over to kiss her cheek. "You take care now, Polly, and don't worry about that business we were talking about before. I'll be in touch."

She fled the house at a fast-paced walk that threatened any moment to break into a run. Not until she had wheeled the truck out of the long driveway and was heading back up the mountain toward home did she begin to feel easier, and then only marginally.

FIVE

Oddly enough, Mark was keen on the idea of paying a visit to the Church in the Wildwood. "Why not?" he said. "We've only seen these people in the middle distance so far—shopping at Minter's, picking up their mail, nodding hello on the street, or waving when we pass them in the truck. This will give us a chance to study them close up. And who knows, they may turn out to be damned interesting."

"But I mean," Laura said, amazed, "the Church in the Wildwood? The surgeon general warns that too much saccharine can be dangerous to your health."

"Don't be such a snob." Mark laughed. "Look, we've spent most of our adult lives among agnostic or outright atheistic sophisticates. Except when they were into Zen or Tao or acid-Zoroastrianism. Arty-smarties in most cases, if the truth be told. Sure, Manhattan may be the omphalos, but it isn't the whole darned world. It's as if there were an impenetrable fogbank on the Hudson River that New Yorkers can never see through. The rest of America doesn't exist. But it does, and it consists of millions upon millions of just plain folks who work and watch TV and bowl and hunt and fish and cut firewood and go, by God, to church every Sunday. That doesn't make them subhuman. In fact, it makes them a whole hell of a lot *more* human than some of the smart-ass creeps we used to hang around with."

"You just want to find some local good-ol'-boy to teach you all about guns and chainsaws," Laura said, but in the end she agreed to accompany Mark to church that Sunday. Feeling guilty still about having abandoned Polly Boggs, and recalling that Polly's truck was out of commission, she called and arranged to take the Boggs brood to church with them.

It was a bright and dulcet morning, full of birdsong and the hum of bees. The Boggs children were dressed in their Sunday best (as they had been, Laura recalled with a twinge, at the funeral), squeaky clean and every hair in place. They might have stepped out of an ad in a 1947 issue of *Life* magazine. Even Polly looked much more "together" in a crisp pink and pale blue frock, white patent leather pumps with purse to match, and a veiled, rather chic little pillbox with plastic flowers sprigged over one ear. Her hair had had a good wash and set and she wore just enough lipstick and eye makeup to bring up her naturally pallid color to a richer, almost ivory and peach-bloom hue. She was indeed a beauty when she tried, as even Mark's eyes attested. (Laura would needle him later about that look, but she wasn't really jealous.)

The parishioners' shoes echoed hollowly on the old pine floorboards of the church as they filed in to their pews. The air was cool, scented with the odor of Saturday bath soaps and Sunday after-shaves and colognes not of the highest quality. Laura noticed many heads turning curiously as Mark led them down the aisle to a pew near the center of the plainly adorned, well-carpentered cavern. Down at the front Laura noticed the tall, courtly old man she had seen at the funeral. He turned and looked her in the eye again, but this time he smiled as he nodded: a smile so bright, so luminous, and at the same time so graciously welcoming that she felt guilty at recognizing the fact that he obviously wore false teeth. He was clad in an expensively tailored gray double-breasted suit and a sedate but elegant bow tie, clearly not of the clip-on variety. She wondered again who he might be. Plainly he wasn't, as she'd thought at first, any kin of Polly's. Well, she'd find out soon enough, she reckoned. Huldy Munro came bustling in late and smiled a gap-toothed hello at the Averys as she took her place in the pew beside the tall old man. They chatted briefly and the man turned again to smile at Laura. Then Pastor Thorpe, clad in a red-trimmed surplice, stepped to the pulpit while the organ, which all this time had been humming and moaning vaguely remembered hymn music, rose to a shrill, peroratory crescendo.

"Brethren," he intoned solemnly, then added with an arch twinkle: "And Sistren as well, I might add." Everyone chuckled, as if such a stage direction had been indicated in their hymnals. "Oh, what a glorious Sunday morning—the sort of day Our Lord Himself might have played hooky from services and strolled bemused among his loved hills and byres. For Our Lord, we are told, loved nature more than the sorry haunts of man, the wildwood and the scent of the wildwood flower more than the dim temple and the reek of incense. Birdsongs rang sweeter in his sacred ear than the din of organ or the chant of choir. To his blessèd tongue the taste of bread and wine smacked pallid beside the tang of blood. . . ."

Wait a minute! Laura said to herself. Did he say

"blood"? She looked at Mark to see if he'd picked up on the word but he was busily scanning the faces of the foregathered worshipers with that intensity she recognized as his artist's eye in action. No one else looked startled. I must have misheard him, Laura concluded. And yet . . .

". . . said of Ahaz that he sinned in worshiping under the leafy bough of the greenwood. No, say I. And no, saith Our Lord in a loud and angry voice. As the poet William Cullen Bryant so sapiently wrote: 'The groves were God's first temples.' As indeed they were, and are yet today. In our own time we are seeing the young of this once-mighty nation turning away from the decaying cities, the drugs and diseases of the flesh, to return in ever-increasing numbers to the true worship of God-in-Nature—happy backpackers, runners of the dawn and dusk, pitching their bright tents and offering their silent prayers in God's vast and leafy temple. . . ."

The balance of the sermon continued in that lyric vein, extolling the virtues of a good, clean, healthy ecological consciousness. The pastor, for all his rubelike manner out of the pulpit, was a fine speaker, though a bit too Wordsworthian for Laura's taste: the English major in her preferred the hard elegiac imagery of an Eliot or a Roethke. The service, after a few forgettable announcements regarding sewing circle and youth group meetings, concluded with a hymn she had never heard before:

Home, boys, home,
That's where I want to be,
With the apple in the orchard
And the weeping willow tree.
Green grow the grasses
Of North Amerikee.

It was a sweet and lilting tune, and it moved her oddly, more like a sea chanty or a marching song than simple church music. At the final verse, however, Jamie Lynn Boggs broke into a hymn of her own—the perennial plaint of wet or hungry babies rudely awakened by whatever alien perceptions babies feel. Polly shushed and comforted her, blushing furiously as she hurried out of the church ahead of the congregation. Laura hurried after her. They were both cooing and tickling at the bawling babe when Huldy Munro came up with the tall old man in tow.

"Well," he said in a booming voice, "I see that my patient's lungs are in good working order." He bent over Jamie Lynn with a wide flash of his luminous dentition. She responded with an even heartier howl.

"Doc," said Huldy, "I'd like ye to meet our new neighbor, Miz Laura Avery. Laura, this here long drink of water is our local sawbones, Doc Peggs."

The doctor bowed formally and deeply, with a merry twinkle in his ice-blue eyes. "Delighted to make your acquaintance, Mrs. Avery," he said. "I hope we'll never have to meet in a professional capacity."

Mark, who had come up during the introductions, put out his own hand. "I'm Mark Avery, Doctor. If you handle maternity cases, though, you may indeed meet my wife in that manner." Laura stiffened: she wanted to kick her husband.

"Oh, are you *enceinte*?" Doc Peggs turned a benign smile on Laura.

"Not . . . at the moment," Laura stuttered. Damnit, I must be as red as Polly gets, she cursed. "But we do intend, *at some time in the future,* to have children. But enough of us. I didn't realize a town this small would have a resident M.D. I think it's just wonderful."

"Well," said Doc, "the Gore wasn't always as small as it is today, and I've been in practice here ever since I graduated from Harvard Med School in 1928. Back in those days most folks would rather have died than drive forty miles to the nearest doctor, as so many Vermonters must today. Besides, I love the Gore, and without sounding too durn gushy, I even have a mite bit of affection for some of its rascally residents." He put a proprietary arm around Huldy and another around Polly Boggs. "Tell me, what did you think of our simple little church service?"

"I wasn't paying too much attention to tell you the truth," Mark said with a grin. "Too busy watching the parishioners—I'm a painter, you see. But what I heard sounded outdoorsy and highly contemporary, if not indeed downright poetic."

"Thank you, kind sirrah," broke in Pastor Thorpe, turning away from another small group of worshipers. "I take it you're the new arrival in town, Mr. Avery. I've already had the pleasure of meeting your wife." As Mark and the padre chatted, Laura turned back to Doc Peggs.

"A bit lush on the nature number," she said, "but certainly short. The sermon, I mean. No frills. I loved that closing hymn, or whatever it was. I'd never heard it before."

" 'Green Grow the Grasses,' " said Doc. "It's actually an old marching tune, quite popular back in the early nineteenth century. Interesting bit of linguistic history goes with it. The American troops who invaded Mexico in 1848 sang it all the time on the road to the Heights of Chapultepec. The Mexicans, hearing the 'green grow' part over and over again, took to calling the Americans 'gringos.' Hence today's pejorative."

Polly Boggs pulled on Laura's sleeve and whispered: "I'm awful sorry, Laura, but Jamie Lynn needs a fresh didy, and real quick too. Do you think . . ."

Laura collected Mark and made her good-byes to Huldy and Doc.

"You might want to come by my office someday," Doc said, taking her aside. "If you do intend to have children soon, and you'd care to consult me, I'd best give you a good once-over. My specialty, if a country doctor can be said to have one, is obstetrics and GYN. And believe me, in a town this size you'll never have to wait for an appointment." He smiled again, and Laura began to wonder if she hadn't misjudged his appearance. He looked now not so much like a hawk, but rather a kindly old stork—or perhaps that was the wrong avian image. More an attenuated, elegant old gray owl of the sort she found in her Peterson's.

"What did you really think of it?" Mark asked when they got home.

"Makes the Unitarians look positively High Church," said Laura. "But certainly it wasn't as freaky as I was afraid it might be—after what Bill McGregor told us."

"Yeah. I kind of liked it. Very simple, no bullshit."

"It *did* seem awfully austere, except for the organ music."

"Did you notice?" asked painterly Mark. "There wasn't a religious symbol anywhere in the church. No stained glass, no holy-water font, not even a single, simple cross. Except on the ends of that scarflike thing the padre was wearing around his neck—what do they call it? A stole? And it wasn't even a cross, come to think of it. It was the same gizmo that's in that portrait you found in the attic. Like a basketball wearing Greek talaria."

He sketched the device quickly on a sheet of loose paper:

BLOODROOT

Laura's garden had been invaded. One morning when she went out to peruse her peas and lettuce, she found two whole rows missing. On closer examination she saw that the plants had been eaten right down to the roots. Rabbits? she wondered. Giant bugs? As she cursed and fretted, she caught a movement out of the corner of her eye. There, at the far end of the garden plot, sitting up on its fat brown haunches, sat a plump and insolent animal with tiny ears and yellow buck teeth.

"Groundhog," said Billy Munro when she called him for a consultation. Since the day he delivered the manure, Billy had become her personal gardening expert. So far everything he prescribed had worked to perfection. "There's some as call it a 'woodchuck,'" he said, "but I ain't never seed one eat no wood. What he likes is fresh greens."

"What can I do about it?"

"Give 'im a lead headache's the best cure," said Billy.

"A lead headache?"

"About a twenty-two-caliber lead headache should do the trick."

"Shoot him?" Laura was horrified. "I could never shoot an animal just for eating what I like to eat!"

Billy chuckled. "Then you'd best plant two gardens, Miz Avery. One for him and one for you."

"Won't a fence keep him out? We could buy some wire. . . ."

"Cost you more'n you'll save on vegetables over the

next two, three years. And chances are Mr. Groundhog would just excavate right under it. They're a diggin' critter, the groundhog. Nope, a bullet's best. But there's some who say that if you spread blood meal around the edge of the garden, the groundhog won't come in. Never tried it myself, since I like to eat the critters once I've shot 'em. But old Miz Markham down to town, she can't shoot so good no more and she tried that 'ere blood meal, and claims it works."

"Where would I find some?"

"I seed a big bag of it in your barn last time I was over. Right under where I hung the pitchfork. You'll know it by the smell when you open the sack."

Mark was busy on a painting in his new studio on the north side of the house, so Laura went out to the barn accompanied only by Bone, the cat. He had filled out nicely over the past few weeks (and indeed the sounds behind the walls had diminished even as he fattened); he followed her everywhere when she was working outside: more like a dog than the other cats she had known. He even came when she called him, bounding over the meadow grass, tail erect, with an eager "Merp-merp-merp!" Light filtered into the barn through the gaps left by missing battens, and motes of straw dust hung in the golden beams. Laura found the bag just where Billy said it would be, and when she opened the top, he proved correct once again: What a hideous stench! Dark, sweet, and sickly cloying—the smell of blood rotted into deep brown dust. When she shoveled the first scoop into the garden cart, Bone's ears and tail perked, then flattened. His yellow eyes probed the corners and his nose twitched, seeking the source of that meaty odor. Baffled, he stalked into the gloom, still hunting.

As she pulled the cart out of the barn, heading for the

garden, she heard a loud explosion from the south side of the house.

Ker-pow!

She dropped the cart handle and ran toward the house. Then she saw something flopping in the grass beside the garden and heard Mark's jubilant whoop from the upstairs window. He was leaning down, halfway out, waving the shotgun at the sky.

"Nailed the bastard!" he exulted. "One shot! Wild Mark Avery, fastest gun in the East!"

He had killed the groundhog, sure enough. Its shot-torn body, when he retrieved it by one dark, handlike paw, oozed blood and intestinal fluid. The reek of it, as he held his trophy aloft, reached her nose and for a moment she felt her stomach heave. It smelled almost as bad as the blood meal, which she now realized, almost sadly, she had shoveled in vain.

Mark's face was alight like that of a small boy—the sort who's just hit his first scratch single in Little League, she thought. He had been pacing the upstairs rooms as he pondered a color problem in his new painting and had noticed the woodchuck munching away in the garden. It was only the matter of a moment before he had taken his recently purchased shotgun from its case in their closet, fed in a few loads of heavy birdshot, eased open the unscreened window, and fired. "He ran a few steps and then rolled right over!" Mark said again and again. "Smacked him fair and square. I didn't want that son of a bitch ruining all your hard work in the garden, honey. Well, he's had his last free lunch, I guess. Now you know why they call it 'Mark's Manship.' "

She told Billy Munro about it next time she saw him, and about Mark's pride in his shooting.

"Kilt it with a shotgun, did he?" said Billy. "Scattergun shoots a wide pattern at that range. Could hardly've missed him. Also you ruin a lot of good meat that way." When she relayed this expert opinion to Mark, he grunted noncommittally, but at least he stopped bragging about his gunplay.

Worse, though, was the smell of the blood meal. It remained with her for days afterward. Even after she had washed her hands repeatedly, the deep, dark echo of old blood remained with her.

SIX

By the beginning of June, Laura realized that they had done the lion's share of the fix-up work on the house. The roof was mended, the chimneys repaired, the rotten clapboards replaced, the plumbing in leak-less good order. They had installed two brand new wood stoves to supplement the Dutch oven and heat the house through the winter without burning a drop of what Mark now called "that durned Ay-rab oil." The Eldridges had left what looked to be a good five cords of well-cured firewood stacked neatly in the shed beside the barn. Anything more they might need, they could buy from Billy Munro, or Mark could cut it himself (he insisted).

Laura realized as well that there was nothing left to delay having a baby. Nothing, that is, but a certain deep, internal reluctance: a fear, perhaps? Why not? All women must feel some trepidation at the thought of having their first child. A new experience, and much much more. A total commitment to a new life—both the child's and her own. And Mark's, too, for that matter. In a way she envied the girls she had known (at least three of them in high school alone) who had "gotten in trouble" or found themselves pregnant after marriage because of some carelessness with the Pill. It seemed so cold-blooded to say, okay, now we have another chore ahead of us to complete our new home. Let's make a baby. Yet if a woman were seriously to control her own life, she must control her own body first. It was only good, solid, liberated sense.

She made an appointment with Doc Peggs.

Doc's office was in his home, the only brick-built residence in town, a sturdy, four-squared structure in the Federal style. Tall shade trees and neatly trimmed shrubbery filled the yard and a neat brick walkway led to the front door, where a foot-worn paving stone bore the inscription: 1814. Doc answered her ring with his sky-blue smile and led her through a center hallway hung with austere etchings, past a room in which reposed what looked like a spinet, into his parlor-office. A tea service stood on an elegant oak sidetable and he poured for them from china as translucent as his dental work. Laura thought wryly of the Park Avenue gynecologist's office she had visited annually for her Pap test—the surly, contemptuous receptionist, the bored women waiting half an hour or more past their appointment time, the doctor himself who regarded her as just another sprawl of thigh: cold meat with fur around it.

Even as he asked her the routine questions—childhood diseases, personal habits, regularity of menstrual cycle, kind of birth-control pill she used—Doc Peggs kept up an easy, homey banter, commenting wryly about the town and the Vermont way of life. For all her urbanity Laura still hated those impersonally intimate internal examinations, the poking and probing of rubber-sheathed fingers into her most privy of orifices. Yet when Doc put her "up on the blocks," as he jokingly put it, and she lay helpless there with her feet in those ugly stirrups, like an upside-down horsewoman who'd dropped the reins, she felt fully at ease. Here, wonder of wonders, was a doctor who actually, warmly felt for her as a *person,* who knew her as Laura Avery, not just "the three o'clock appointment, and we're running a bit late, Doctor."

"Well," he said happily when they had finished, "you're in A-number-one shape, Laura. No reason why you shouldn't bear a healthy, full-term baby. Neither you nor your husband have any family history of, well, idiocy or birth defects, do you? No? Just Mark's allergy to strawberries, and that's his misfortune. No problem. Still, you're nearly thirty years old and you've spent a lot of time in cities. What with all those pollutants and the genetic damage they can do, even though you personally don't smoke or drink to excess, you might want me to run an amniocentesis on you once you *have* conceived. It's a simple test, just a sampling of amniotic fluid that can tell us whether the fetus by any remote chance has Downs syndrome—that's mongolism—or any of a wide range of possible birth defects. Not that I think for a moment it will. But better sure than sorry, as I always say."

"That's where you run a needle into the womb, isn't it?" Laura said hesitantly.

"Doesn't hurt a bit," Doc reassured her. " 'Course, I've never had one myself, ho ho, but I've done any number of them and never once knew a woman to so much as flinch. I can do it for you right here in my office. No need to drive clear to Rutland or Burlington. And the nice thing about it is, it tells you the sex of the baby as a kind of bonus. You can get a head start on the color scheme for your layette."

"I guess I don't want to know the sex beforehand," Laura said. "Makes it more of a surprise. A friend of mine in New York City, Judy Monkhouse, had the test and was told the baby would be a boy. She was delighted. But to me it'd seem too much like opening your birthday or Christmas presents a week early."

"Anticlimactic, yes. I can see that," Doc said. "So if you decide to do it, I won't tell you. I'll be the only one to know, once the lab results come in from Burlington, and I won't let on to a soul. Now then, where are we? The third of June, and you have four days' worth of pills left for this menstrual period. There's a strong rebound effect when you stop using them, so if you go off the pill as of the seventh, you should ovulate next on . . . let's see . . . the twenty-first of June. Two or three days bracketing that date would be the most likely time for you to conceive. I know it sounds a bit cold and heartless"—her very own words, Laura thought—"and it may take some of the wonderful spontaneity out of that most loving of human interactions, but then again it's calculation in the best of causes: the creation of another human being, who will be loved and cherished beyond price. There, that's my little sermon for the day."

As he ushered her toward the front door, Laura asked if she might look at the spinet in the drawing room. The delicately legged instrument glowed warmly with lemon oil; lace doilies and vases adorned its lid. As Doc sat at it, tinkling the keys in that tinny, old-timey sound, she noticed a painting hanging on a far wall. It was a portrait of the same woman whose likeness Laura had found in the attic: The Lady in Weird.

"Who's that striking woman?" she asked.

"Oh, that?" said Doc, rising from the keys. "That's old Cassie Eldridge Ashburn, the grandest dame the Gore ever produced. She grew up a humble farm girl in the very house where you're now living. But after she married Daniel Ashburn in the early 1800s, she came into her own. Founded Ashburn's sawmill and put the town on the map by producing some of the finest hardwood furniture and construction materials in New England. She and her son, Ahaz, really kept this town from going under once the sheep farming failed. In fact, if it weren't for the mill, Hubley's Gore today would be just a wide spot in the road, with long grass growing where we stand at this very moment."

"I found a painting of her up in the attic," Laura told him.

"You did?" Doc's eyes lit up with delight. "I'd like very much to see it. Town history is my true avocation —I'm writing a book about it, in fact. Between my many medical appointments, of course. Ha ha."

"Well," Laura smiled, "just drop by anytime, Doctor. Mark and I would be glad to show you what we've done with the house. And we're both very interested in history."

"Ah, history," Doc mused fondly. "The marvelous thing is we're all part of it, yet it never ends."

Rain marched into the hollow on thunder-booted feet, then settled down for a dreary, longish stay. Mark, always secretive about his artwork, remained secluded in his studio, emerging at the end of the day to flop flaccid and glassy-eyed in front of the television set they had reluctantly bought "to keep up with the news." He watched all manner of schlock—*Gilligan's Island* and *Batman* reruns, *I Love Lucy* and *The Honeymooners*—claiming that it allowed his mind to freewheel in the unconscious and thus solve in advance the next day's painting problems. Laura at first worried that the rain would reduce her burgeoning garden patch to a muck of limp, drowned groceries. But the plot was on a slight slope and drained readily: though her radishes went woody fast, the rest of the growth held on, doggedly awaiting the return of the sun.

When it did, finally, it brought Doc Peggs and Huldy Munro with it.

"Rise and shine, you slugabeds," called Huldy as she emerged from Doc's carefully restored 1937 Plymouth "woodie" station wagon. She carried the same wicker picnic basket she had brought on her first visit. "Me and Doc are gonna take a hike up into the Cauldron and have us a picnic. I figgered you two 'ud relish a bit of a outing, after all that rain, so I made enough food for all."

"That's very thoughtful," Mark said as he and Laura greeted them on the stoop. "But I'm in the middle of a painting right now, and I really—"

"All work and no play," Huldy broke in. "I won't hear of it, and the doc'll tell you that a little sunshine and woods music is the best tonic a body could have to keep the cree-yative juices a-flowin'. Right, Doc?"

"You bet," said the physician. "Surely you can afford a day off from your labors, Mr. Avery. A beautiful day like this!" He gestured around the valley, fresh-washed green and sweet with the smell of wet flowers. "And I had it in mind to show you a spectacular view from the Cauldron which I've always thought would make an ideal vantage point for a landscape painter."

"Oh, Mark, let's do it," Laura pleaded. "I've been feeling so cooped up."

"Well," Mark said, relenting, "it'll certainly be better than Gilligan, Ricky, Ed Norton and the Joker."

"Besides," added learned Doc, "it's Midsummer's Eve, and the ancients viewed this as one of the best-blest holidays on their calendar. We might do well, in these hedonistic, materialist times, to follow their example. 'Getting and spending, we lay waste our powers: . . .' as the poet so aptly said."

" 'Little we see in Nature that is ours; . . .' " Mark completed the couplet. "Let's do it."

They hiked up a path that flanked Cauldron Brook, which plashed and leaped rowdily from pool to crystalline pool in its headlong spill down the mountain. At one point they flushed a long gray-brown bird from a clump of young spruce. It rocketed away through the woods with a roar of wings that made Laura start.

"Ruffed grouse," said the Doc. "*Bonasa umbellus*. Also known as pa'tridge, woods pheasant, and, in the days of the market gunners, 'white-flesher,' for its succulent breast. I used to hunt them as a lad. Now I'd put them all back in trees if I could."

"I don't know," Mark said. "I plan to take a poke at them this fall, soon as the season starts."

"Hunting's a young man's game," Doc said. "The closer a man gets to the grave, the dearer he values his fellow creatures and the sadder he feels at taking their lives. Yet it's mighty fine sport, partridge hunting. They can walk your legs off for you—good for the ticker. I hope you're an accurate snapshot, though. They don't give you much time to aim, as you can see."

"I'm working on it," Mark answered. Laura was glad to see he didn't launch into another big brag about his marksmanship on the poor woodchuck.

Doc, leading the way, angled off the main path halfway up the Cauldron and took them into the deep woods. They were heading for the oak grove.

"Didn't you say the oak grove is dangerous?" Laura asked Huldy.

"Only if you're plannin' to cut in it," the old woman replied. "If you come peaceful-like, it's the most hospitable place on the mounting."

"I've been through it plenty of times, fishing the different brooks up here," Mark said. "No bogeyman so much as said boo."

Doc chuckled and kept on climbing.

A cool green light pervaded the grove, and as she entered it, Laura felt the same sense of austere, solemn sanctity she had felt in church that Sunday. The thick gray boles of the oaks rose like the pillars of some ancient cathedral. It was quiet: the birdsong that had surrounded them on their climb evaporated as they entered, and even the background babble of falling water was muted by the giant trees. The floor of the grove was parklike, grass and matted leaves and an occasional sapling soaring up where light penetrated the dense canopy overhead. There were not even the usual twigs and branches one might expect to find littering the ground. It was as if someone had policed the area only this morning. Perhaps the nymphs and dryads, she thought with a silent giggle. Still, it was passing strange. . . .

Suddenly Laura felt something crunch beneath her feet—a wet, crackly popping. Looking down, she caught her breath. Blood! The greenery was spattered with it. Had she cut herself? Then she looked more closely and saw that what appeared to be blood was actually the sap of a short-stalked wildflower, a myriad of them that covered the floor of the glade. She had crushed a few while walking.

"Bloodroot," said Doc, coming up silently beside her. "*Sanguinaria canadensis,* a member of the poppy family. When they bloom in the early spring, they produce a lovely white flower. They grow only in deep, rich, well-fertilized woods." He smiled his odd blue smile. "These woods are rich indeed, Laura, graced as they are today with your fair charms."

She stifled a giggle, yet his old-timey eloquence was somehow touching.

Doc led the way into a wider, more open place, almost a clearing, then halted as they caught up. Clearly they were meant to see and feel something here. He did not say a word. Then Laura saw the Bull Oak. It soared from the center of the open space like some giant gray arm of God, reaching gnarled fingers toward heaven. Its mass, its sheer size, its . . . density! She felt a momentary thrill run through her, as if she stood in the presence of something so old, so sentient, so awful in its majesty that it made her own life shrink to insignificance.

"My God!" she whispered.

Doc turned his head and smiled upon her: that wise, that luminous smile.

"What's this old foundation over here?" Mark asked. He had walked under the tree and was squatted beside a cellar hole that lay some yards away.

"Used to be a cabin stood here," Doc said, joining him. "Belonged to a woodcarver named Obediah Magrute, who came here in the early 1800s. Bit of a loner, he was. Or so they say." He grimaced. "Came to a sticky end."

In the center of the cellar hole rose a big stone pier, flat-topped and moss-grown, like some primitive altar.

"What's that structure in the center?" asked Laura.

"Oh, that's where the chimbley rose, kind of a footing for it, I guess." He walked up beside her to study it. Laura saw, on a stone near the top and center of the pier, a symbol scratched, or rather graven, in the rock. It was the same circle device with arms that marked the portrait of Cassie Eldridge Ashburn. She looked at Doc and he nodded.

"I'll tell you a story," he said. "Obed Magrute, as

I mentioned was something of a lone wolf. After he got here in 1809, nobody knows where from, he prowled these hills for a couple of years, looking for God only knows what. He apparently found it—peace, perhaps—in this ancient oak grove. Yes, it was ancient even then, more than a hundred fifty years ago. That big tree, what we call the Bull Oak, must be close to four hundred years of age: the daddy, granddaddy, and great-great-granddaddy of all these trees that surround it. How did Faulkner put it? 'Old Priam reft of his old wife and outlived all his sons.' Well, this land in those days belonged to Noah Eldridge, and Magrute bought these few acres from him. Built the cabin that once stood on these stones. Kept to himself, carving oak artifacts—mantelpieces, scythe snathes, and the like—and selling them in town. A harmless man. Until he met Noah's daughter, Cassie Eldridge—yes, that same Cassie you and I have paintings of. Obed loved her, wooed her, got her with child. But she refused to marry him, even though she was in that condition. He threatened her, pleaded with her, swore his life meant nothing without her. Yet she could not marry him. So, one night, he set fire to his cabin and burned himself up with it. End of tragedy. Cassie, of course, went on to become the savior of her town by starting the lucrative sawmill, the wood of which was cut in this grove and its outlying arms—in the town forest. Where it's still cut to this day."

"What about that symbol that's in her picture and also on that rock over there?"

"Oh, I expect some school kid carved that in there," Doc said offhandedly. "One of Ben Thorpe's youth group members. He often brings them up here for an outing, or to camp under the Bull Oak. I know it's your property, rightly, and I hope you don't mind the trespass. But the town has always felt that this grove was something special. The symbol itself is something Cassie's son and only child, Ahaz Ashburn, dreamed up. He was a very religious man, and founded the Church in the Wildwood down to town. Probably found the symbol in some old book or other. According to those who knew him—he didn't die until 1890, at the ripe old age of eighty-six—Ahaz always had his nose in a book."

"Ripe old age, my wrinkled ashplant," hooted Huldy. She had been spreading the picnic things on the greensward under the Bull Oak, and now she beamed at them with her toothless grin. "I'm durn near that old m'self, and I can still outhike and outclimb you, you old geezer. C'mon, dinner is served."

Cold chicken and baked ham; home-baked crusty bread; crisp and fiery radishes from the Munro garden; spiced apples, sweet pickles and mouth-puckering sour ones, and corn relish, coleslaw, cold soldier beans and "sparrow grass" in a vinegary sauce; all washed down with ice-cold fizzy cider from a gray stone jug: Huldy had done herself proud. "The sweet butter's of my own churnin'," she said proudly. "Keeps the shoulders strong and the tiddies firm. I'm a old lady that's proud of her figger."

For dessert she produced a compote of wild strawberries picked in her own meadow. Mark's allergy precluded his eating them, but Laura more than made up for his lapse. "What's in this besides the strawberries?" she asked as she worked on her third helping. "It's got kind of a liquory, herbal flavor—delicious!"

"That's my secret, Laura Avery," chuckled Huldy. "Mebbe if you're a real good girl to me, I might let you in on it in ten or twenty years."

"Well," said Doc, letting a notch out of his belt

buckle, "I think a leetle constitutional is in order. Best thing in the world for the digestion, and to keep the belly flat."

"You'd said something about a particularly beautiful view," Mark said. "I'd be interested in seeing it."

"No sooner said than done, my boy."

Laura, resting with her back against the bole of the Bull Oak, felt full and drowsy, almost as if she'd been doped. Once, on hashish, she'd felt this way. But no. She'd only overeaten—really pigged out, she chided herself—and doubted she could walk a hundred yards uphill without collapsing in her tracks.

"If you don't mind," she said, "I think I'll just stay here with the picnic things and guard our leftovers against bears, or whatever."

"And catch forty odd winks in the process." Huldy laughed. "You been workin' so hard, honey, that I reckon we can forgive you. Come on, fellers, I'll race you to the top of the Cauldron."

With a wave and a smile the three others set off up the mountain. They were hardly out of sight before Laura's eyes were closing involuntarily and she sank into a warm, wind-washed sleep. Her last image as she nodded off was of the thick branches of the Bull Oak spreading over her like giant arms, light glinting in a million mini-novas off the waxy green foliage above.

"Do you think you can do it?"

"Yes."

"You used to could do it, that I know. You used to could do it the best of anyone."

"Of anyone *you* knew, you wanton strumpet."

"Oh, get on with you. You know what I mean. But can you still?"

"I'd better. If I don't, we're all finished."

"She's a beauty, that's certain sure. Sometimes that can put a man off."

"Not me. I know I can do it."

"Then you better. What about tonight?"

"All set."

"How?"

"It's easy. So young."

"This is a good night for it. The only night for it, really. But a good night for it anyway. I can feel it."

"Yes. The timing is perfect, especially the moon."

"This is our last chance, I reckon. It's a shame the other didn't turn out."

"It's always a fifty-fifty chance. This one will work. I'll check on it along the way, and if it doesn't we can still move fast. Still save it."

"It better work. You sure you can do it?"

"I'm sure."

"Old."

"Yes, old. But not too. I tell you, I'm sure."

SEVEN

Laura woke with a start.

It was cold, and a thin breeze hissed through the leaves overhead like knives through tissue paper. The sun had disappeared behind the ridge to the west; only a pale purple line of fading daylight back-lit the hunch-backed top of Abednego Mountain across the way. As Laura clambered to her feet, her legs felt stiff, almost paralyzed. Where were the others? How long had she slept? It was too dark in the shadows to read her watch.

She walked stiffly around the Bull Oak, her legs feeling as if they were caked in heavy mud, the cold sparks of incipient panic kindling in her belly. Where was Mark? And Huldy and Doc? Had they fallen off a cliff somewhere up there in the rapidly thickening darkness? Were there avalanches in these mountains?

Something rustled in the brush ahead and to her right. A quick, scuttling scurry—probably just a rabbit, she reassured herself. Nonetheless she edged toward the opposite side of the Bull Oak, her eyes probing ineffectually the murky dark. The moon stood high overhead, pale and ethereal and almost at the full. It cast no shadows: the whole grove was shadow. Should she head home and call for help? To whom? Polly, or Ike Minter—the state police?

Her tongue felt dry and thick against her palate: thirsty, very thirsty. She picked up the stone jug of cider but the cork was stuck and she broke a fingernail trying to pull it. There wasn't much left anyway, judging by the weight of it and the minimal gurgle when she sloshed it back and forth.

From a tree to her left something flapped into a sudden, feathery roar—two dark shapes lined out and away into the night woods. Her heart leaped, then settled back to a rapid thudding. Ruffed grouse, she told herself. Like the one we flushed this morning—years ago! A pair of pa'tridges feeding on young acorns. I probably scared them worse than they scared me.

But her legs would not seem to warm with the walking; they remained stiff, heavy, slow. She walked and walked, in a big steady circle, pausing occasionally to listen for the sound of footsteps coming down the mountain. All she heard was the working of wind in the treetops, a sibilant, murmuring, muttering hiss.

"Lauuuuuuu-ra? Laura Pierce?"

She stopped short. The voice came from the inky black shadows just ahead. A low, hissing voice, like the wind on the ridges. She realized with a start that it had called her by her maiden name. Who . . .

"Laura Piersssssssssss?"

"Who is it?" Her own voice was cracked, dry with her overwhelming thirst. "Is that you, Mark? Doc? Huldy?"

"Over here, Laura. Lauraaaaaa?"

Soft, smooth, deep.

She found herself walking into the darker darkness at the edge of the grove. A figure stood, small and dense, among the trees. She should stop, run down the mountain, anything but walk forward like this. But her legs would not obey.

A short, skinny figure, wearing a baseball cap. Billy Munro? Something glinted near its feet, something hard and shiny: metallic.

"Who are you?" she croaked, her voice breaking. "Is that Billy? What do you want?"

"It's just me—Dolph," the voice whispered soothingly. "Just old Dolph Rooney. Do you have a light?"

"A light? What for?"

"I want to show you something, Laura. Lauraaaaa?"

Her hand numbly sought the metal match-safe in the breast pocket of her flannel shirt. Numbly she unscrewed the top and withdrew a sulfur-tipped match. She was close to the figure now, within arm's reach. The features under the bill of the baseball cap were dead black. Death black. She struck the match.

Light flared and guttered, enveloping them in a sulfurous halo. The deep-set eyes burned into hers.

"Did you ever," said Dolph Rooney, "see teeth like these?"

His gargoyle lips began to spread.

And spread.

And spread. . . .

Inside those lips, the curved and whirring teeth of a rusty chainsaw!

Laura screamed, screamed, screamed until her lungs were empty. Then she screamed again because she could not hear herself.

"Honey! Honey!" Someone shaking her by the shoulders. "Laura honey, wake up!"

Her eyes snapped open, unfocused and laden with panic. The blur in front of her hardened, refined itself as the shaking continued—it was Mark. She was sitting up in bed, shuddering in the welcome light of the reading lamp. Snug under the goose-down quilt, wrapped safely in her husband's warm, strong arms.

"Oh, Mark! Oh, my God—it was horrible, horrible!"

"Easy, honey," he said, hugging her tight to his nightshirt-flanneled chest. "Just take it easy. It was only a bad dream. Calm down now, baby." He kissed her wet forehead.

She pushed back from him and tried to smile. He looked gravely into her eyes.

"Tell me about it," he said flatly. "If you tell me about it, it'll go away. Won't it, my honey girl?" There was something hollow and hissing to his voice, an echo of the voice in her nightmare?

She told him the dream, disjointedly, in short, gasping sentences and phrases, confused now about the reality of the first part—the picnic on the mountain. How did she get back? Or had they gone at all? She came to the part about Dolph Rooney. And the gruesome, never-ending chainsaw smile.

Mark sat back from her, his shoulders hunched, his head moving out of the light and into the darkness. A sudden chill came over her again and she shivered.

"Teeth," Mark said. His voice was hollow as a grave. "You mean, like . . . these?"

This time, as the chainsaw whirred, she could not scream. . . .

And this time she awoke for real—she was sure of it. Yes, it was dark. Yes, cold. She was on the mountain, in the grove, under the Bull Oak. And there were footsteps coming down the mountain toward her. She could hear them crunch in the dry oak leaves. A tall, thin figure took shape in the darkness, paused as it studied her where she lay, immobile beneath the tree, then came on: it was Doc Peggs.

She could not speak. Could not move her lips. Only

stare up at him as he stood there, looming rakelike over her, leaning on a strangely carved staff, his head haloed in the silver fluff of his old man's hair, his eyes brighter than moonlight as they gazed deep into her own. Then he began to smile—no chainsaw this time, just those pallid, almost phosphorescent teeth, blue and glowing: a smile she would never forget. She felt paralyzed completely now, like a mouse before a snake. Doc knelt and began to undress her. Her head spun as his strong hands laid her naked, then turned her over, facedown on elbows and knees. She could feel his hands lifting her hips, then the push and slide of him entering her.

He's raping me, she thought. And I love it.

No—no! I hate it! I can't stand it! Yet . . .

I love it. He loves me. The Bull Oak . . .

She pushed her face deep into the cool grassy earth between the roots of the tree. Her nostrils filled with the dark, sweet, cloying odor of the earth—of blood meal, she realized distantly. An ugly smell, yet a good smell, rich, wild, and pagan. She lifted her face as he worked toward his climax. Stared up at the tree looming vast and dense ahead and above her. The rough bark seemed to stir as her passions churned: a shape began to emerge from the crenellated gray, a skull that slowly took on flesh: a strong, bearded, patriarchal face, the stern face of a prophet or a priest: then the beard fell away and she was staring at the features of a woman: The Lady in Weird—Cassie Eldridge. Which in turn was succeeded by another face, wild-eyed, fanatical, hell-driven—who?

And then as she slid down into a deeper darkness she saw Doc's face before her: Doc, serious, solemn almost, gentle of eye, watching, watching, watching. . . .

How she made her way down the mountain in the dark she never knew. All she could recall was her panic-stricken flight, the whip of branches on her face, the rip of flannel as briars tore at her shirt sleeves, falling and bruising her elbows, her knees. Halfway down she ran smack into them: Mark and Doc and Huldy. She fell weeping against Mark's chest.

It took a while to calm her.

Halfway up the mountain to the lookout, it seems, Doc had felt pains in his chest—a touch of angina, he said. Nothing serious. He would find his way back to the grove and wait for them while Mark and Huldy continued. But on the way down they had heard him calling from a thicket well off the path. He'd gotten "turned around," he said: the forest had changed since last he was up this high. It took them a long while to find him, and then they in turn had found themselves floundering in unfamiliar woods. They were only now back on the trail, heading up to retrieve Laura.

She heard the explanations in silence, her eyes flat as she watched Doc's face. But there was nothing there to confirm what she knew had happened—unless . . . Unless what? Unless it had all been a dream within a dream.

Yes, that must be it. She certainly didn't *feel* raped, not down there where it counted. Or did she? She couldn't tell, she was exhausted, sick at her stomach with fear, the panic only slowly ebbing away as she held Mark's hand tightly and they threaded their way down to the meadow and the house.

All the next day she felt low and edgy, unable to think coherently, as if she were recovering from an overdose of some heavy downer. She felt on the brink of tears. Then at dark on the twenty-second of June, staring out the kitchen window, she saw what looked like a bonfire flickering in the trees of the oak grove, high on the mountain. She went outside. From the distance came an ululating, keening sound, alternately deep-throated and high-pitched, as of voices chanting from the fire. An image flashed into her mind: of Obediah Magrute, writhing in the flames of a sacrificial funeral pyre.

She wept.

Then Mark was beside her, his arm around her shoulders.

"Coyotes," he said. "It's just coyotes howling. I've seen sign of them up there. The hills are full of them."

"It's not, though, you know," Laura sobbed. "It's something awful, something strange and evil up there. Some awful rite or sacrifice."

"Now, Laura . . ."

"Don't 'Laura' me," she snapped, suddenly raging. "Yesterday afternoon up there, I don't know what happened. I dreamed . . ." Could she tell him? She did. "I dreamed I was being raped. By Doc Peggs. First doped with that damned dessert of Huldy's and then raped by Doc."

Mark laughed aloud and held her at arm's length. "Now you are being silly," he said. "Doc was with us while you slept. And anyway the old geezer's too far gone to get it up, even for someone as delectable as you." She bristled at his insensitivity. "Look," he said, "maybe you're pregnant. Aren't pregnant women supposed to get kind of nutsy? Anyway, you've always been super-sensitive, and this is just another sign of it. Now calm down, honey."

At that moment the moon rose behind the shoulder of Widdershins: bulbous and red in its fullness. She felt herself suddenly grow calm again. Maybe Mark was right—maybe she was pregnant and imagining things. The moon must be what she'd mistaken for fire. Just the rising moon. She felt a shudder of relief sweep through her, and hugged Mark back as hard as she could.

But the dream . . . The dream. If she was indeed pregnant, maybe Mark wasn't the father. Maybe it was Doc?

The "coyotes" howled until midnight.

That was the night Jamie Lynette Boggs died.

BOOK TWO

Summer

ONE

"Sudden infant crib death," said Doc Peggs. "No one knows what causes it. Odd thing is, I'd been by the house that afternoon to look in on Polly, try to cheer her up some, and I'd given the baby a look-see. Perfect health as far as I could tell. Burbling and smiling to beat the band. Polly put her down for her nap about three. When she checked her at five thirty, she was . . . gone."

Laura had heard the news the following morning, from Huldy Munro. She was in the middle of baking some bread when the old woman called. Shocked and horrified, she had let the first two loaves burn beyond salvage, then pulled herself together and baked the rest to bring over on her condolence call that afternoon at the Boggs house. It was the custom in that country to bring food to bereaved families.

Doc answered the door when she and Mark pulled up in the barnyard. He took them aside to explain how the baby had died. Three townswomen Laura didn't know by name were just leaving, dowdy and solemn in outmoded summer frocks and too much makeup. In the gloom of the kitchen she saw Huldy busy at the stove, while the Boggs brood hunkered as usual around the television set, its volume mercifully reduced to a mutter.

"We just stopped by to see if there was anything we could do," Mark explained after saying "Hidy." "Laura baked some bread, you see, and I thought I'd go out and do some work on the woodpile, if that'd help."

"I'm sure Polly will appreciate it," Doc said. "Jermyn here will show you what needs to be done." He gestured to the gangling pre-teener who turned sullenly from the TV set. He and Mark went silently out the door. Laura swallowed hard and turned to Huldy.

"It's a four-grain bread," she said a little loudly, "white flour, whole wheat, rye, and oatmeal. We love it, and it's very healthful. . . ."

One of the children made a muffled yucching sound and the others tittered.

"Hush now, you younkers," Miz Munro said. "That's fine, jest fine, Laura," she continued. "It's about time these whelps got weaned off of Wonder Bread. Polly never took a shine to bakin'."

"How is she?" She asked the question quietly. The children's attention was riveted on the blue-green glow of the boob tube.

"Pretty depressed," said Doc. "She takes nourishment all right, and moves her, well, inwards quite regular, but she's yet to say a word about it, even to the children. In fact she hasn't talked at all since she called me last night."

"She'll snap out of it," Huldy said, stirring a flame-darkened pot full of savory stew. "Same thing happened to old Granma Talbot years ago when her youngest, Abel, fell under the harrow. You remember, Doc? Didn't talk nor budge from her bed for a month. Then one morning she snapped right out of it and was up fryin' doughnuts before dawn, singing to herself as if nothing had happened."

"I'd like to see her," Laura said.

"Well, I don't know," Doc said, worried. "She really ought to have quiet."

"She's always talked with me," Laura insisted. "Kind of like we were city sister and country sister. It would do her good, I'll bet, to have someone her own age to console her. Not that . . ."

"Mebbe she's right, Doc," said Huldy. "So long's you're in there with Laura in case Polly gets to, well, you know, babblin' or whatever?"

"Babbling or bawling, what difference does it make?" Laura was suddenly angry. It was as if these two were trying to keep her from her friend. Probably just their old-fashioned medical beliefs. "But the best thing for her would be to get the grief out of her system, not let it fester in there the way it did over her husband. I'm going in there." She brushed past Doc toward the corridor that led to the bedroom, but Doc grabbed her arm. He had an amazingly powerful grip.

"You're right, Laura," he said with sudden compassion. "But just let me go in first, to see how she's feeling and prepare the way." He picked up his black leather bag and preceded her into the corridor. Laura waited outside the bedroom. The smell of dirty diapers, suddenly poignant to her, still lingered in the hallway, and the Brothers Kennedy still glowed in the dark, with the Beatle Martyr grinning madly over their shoulders.

To hell with this, Laura thought. Who needs it? She pushed the bedroom door open and walked in. Doc rose hastily from a kneeling position beside the bed, a hypodermic needle in one hand and a dab of dripping cotton wool in the other. Polly lay bedraggled under a heavy quilt, her eyes focusing suddenly and hopefully on Laura.

"Oh, Laura, Laura!" she said in a drowsy voice. Her face knotted and her eyes filled with tears. "They took my baby!"

Laura knelt beside the bed and hugged her, looking up at Doc, who shook his head with weary mystification. Polly sobbed and wept, and Laura tried to comfort her. Then she slumped back on the pillow. Her eyes were glazing. She smiled weakly at Laura.

"Thanks for coming," she said in a near-whisper. "You don't have to bother going to the funeral. I'm not. Jamie Lynn won't be in the coffin."

"Now now, Polly," said Doc, chidingly. "You know I took her away last night for good medical reasons." Then to Laura: "She seems to think I made off with the baby for God only knows why." Then to Polly: "That shot I just gave you will make you feel much better, Polly. Your friend is here now and you can rest. She'll take care of the other children, and Pastor Thorpe will be here soon to take them down to his house for the night. You just relax now. . . ."

Polly, with sudden strength, pulled Laura's head down close to her mouth. Her eyes were sly and yet fearful at the same time. "Laura," she whispered, "don't believe him. He killed her. I know it." She pushed Laura away and smiled shrewdly, nodding and nodding until her eyes began to close. Then she eased back into the pillow and began to snore. Doc ushered her out of the door and closed it quietly behind him.

"She's a little paranoid," he said when they got back to the kitchen. "Not surprising for a woman who's lost both a husband and a baby in the space of three months. But at least she's talking now. That's a good sign. The paranoia will ease as I wean her back off of the sedative and I reckon in a week or two she'll be good as new."

Laura wondered.

* * *

"I agree with Doc," said Mark. "Sure, Polly's going crackers. She's had a hell of a jolt. And he had to take the baby's body away for fear that whatever disease it had might infect the other children. Polly, in her grief, saw it as a kidnaping. The human mind is extremely reluctant to admit the death of a loved one. That's her defense mechanism, is all."

"I guess you're right," Laura said, "but I'd still like to know what's in there."

They were standing in a small group of mourners—Doc, Huldy, Dolph Rooney in a moth-eaten, 1940s pin-stripe suit with hugely padded shoulders and pegged trousers, a regular bebop outfit, and a few people they didn't recognize by name—at the edge of a freshly dug grave in the Hubley's Gore cemetery. Laura was looking at the tiny coffin that contained the mortal remains of Jamie Lynette Boggs. Or did it?

Of course it does, she chided herself. Don't be nutsy. You'd be acting crazier than Polly if someone you loved died so suddenly, Mark for instance, or a newborn baby. She shuddered at the thought. Polly, as she'd said, was not there. But the Boggs children stood, bored and fidgety in their Sunday-go-to-meetin' clothes, listening to Pastor Thorpe deliver a meaningless eulogy. Laura noticed Ike Minter in the crowd as well. He too looked infinitely bored, as if the burial of an infant was as routine a matter in the Gore as another delivery from the Genesee Beer truck.

Even Mark was paying more attention to the surroundings, human and funereal, than to the solemn matter at hand. His artist's eye, she thought bitterly. What a blessing it must be—an automatic out from feeling unpleasant emotions. Just shift into objective gear. For a moment she hated him and his inhuman objectivity. As if it was going to produce his equivalent of Goya's *Los Desastres de la Guerra* or something. Then she relented: After all, it *was* a compellingly poignant scene—the old time-worn gravestones tilted this way and that by decades, no, centuries of frost; the lush summer trees blooming green and indifferent in the background; the thin white spire of the church, the red-cheeked children, the lined, work-warped faces of the elderly; the preacher pontificating over so mortal, so human a loss, as if words and rites could help. The cheap and tiny coffin. Maybe it *was* a painting.

"Norman Rockwell with balls," Mark said as they were driving home. "I'm going to paint it. Death in life." He was very excited, pounding his palms on the truck's steering wheel as he drove. "Did you see the light, the geometry of it? Spire and headstones, blooms and wrinkles? I don't even know if I'll have the coffin in it—too sentimental, maybe. But implied, you know? By the angles and the shadows, the whites and greens and yellows against the dark grays. It could be the big one, honey." He hissed through clenched teeth. "If I can just catch the sense of time, the fangs of frost waiting down in the rich brown earth, the worms and the swoop of it. . . ."

He had tears in his eyes.

And she loved him again.

There was always someone else present when Laura visited Polly Boggs. Usually it was Huldy or Billy Munro, but sometimes Pastor Thorpe, the Pastor's mousey wife Meredith (queenpin of the sewing circle), Liz Markham (a peppy, gum-popping blonde, wife of the town constable and distaff driver of the school bus), Sibyl Mortimer (town librarian, neo-Hitlerian book-banner and Chatty Cathy lookalike) or even Doc Peggs and his sidekick, Dad Sweet, chief of the Hubley's Gore Volunteer Fire Department. Dad was portly, dim, and possessed of a belly-bouncing cackle—especially when he "kinged" Doc in their never-ending checkers games —that would have done justice to Edgar Buchanan on *Petticoat Junction* (a new Mark Avery discovery in the ongoing war against postpainting blues).

"Busybodies!" Laura complained after these visits. "I can't talk to Polly without someone looking on solemnly over my shoulder, as if I might say something that would turn her into a pumpkin."

"Look, it's the country way," Mark would reply reasonably. "In these rural communities people look after each other. Ask Bill McGregor about it. It's the social cement of a frontier society, where in the nineteenth century people lived miles apart, far from any help but what they could offer one another. It's of a piece with quilting bees and barn raisings and movements like the Grange, which fought off the railroad and timber barons and the gunslinging Cattlemen's Associations."

"Yeah," said Laura, "and of witch hunts and vigilante justice as well."

"Can't have everything," Mark said.

What was more frightening to Laura, on the few occasions she did manage to get Polly alone, her friend was so heavily drugged she was almost incoherent. One afternoon when Billy Munro had "the duty," she prevailed on Mark to call the Boggs house after she got there and engage Billy in a long technical discussion on the merits and drawbacks of various chainsaw models. Mark was delighted to abet her: he had finally overcome (he thought) Laura's resistance to his purchase of a saw.

As Billy's attention disappeared into the Dismal Swamp of abstruse weight-to-chain-speed ratios and Stihl versus McCulloch, Laura slipped quietly out of the kitchen. She found Polly in a small side bedroom no bigger than an outsized closet—the baby's room—rocking listlessly in a tiny chair stenciled with bunny rabbits and "Smile" symbols. She was staring at the empty crib.

An open pad of cheap manila paper, probably belonging to one of the older kids, lay on her lap, and in her right hand she held a red Crayola, the butt end of which was chewed ragged. Her lips looked makeup-bright. There were red smears as well on the neck of the square bottle, half empty, that stood on the floor near her feet. The label read "Old Duke White Grape Wine" and it had been bottled in Canandaigua, New York. Judging by Polly's breath when Laura bent to kiss her, it had not been a good vintage year.

"Care for a sip?" Polly asked with an askew smile. "I can ask you that without feeling embarrassed. Nowadays it's downright upright." She giggled brightly.

"Polly, you shouldn't be drinking on top of those pills you're taking," Laura scolded. "You could . . . hurt yourself that way."

"So what? They're gonna get me anyways." She took a deep swallow from the bottle.

"Oh, Polly! Nobody's going to do anything to you. Everyone is very concerned for you. They just want to help."

"Then why did they switch the cribs?" She stared at the crib in front of her. From one chipped end a pop-eyed clown stared back.

"What do you mean? That's the same crib it's always been."

"Like heck it is, Laura! The night that . . . The night it . . ." She took another slug of Old Duke. "The night I found her, there was a special mark on the crib. Right next to the clown's head. It's not there anymore."

"A special mark?"

"Like this." Polly turned back the blank page in the sketch pad. On the previous page, waxy red as new-spilled blood, she had drawn the symbol:

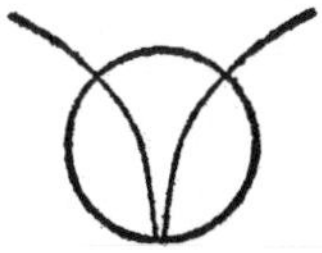

Laura stared at it for a long, a week-long minute.

"That's just the sign they use in Pastor Thorpe's church," she said finally. "There's nothing special about it, really. You must have imagined it once you saw that Jamie Lynn was . . ."

Big fat tears welled instantly in Polly's blear eyes, hung shivering for a moment, then spilled down her pale cheeks. Laura noticed she had zits at each corner of her crayon-smeared mouth. Of course, Laura thought wildly, when Polly realized the baby was dead, her mind flashed immediately to the church, and to the funeral that would have to take place. Of Ben Thorpe in his surplice and stole marked with the symbol of the Church of the Wildwood. And in that very instant Polly must have freaked out.

Comforting Polly with hugs and murmurs, Laura caught movement out of the corner of her vision. Billy Munro stood leaning in the bedroom doorway.

"She hadn't oughter be drinkin' that wine," he said solemnly. "That there wine ain't good for her, Doc says. You hadn't oughter of brung it, Miz Avery."

As Laura fulminated and denied, Billy crossed the room, grabbed up the bottle and Polly's sketch pad, and retreated to the kitchen. Laura led Polly to her bedroom and tucked her in. Polly fell asleep as soon as her head hit the malodorous pillow.

"You ought to change that linen in there the next time she's up and around," Laura snapped as she blew through the kitchen toward the back door. "And I *didn't* bring her that wine."

"Sorry, Miz Avery," said Billy.

The next day when Laura called the house, the operator came on the line to say that the phone had been disconnected.

TWO

As in most New England communities the Fourth of July in Hubley's Gore was the biggest, noisiest, gaudiest holiday of the year. Marching bands and volunteer fire companies, replete with old-timey engines, came from neighboring towns, some as far away as the Berkshire Hills of Massachusetts, to take part in the big parade. Latter-day Green Mountain Boys polished their muzzle-loaders, replenished their horns of black powder, and patched the moth holes in their fringed, green-dyed "buckskins" (actually store-bought cotton). Local organizations from the Four-H Club through the Men's Choir & Down-Home Shitkicker Band to the Women's Sewing Circle prepared floats and display booths. There would be a pie-eating contest, a greased-pole climb, a livestock show, and competitions for the best preserves, relishes, bakery goods, and home-grown vegetables in the Gore. The *pièce de résistance* of the day would be a whole roast ox, contributed this year by Bobby Morton, the town's biggest and only successful dairy farmer, who also fattened beef critters as a sideline. Wives throughout town did their bit with accompanying dishes:

breads and rolls, slaws and salads, casseroles and condiments, and a quarter acre of fresh-baked fruit pies. Laura, at Huldy Munro's request, contributed half a dozen loaves of her four-grain bread. She wondered how much of it would be eaten.

As far as Laura could tell, most of the men in town donated little more to the big day than a lot of organizational advice and a group effort at growing chin whiskers—an old tradition in the Gore. Mark's beard, after a slow start, came in full, dark, and sleek as a prime otter pelt.

"My God," she exclaimed on the morning of the fourth as he came into the kitchen, "you look like Ivan the Grungible!"

"I don't know," he said with mock vanity, "I thought it made me look like a younger, tougher Hemingway." He posed before the oval mirror at the foot of the stairway and mustered his sternest Ernest. *"Il faut, d'abord, durer,"* he gritted through clenched teeth.

"Il faut, après tout, shaver," she laughed. "As soon as it's over, that is. I think you stand a good chance of winning the L'il Beaver contest hands—or jowls—down."

It occurred to Laura that in many more ways than she, he had really become part of the town and in truth she wasn't sure how she felt about that.

The day was cool as they left the house, but the cloudless sky, without a breath of wind, promised a scorcher before it ended, Laura thought. (Later she would recall the cliché and regret it.) They stopped at Polly's on the way down the mountain, hoping she would feel well enough to accompany them to the festivities. Getting back out into the world, even so small a one as the Gore, would be the first step to recovery, they both agreed. Doc's wood-sided Plymouth wagon—

"his Plywoodie," Mark called it—stood in the barnyard as they pulled in.

"I really don't think she should go," Doc said when they came into the kitchen. "She's resting now. All the excitement, the music and firecrackers and kids playing, the women with babies in their arms—it would be too much for her. The kids are with Ben Thorpe, and Billy Munro said he'd look in during the afternoon. Unfortunately I won't be able to. I have to judge the floats in the parade—part of my civic duty as senior selectman."

"It's chilly in here," Laura said, wrapping her arms across her chest. "This is the coldest house I've ever been in. The Fourth of July and frost on the draperies."

"It's all those shade trees planted around the house, especially the old 'husband and wife' trees at the corners," Doc said. "Maybe we'd best start a little fire in the stove to take the chill off."

"What happened to her woodpile?" Mark asked. "It's practically gone. A week or so ago when I was over here, she must have had four cords out there."

"Had to sell it," Doc said sadly. "She's fast running out of money. Jim's workman's comp from the job he had at the mill didn't cover his accident up here, and her Social Security check is hardly enough for them to eat on. If it weren't for you kind friends and neighbors . . ."

"She should sell the place and move back with her folks in Shrewsbury," Laura said.

"They're too crowded and poor to have her," Doc said. "Anyway, she couldn't handle an uprooting like that right now. As to firewood, I brought a load up in the back of my station wagon. Good, long-burning, well-cured oak. Maybe Mark could help me bring it in and we'll get a fire started."

While the men went out to the yard, Laura looked into Polly's bedroom. She lay death-quiet under the heavy patchwork quilt, but her eyes were open. She was staring blankly into a far, dim corner of the bedroom.

"Hi, Laura," she said when Laura sat down on the edge of the bed. "Did you see what Ike Minter brought me?" She pointed listlessly to the dresser against the wall, but her eyes stayed fixed in the corner, her voice flat and lifeless. On the dresser stood a new Sony casette player and a stack of tapes.

"Oh, how nice!" Laura said. "Have you been listening? Is there anything I can put on for you? Look—you've got Buddy Holly and Little Richard and Elvis and *Sergeant Pepper*. . . ."

"Yeah." Polly tried to laugh. "Classical music, my kids call it. Oh, shit." She started to weep. "The first time I heard the Beatles was with Jimmy. At the prom, my junior year. I got drunk on white wine spritzers and Butchie Bellhouser had some pot that we smoked out back of the gym, and I threw up on my party shoes but Jimmy he didn't care, he said he loved me, and we went in the back of the car out there in the parking lot and he made love to me, the first time it was, too, no matter what the other girls thought . . . and when we went back in they were playing 'Yellow Submarine' on the juke and I just stood there in my pukey shoes feeling so happy, Laura, so spread out and thinned out and happy with Jimmy's arm around me, just smiling there in the music, Laura, in the town where I was born. . . ."

Her eyes snapped out of the corner and into focus, burning into Laura's own.

"They're going to kill me, Laura. Now! Tonight! I know it. I can feel it. Sometimes I can hear them talking about it, through the windows and the floor overhead, and sometimes out of the toilet at night."

"Polly . . ."

"And you too, Laura. They're going to kill you too. And Mark. And if you have a baby, they're going to kill it worst of all. The woods, Laura, the woo-uds!" She sobbed in great, racking jolts like someone hauling boots out of deep spring mud. "They kill outsiders. Every one."

"Polly, please. . . ."

Doc came into the room with his black bag.

"You'd better go into the kitchen, Laura," he said. He unbuckled the bag. Laura saw him reach for the hypodermic.

Mark had a good pile of oak stowed in the woodbox and a fire crackling in the stove. Laura checked it, fed a few more split sticks into the blaze, and closed the stove door. She dogged the handle down tight and set the adjustable draft dial at three—enough for a good, long burn, enough to warm the house up for the rest of the day and the night as well. Doc came out and said Polly was asleep.

They followed him down the hill into town and the carnival.

Where they had a marvelous time. They ate cotton candy and home-stuffed kielbasa and sipped white lightning from a jug Dolph Rooney kept chilling in the brook behind the big field near the firehouse where the fair took place. The Green Mountain Boys let Mark fire their muzzle-loaders—great whooshing roars of slow, white, sulfurous smoke—and Laura almost won the egg toss for women, teaming with Huldy Munro and going out only at twenty-two yards with yolk on her Olof Daughters clogs. Mark entered the greased-pole climb, stripping to the waist and wearing an outsized set of Oshkosh B'Gosh bib overalls loaned him by Chub Markham, the town's burly constable. But he got only halfway up the pole before he lost traction, skidding and scrabbling back down like a distraught gibbon. So Laura put on the overalls—lots of laughs and applause from the crowd—and made it to the top. She finished third among the women, beaten out only by the anthropoidal Minter twins, Ilona and Ramona, Ike's nieces. Her prize was a real medal, inscribed with the date and the event, that hung from a red, white, and blue ribbon. It was the first thing she had ever won, athletically or otherwise.

"Talk about hot monkey love." Mark laughed, his cheeks flushed under his beard. "You take the cake, baby! Christ this is fun! It's better even than that Feast of San Rocco down in the Village. Or is it San Gennaro? I can't keep those guinea saints straight, by Gaw-ud!"

He's even starting to talk like a Vermonter, Laura thought.

There was contra-dancing as well, to the lively music of a string band called Applejack from across the state. Laura was fascinated by one of the girl fiddlers, a long-haired honey blonde with wire-rimmed glasses whose stern and serious mien provided a perfect visual counterpoint to the peppy, infectious strains of the Irish jigs, reels, and hornpipes the group played. While Mark went back to the truck for his sketch pad, Doc Peggs asked her to dance.

He must have stopped at home to change, for now instead of his customary vested suit and bow tie he was wearing casual clothes: Wellington boots, tan corduroy jeans, a clean but faded chambray shirt held at the throat by a black string tie with horn clasp, and a buckskin vest with horn buttons. On his long head perched a wide-brimmed panama straw with a pheasant feather band. He bowed to her in a courtly manner, smiling naughtily, and they launched into a schottische.

My how the good doctor could dance! Back and

forth they stormed and turned, stomping and spinning to the music, Doc as vigorous as a frisky twenty-year-old, with all eyes on them as they went. At each turn and stop Laura could see the eyes of the blond girl fiddler fixed on hers: she did not smile, even when Laura waved gaily to her and laughed. Then the band shifted gears into a slow country waltz and they kept on dancing, Doc very proper now, almost *fin de siècle* Viennese in his whirling precision.

"You're a marvelous dancer," Laura said. "Since the Frug came in, Mark absolutely refuses to dance."

"Oh, I've tripped the light fantastic toe a few times in my day," said Doc. "Anytime you feel the need of a partner, just look me up. There's nothing I enjoy more than to put my arms around a lovely, lissome lady of surpassing grace such as you, my dear. And in public, to boot!"

"Thank you, kind sir," Laura laughed. "You know, I had . . ." She stopped.

"What?"

"Oh, nothing. Just I had a dream about you the other day." She felt herself blushing and moved her head in closer to his chest so he wouldn't see.

"A nice one, I hope. Nothing cold and clinical and obstetric in nature?"

"Oh, no, just a plain old dream. I can't even remember the details, except that you were in it." It was a harmless lie.

The waltz ended and he held her away from him at arm's length, smiling down at her with a warm, almost a loving twinkle in his eyes. In this summer light they looked more green than blue. He was a handsome man, sure enough. She wondered why he had never married. Could he be gay?

"I was married once," he said as if reading her mind again. "To a girl very much like you, in appearance at least. I loved her very dearly in the short sweet time we had together. Unfortunately she was taken from me in her twenty-fourth year. Those were the days before antibiotics."

"I'm so sorry."

"Enough *tristesse,*" he said emphatically. "This is a day of joy! Our mighty nation's birthday—long may she live! May I offer you some sippin' whiskey, Laura my love?" He produced a hammered silver flask from the inside pocket of his vest. Mark joined them and they toasted the Lady Liberty, Tom Jefferson, Sam Adams, and finally, at Doc's behest, Captain Daniel Shays.

"You know," Doc said, wiping his lips with a red bandanna, "Captain Shays and some of his supporters in the failed rebellion ended up here in Vermont, not far away, actually. Up in the town of Sandgate. He and his men were opposed to high taxes, high government salaries, and banks and lawyers generally."

"A shame he's not alive today," Mark said. "He'd have quite a following."

They walked over into the shade where two-man teams were competing in a sawing and log-splitting contest. They used old-fashioned, two-man crosscut saws rather than chainsaws, then picked up heavy splitting mauls to whack what they'd sawn into stove chunks. A judge rated them in both evolutions. Doc suggested that he and Mark team up.

"I don't know beans about this stuff," Mark said. "Yet."

"No time like the present to learn," said Doc. "On the sawing you just bring the saw back to you as straight as you can. Don't push when I pull or the blade will buckle and we'll lose time. Leave the power strokes to me."

They took their places and Doc stripped off his vest. He placed his straw hat on Laura's head, then rolled up his sleeves. She could see that he had tattoos on either forearm but couldn't make out the pattern. The judge gave the signal and they began sawing. A crowd of townsfolk had gathered and cheered them on. Once again Doc's vigor denied his age: the sawdust fell like the blizzard of '88 (as Huldy put it aloud to the multitude) and when the cuts had been completed, they had the best score of the afternoon so far, on the sawing segment at least. Now each man had to split one of the two-foot-long logs they had sawn. The wood was oak from the town forest—cousins to the wood in their own oak grove—and it was both green and knotty, ten inches across at the butt ends.

"This is the tricky part," Doc said. "You have to find the fatal crevice in the face of the log, the crack that runs clear through the piece. Hit it smack on with your hammer, and she'll go." He pointed out the cracks on both logs that he felt would work best.

"Best mark so far is three hammer blows for the two logs," said the judge.

"I'll take my log first," said Mark. He stepped back, spat on his hands, then hefted the eight-pound maul. He narrowed his eyes, sighting in on the crevice, then swung—and missed the log entirely.

"One," said the judge.

Mark lined up again, shook his shoulders, lifted, and swung. This time the cutting edge of the maul bit into the log face—but a good two inches from the "fatal crevice."

"Two," said the judge. "You cain't win now, not on the splitting leastways. Four strokes between you and you'll tie for the lead, sawing and splitting combined."

"Leave your maul in the wood," Doc ordered. "I'll free you and split it at the same time." He reversed his maul so that the flat, hammerhead side was downward, then with blurring speed swung and hit Mark's hammer end with a tremendous clank. The log flew apart. The crowd applauded.

"Three," said the judge.

Doc turned on his heels, took a quick look at his own log, then blurred the hammer again, cutting edge downward. There came a whacking popping sound and the second log lay severed on the grass.

"Hooray for Doc Peggs!" the crowd huzzahed. "King of the Woo-uds!"

They celebrated with more of Doc's whiskey. By the time the sun was sloping redly toward New York and the ox had been pronounced roasted, Laura was woozy with sun and hooch and the unaccustomed crush of people, people, people. In the city she had hardly noticed the presence of humanity on all sides. Now, after scarcely three months in Vermont, a crowd of less than a thousand felt like Yankee Stadium with a rock concert in progress.

After they ate—the beef was delicious, blood red, and marbled; at least a dozen townsmen came up to congratulate her on her bread—they watched the parade roll past: antique cars and fire engines; sewing-circle ladies in Colonial costume; marching bands playing patriotic tunes; Four-H Clubbers leading sweet-smelling, spotlessly clean heifers, sheep, milch goats, and huge white idiotic-looking turkeys; even a float from the church on which stood Pastor Thorpe in his clerical garb under a papier-mâché oak tree while the men's choir chanted hymns and country music. Then came the fireworks.

"Ooooooooooh!" and "Ahhhhhhhhhhh!" went the crowd as the rockets soared and burst. . . .

In her airless bedroom Polly Boggs lay dreaming. She was in Vietnam with Jim. They were hiding from something—the Viet Cong? It was terribly hot. She was soaking with sweat. . . .

"Ahhhhhhhhh!" and "Ooooooooh!" went the crowd. This one was red and white!

The stove in the kitchen glowed red hot. A guttural roar echoed up the stovepipe. Beads of melting creosote oozed from the joints in the pipe. The smell of it filled the kitchen. Polly dreamed that jets were passing overhead. They were spraying something foul and poisonous on the jungle canopy. She and Jim cowered deeper into the wet, hot undergrowth. . . .

"Ahhhhhhhhhh! Did you see that one?" The crack and crackle of the fireworks rolled out to the wooded hills, then returned in a muffled roar as the false stars novaed close overhead. . . .

Polly and Jim were running now, running through the swampy forests of Asia. She could hear popping noises—gunfire? She tripped and fell, and lost her grip on Jim's hand. She couldn't get back to her feet.

In the kitchen the handle on the stove door began slowly to turn. The draft control clicked up from the nearly closed position at which Laura had left it and inched its way toward wide open. Creosote dripped fat and black and boiling hot onto the stovetop, to sizzle and smolder there, filling the room with a burnt-tar stink. . . .

Bam! Bam! Bambambam! Big bursting flowers painted momentarily against the velvet blackness. Green and blue and fiery orange! The kids squealed in fearful delight. . . .

The stove door swung open, slowly, glowing, its hinges silent under the rising roar from the stovepipe and the chimney flue. The stove's square mouth was filled with flaming red teeth, translucent coals so hot they were shading toward white. Waves of heat rolled up from the stove top, out in billows from its pulsing sides. The linoleum around the brick hearth began to soften and melt. Polly looked up from the jungle mud. Over her towered a huge tree. A massive, gray-barked tree with crooked, threatening limbs. The big oak, it was—the Bull Oak from the Woo-uds. . . .

They were firing volleys now—starbursts and cannon flashes, screaming meemies and repeaters, a flaming, corruscating barrage of fierce beauty that turned night to day. . . .

Blazing coals spilled out of the stove's mouth, onto the wide ash lip, then down onto the hearth. And more kept coming. It was as if the fire, in burning, were actually growing: as if more fuel were appearing and igniting inside the box even as it grew hotter. A regular river of fire now cascaded onto the hearth bricks, piling and spilling finally onto the already preheated linoleum. Flame crept across the floor, accelerating as it went, then began to climb the flimsy wooden walls. At the same instant the chimney fire ignited. The sound of jet engines filled the house. Flames shot high into the sky from the chimney top.

In her bedroom Polly Boggs finally awoke. . . .

THREE

It was Laura who spotted the glow as they drove up the hollow toward home. At first she thought it was just another brilliant moonrise, until she remembered that they were now in the dark of the new moon. The glow danced and flared behind the trees of the ridgeline: red and yellow and a pale, eerie loom of blue-green.

"My God!" she yelled as it dawned on her. "It's a fire! A big one! Polly's house is on fire!"

Mark speeded up, whipping the truck through turns that got them sideways at times, the gravel of the road-bed rattling against the truck's belly bash plate.

"Her phone's disconnected," he said tensely. "I'll jump out at the driveway and run up there. You head on home and call the fire department. Then get back down here fast as you can. The number is pinned to the paneling right next to the kitchen phone."

He skidded to a halt and leaped out, disappeared with long strides up the dark driveway—up toward the ballooning flames whose roar and crackle filled Laura's ears. She fumbled the truck into gear, stalled it, re-started, and sped up the hill. Her mind was blank confusion. Calm down, calm down, she ordered herself. Think clearly now. She felt confused, spinning with the same nightmare disorientation she'd felt up on the mountain, the day of the picnic—and the dream. Get a hold of yourself, you silly thing. . . .

The phone number was where Mark had said it would be. But the fire emergency number just rang and rang.

"Damnit! Where are you? Answer you bastards, answer. . . ."

On about the thirtieth ring Dad Sweet's voice came on, cranky and slurred from too much of Doc's whiskey.

"Dad, it's Laura Avery. The Boggs house is on fire. Blazing! Mark's up there now. Please, please hurry."

"Boggs," he said, suddenly sober. "Got it. We're on the way."

As Laura raced back down the hollow, she could hear the big fire siren hooting down in town. It added to the nightmare feeling: she wanted to keep speeding down the mountain, turn south and head for the safety of New York. The safety of calm, quiet Bill McGregor. Instead, she wheeled up into the drive, crashing through bushes on the roadside, bouncing so high on one pothole that her head clanked against the cab roof. The sickening hot fire smell filled her nostrils—the breath of some dreadful dragon—and she could feel the pulse of the heat against her face through the open truck windows. Flame and shadow writhed together, an obscene dance of light and doom. At any moment she expected to see a grim figure coalesce from the flames—Dolph Rooney? Or maybe Doc? The whole house was engulfed, she could see as she stopped in the barnyard. Too bright to look at directly: it hurt her eyes. Where was Mark?

Roofing slates popped and exploded, sending sharp shards of hot stone whirling down into the barnyard. She saw the kitchen window glowing white-hot, bulging inward like a blind, fire-filled eyeball. Then it too exploded, a slow spinning white wave of glass that starred and fragmented as it burst. She ducked behind the protective hood of the truck.

Where was Mark? Polly? Oh, God—in there? Her heart seized, then pounded madly. Her lungs felt on fire. Mark!

And then she saw them, the nightmare shapes of her dream state: two figures near the blazing side of the house, one flat on the ground, facedown, the other standing over it. Something that held an ax!

It was Mark on the ground.

And Dolph Rooney bending over him now, axhead glinting in the flames.

She ran toward them.

"Easy, Miz Avery, easy!" Dolph ordered as she piled onto him. He fought her off and dropped the ax to pin her arms at her sides. His face writhed red in the firelight. "I had to coldcock him to keep him from going in the house. Just a tap on the bean, that's all. He's coming around."

Dolph released her and bent over to grab Mark under the shoulders. Together they dragged him, groaning, away from the falling, flaming debris. Then the fire truck arrived, its siren drowned under the scream of burning timber.

"Polly!" Laura screamed. "Where's Polly?"

At that moment a figure appeared at the upstairs window—Polly! Her hair a halo of flame. Her eyes, mad and fire red, locked on Laura's. Then Polly screamed, long and lorn and loveless.

Just then the roof fell in. . . .

"I wish we could have avoided it."

"But we couldn't. She was talking too much. She was scaring Laura."

"Still, such a waste."

"It was that, now, or waste the whole thing."

"I guess so, but still . . ."

"We had to."

"What do we do now for September? It was her turn."

"We'll figure something out. Somebody must know someone."

"Still, it's such a shame we couldn't avoid it."

"I suppose so. But we couldn't, could we?"

"No."

Laura could not bring herself to attend the funeral. Mark went alone and made her apologies to the Boggs children. They stared at him blankly. Then they went off with Pastor and Mrs. Thorpe, who said they were considering adoption.

Laura sat all day in the living room with a book in her lap, but she could not read. At night in bed, when Mark tried to love her, she lay quiet, passive, lost in cold thought. She knew she was hurting him but she could not respond. He lost himself in his painting. For more than a week she was quiet, dry-eyed, remote. Then one afternoon she went into the garden and began to weep. She wept all afternoon, until Mark saw her and came out, and when he took her in his arms, she hugged him fiercely and they made love in the lettuce rows. It was only then that she realized her period was a week late.

"Yes," Doc Peggs said later that week. "It's for sure, Laura. You are officially with child." He smiled broadly, eyes twinkling in hopes of kindling some joy in her. It was as if he were the grandfather, she thought with a little sting of resentment. Then she corrected herself: I should be grateful that he cares.

"Well," she said finally, "at least I have that." He gave her a hurt look.

"Laura, you're taking Polly's passing way too hard," he said softly. "I know it was awful, God-awful, and that the two of you had grown quite close. But accidents like this happen all the time in the country. You mustn't let it get to you so. Especially now, with the baby coming."

"Oh, Doc," she said, feeling the tears well. "I'm the one who put the last wood in the stove that day. The firemen say the door on the stove came open and that's what started the fire." She felt the tears grow into sobs. "I'm the one. . . . I killed her."

"Nonsense, nonsense. Who told you that? Dim old Dad Sweet? He should know better. It was a chimney fire that ignited the house. Not the stove. I swear to you. She'd let too much creosote build up in the flue. It happens all the time in wood-burning country. Now I want you to forget this business—get it clear out of your head. You're a strong, sensible woman from what I've seen of you. If you keep thinking and feeling that way, you're just betraying yourself—and much more importantly at a time like this, the life you're now carrying within you."

And so he calmed and cajoled her and she came back into her life, out of the dark hole she had dug for herself deep, deep in her soul. Except . . .

Toward the end of the month Billy Munro showed up on his rickety Case tractor to mow the Averys' meadow. All afternoon he circled and circled through the fields, his baseball cap cocked back on his sunburnt forehead, sipping cans of Genesee from a six-pack that rode with him under the saddle seat. The sweet scent of mown grass filled the house and Laura felt happy. Even the tractor drone sounded cheerful, as if some giant bumblebee were working the meadow flowers. Billy carefully steered around the few white marble outcroppings in the field, so plenty of black-eyed Susans and daisies would still wave their pretty heads in the summer breeze even when he had finished.

Near the top of the meadow the oak grove had sent invaders into the grassland—thin saplings scarcely an inch in diameter. Mark noticed that although Billy cut other suckers of that thickness, he avoided the oaklings. When he stopped near the end of the afternoon to refuel the tractor, Mark asked him why.

"Too tough for the blade on my mower," Billy said gruffly. "If'n I had a brush hog, now, mebbe."

"But you're cutting the aspen and maple and cherry suckers," Laura pointed out.

"Oak's tough," Billy said stubbornly. "Tougher'n anything else in the woo-uds."

"Hell, I don't know," Mark said. He pulled out his Buck knife and proceeded to cut at a nearby oak sucker. The blade, razor sharp from honing, bit into the bark and then skidded.

"Shit!"

Mark jumped up and back from the sapling, dropping the knife in the grass. He shook his left hand. Blood welled slowly from a deep slash across the heel of his palm. "Goddamn Boy Scout trick that was!"

Billy watched with wide-eyed fascination as the blood rolled in thick, heavy drops off Mark's hand. He licked his lips. The blood splashed on the grass and ran down toward the roots of the sapling, where it disappeared almost instantly into the summer-sere earth.

Then Billy keeled over. His eyes rolled back in his head and his thin, wiry body convulsed, twitching in the grass as if he were attached to electric wires. Foam bubbled from his lips and strange words came pouring out of him in a singsong rhythm. His heels drummed the earth in counterpoint. Laura quickly stooped over him to try to retrieve his tongue—somewhere she had read you should do that, and Billy was clearly in an epileptic seizure—but his ragged brown teeth, slippery with froth, snapped and clacked like a rattrap gone berserk and she feared for her fingers. Instead she loosened his work shirt and opened the chest buttons on his sweaty, sour-smelling union suit.

On his chest she saw a tattoo: it took a moment for her to recognize it.

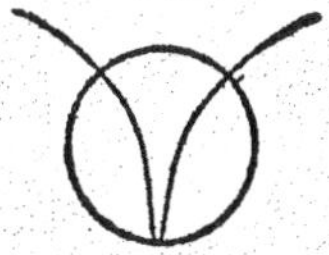

When Billy came out of his fit, he stared at her huffily as he buttoned his shirt. Then, saying nothing, he went back to the tractor and continued mowing.

"If you wouldn't mind, I'd like to go down to New York for a couple of days."

"Oh?" Mark looked up from rebandaging his cut hand. It was evening and cicadas buzzed their saw-song from the warm dark. "Anything the matter?"

"I'd like to start getting together a layette for the baby," Laura said. "But also, you know, just to get a change of scene for a while. See some of my friends, buy some books, take in a show or two." Mark hated the theater. "Mainly, though, just be by myself a bit. You don't mind, do you? I don't have to . . ."

"No, no," he said, putting an arm around her. "I understand. You need your space to yourself for a while. It's okay. It'll help you to get all that bad stuff laid to rest, finally." He kissed her forehead. "I've got plenty to keep me busy and out of trouble while you're away."

She kissed him back thankfully, and left the next morning.

FOUR

Never had she loved the city quite so much. The shoving, scurrying millions on the avenues, the gleam of glass and steel as high as the neck could crane, the honking buses and street-shaking subways and even the tough-guy lingo of the cabdrivers—she loved it all and then some. For an hour that first morning she simply sat on a bench beside a skyscraper-waterfall off Fiftieth Street just watching people pass by. She window-shopped and poked her way through quiet bookstores, wandered the salles of the Metropolitan and the Museum of Modern Art, waited on line for tickets to a new smash musical. She lunched at Lutéce with her modeling pals, getting tipsy on two vodka Gibsons and splurging on black caviar, oysters, a flaky fresh filet of Dover sole. The girls were all squeals at the news of her pregnancy, though Freddie Overstreet wept a bit (perhaps at the memory of her two abortions).

That evening she called Bill McGregor. He was delighted to hear from her and quickly invited her for dinner. Oddly, she felt nervous as a teenager on her first serious date.

"The country girl!" he said as she came through the door. "Let me kiss the roses from your cheeks."

"Or the calluses from my hands," she answered, throwing her bag on the couch. The apartment was, as usual, spick-and-span; he had already poured the customary sherry. "Oh, Bill," she blurted, "I'm so goddamn miserable." She turned and he held her and for just a moment it was the old days again.

"What is this," he laughed, "a scene from *The Sun Also Rises*? Why so drear, Lady Brett?"

"I don't want to go back to that awful place," she wailed. And then she told him—all the things she hadn't told her girl friends: about Polly and Doc and Huldy, about Billy Munro and Jamie Lynn's death, how the town looked and felt, about Mark's growing and repulsive macho-man trip, and finally, her voice breaking toward sobs, about the Fourth of July and Polly's death. Bill listened with his usual sympathy while they ate, nodding and watching her gravely. Suddenly she felt as she had in the old days, when they were lovers. His warm understanding, so unlike Mark's self-centered machismo, showed he had never lost his love for her.

"Do you want my reading on it?" he asked when she had wound down. Then he grinned mock-wickedly. "I know that the best way to get a woman into bed is to let her unburden herself, so maybe I should shut up and just let you talk on."

"No," she said, laughing finally. "Tell me: what's happening to me? Is the place really as bad as I just made it sound, or are my fears just . . . babyish? Those of a spoiled-rotten city brat?"

"Possibly," he said, suddenly serious. "But not quite that extreme. Actually, all the things you've described are part of country life. Nothing mysterious. It's tragic, your friend Polly's death, but I think it's as the doctor said—just another chimney fire. The poor woman just hadn't kept her stove clean. You can't blame yourself for that, Laura. Nor any malevolent force, either."

"So?"

"So, I think what you're suffering from is simple ego loss. When you lived in the city and modeled, you were somebody. You had a career, a reputation as a fine model, a coterie of like-minded friends. When you walked down the street, people turned their heads to watch you. Don't deny that you felt great about that. Remember the time that out-of-town couple came over to us in the park and asked for your autograph? You positively beamed with smugness. But now you're sitting in some jerkwater town where nobody knows you from Eve, Mark rules the roost, you're bored and somehow diminished. Maybe Mark's macho trip is ugly to you, but after all he'd lived and worked in your shadow for a long time. It's understandable. Knowing you as well as I do, though—what is it? ten years now anyway—I'd bet my boots you'll adjust to it finally. And once Mark's he-man number has run its course, you'll settle in there quite nicely."

"Okay," she said, "but what about all this other weird crap? The Church in the Wildwood. The haunted oak grove. Obed Magrute and Cassie Eldridge—Eldritch Cassie is how I think of her. That's not your typical 'country living,' is it?"

"Again, that's the thing I told you about. The winged disk of Ahaz—Ahaz Ashburn was his name—I looked it up. Remember I told you they'd had this religious glitch in America back in the early 1800s, and the Gore came up with its own variant. That's your Church in the Wildwood. Of course it's freaky, just like Father Divine in the thirties, or boogie-woogie in the forties, or Jesus freaks in the seventies. Look at the hippies. America fights the war between Apollo and Dionysus every goddamn generation or two. What you're seeing up there is a played-out version of one battle in that war, a battle that began circa 1810. Not to worry. And certainly nothing to do with the tragic death of your friend."

"I don't know," Laura said. She felt a bit silly, having brought the whole matter up in the first place.

"Look," said Bill, "I'll dig around in the library, see what I can find out about Ahaz Ashburn and that whole damned cult. Send it to you when I've got it. Now, how's about a little Benedictine?" He leered at her with his usual mock-lust. "Get you a little spiffled and—hey presto—between the sheets?"

For just a moment, she thought it a good idea. Why not? This after all was the liberated '80s. But no, she thought, that would be quitting.

She laughed. "Good old Bill. Never say die." They finished their coffee and she prepared to go.

"You're leaving something out," he said as she stood at the door. He looked at her gravely now, his voice a bit tentative. "Aren't you?"

"I'm pregnant," she said at last.

"Well," after a long pause, "that's good. That's just fine, babe." He hugged her and in the grip of his arms she could feel his longing and, once again, his surrender to . . . What?

The inevitability.

Poor, priestly Bill.

"The trapper's last shot," thought Gillie Brunette. "Or better yet, the poacher's last shot." He carefully plied the spring-loaded plunger until the tension felt right, held his breath, and released it. Instantly his hands flew to the flippers on either side of the tilted cabinet. The single steel ball-bearing zipped up the alley, caromed off the curved rubber bumper at the top, and began its random, beeping descent through the guts of the pinball machine.

With tight little grunts, frantic flips of the side-bats, and plenty of body-English, Gillie Brunette worked the ball for all it was worth. When it finally clunked to rest at the bottom, he glanced eagerly at the scoreboard. Twenty thousand and three! *All raaaht!*

He sauntered as casually as possible to the scarred oak bar of the Beech Seal Tavern to collect his fifth free cream ale of the evening. All eyes were on him. Dead cool, that Gillie Brunette. One tough dude. First he wins on the mechanical bull, then he cleans up on the pinball machine. He shrugged his skinny shoulders inside the fashionably faded blue denim cowboy jacket (cost him $32.50 in Rutland, it did) and placed a pointy-toed, hand-tooled imitation Frye boot on the bar's brass rail.

Ooops!

Something soft and gooey between the heel and sole of that boot. He glanced down, flustered.

Goddamn!

Cowflop!

Look out, keed, you're blowin' your cool. As furtively as possible he tried to scrape the cow dung off against the bar rail, but the pungent reek of it announced his failure. He glanced up at the Dewar's White Label clock back of the bar, tucked away between mangy deer heads and the customary cutesy no-credit signs. Quarter to eight. Goddamn it, Bill should've been here half an hour ago if they were gonna make it to the meadow by moonrise. He socked the squat brown Jennie bottle to his mouth in what he hoped would look like "a vicious slug." Instead the hard glass bumped against one of his teeth—one of the brown, sore ones. He nearly yelped with the pain. Out of the corner of his eye he saw Norm Towson, the bartender, watching him with a crooked grin on his jowly hick kisser. Gillie fired right back with a tough-guy scowl. Norm turned away, his fat shoulders quaking slightly.

Bastard! One of these days . . .

A pickup growled to a halt in the parking lot and a moment later Billy Munro walked in. To young Gillie Brunette, he was approximately God: skinny as a skeeter-hawk, dark, hard-faced, walking with that easy Fluid Drive of the born woodsman. At the age of thirty-two, Bill Munro was acknowledged far and wide as the most skillful game outlaw in Vermont—if not all New England. He knew where all the big trout lay and caught them, at night, from the ponds and private holes of the most heavily patrolled land, then sold them at outrageous prices to his restaurateur pals over the border in New York state. He once got sixty-five dollars for a perfect eight-pound cock rainbow from a college prof in New Jersey—a fly-fiisherman *manqué* who wanted it for his study wall—or so the legend had it.

"How's your bowels, kid?" Billy plunked his elbows on the bar next to Brunette and flicked a hand in Norm Towson's direction. The bartender popped a Heineken's and hurried over.

"You told me to be here at seven so's we could make moonrise," Gillie said softly. "I been here since six thirty." There was just a hint of an aggrieved whine to his voice and Munro threw him a sharp glance. Gillie felt the cold worm of fear writhe in those very organs Munro had just mentioned.

"I show when I show," Billy said curtly.

He was not a man to cross, even on the slightest matters. Why, just three years ago a guy had tried to cross him—another professional poacher, from the

Adirondacks—and Billy took him out right bold. The guy had been killing deer in Billy's territory but one afternoon Billy found him in the parking lot outside Minter's store, just down the road here. The New Yorker was sitting behind the wheel of his car. Billy pulled a .44 magnum revolver and laid it against the man's cheekbone. "I'm gonna blow your head off," he said.

The other man smiled.

Billy blew his head off.

And the judge let him go when he claimed he didn't know the gun was loaded. Or so the legend ran.

You didn't fuck with Billy Munro.

"We're not going up to those meadows," he said now. "I got word the warden's staking it out. We're gonna hit that edge up there on Widdershins instead. That one I told you about, above the Eldritch place."

They were going for deer this September night. Billy had received a call earlier in the day from a client in New York City, a Breton restaurateur he supplied year round with venison. A good customer—six deer a year at an average of a hundred bucks the animal. The man had a party of frog eaters coming in from La Belle France next weekend and he needed meat in a hurry. Two plump young does would do just fine. Two-fifty the brace. That's $125 a deer, Gillie computed. And I'll get a whole share this time!

"Whereabouts on Widdershins?" he asked in a throaty whisper.

"Above Eldritches, I told you. That overgrown meadow just below the oaks."

The worm of fear in Gillie Brunette's guts suddenly graduated to cobra class.

"The Oaks?" he quavered.

"Gawdamn right the Oaks. I checked it out this mornin' and there's plenty of acorns fallin'. Deer been usin' in there right and left. Trails like friggin' innerstates, meadow grass mashed all flat from where they been lyin' up."

"What about them flatlanders that bought the Eldritch place?" Gillie asked. "I hear tell they're livin' there year round now."

"Flatlanders," Billy snorted. "What do they know? They'll hear the shots and take 'em for backfires. Prob'ly don't even know it's illegal to take deer this time a year. Anyways they're friends of mine, we can fix it."

"I dunno," Gillie said softly. "Drooker's Woods. A bad-news place."

"Says who? Your maw? 'Drooker's Woo-uds.' " His voice had a buck-saw edge. "All the ole farts around here say it's ha'nted. But it ain't. I been through there since I'm a weaner, tooken more deer out of there'n you've ever even shawt at. It ain't no more ha'nted 'n goin' to church."

"I dunno."

Billy snorted again, just like a big ten-point buck in the rut with his neck all swole—and spun toward Brunette. " 'I dunno,' " he mocked in a falsetto. "Well, Goosey Gillie Brunette, now I know why you got the nickname. Why don't you and your 'I-dunno' jest stay right here in the Seal for a thrillin' night of pinball and Jennies? I kin use that one twenty-five I was gonna pay you for to pay up my new tractor tires." He chugged the rest of his greenie in two swallows and headed for the door.

"Wait up!" Gillie yelled. He fumbled a crumpled bill from his pocket, slapped it on the bar, and waved off the change as Norm Towson came over. He ducked out into the autumn twilight dogging Bill Munro's heels.

Not until later did he realize his magnanimity: the

only bill he'd come out with that night was a ten spot.

"Laura," Mark Avery called softly. "There's something I want to show you."

He heard her get up heavily, almost dutifully, from the living-room couch where she had been reading and pad into the kitchen. She was feeling her pregnancy and he felt guilty. He handed her the 7x40 power Swift Skipper binoculars and pointed up to the top of the meadow. It was dusk and in the low, blue-green light the shapes of six deer stood out warm and coppery-brown. Their graceful necks arched as they grazed at the edge of the oak grove. Laura took the binoculars—dutifully again, it seemed to Mark—and looked at them. He watched her closely. When her lips widened into a pleased smile, he put his arm around her shoulders.

"Oh," she said, "how beautiful! I can see their eyes."

She had been moody since her return from New York two months ago. At first Mark had written it off to the baby—after all, a woman felt the commitment much more deeply than a man, much as he might try to empathize. She hadn't been bitchy, nothing like that. Just . . . remote. He tried to cheer her by taking active, muscular interest in her vegetable garden—weeding the beds and building a rock retaining wall around the lower edge, watering the thirsty tomatoes and talking heartily about how good they would taste when they ripened. But they never did. The first frost, in late August, turned them pale pink on the vine. At night he tried to love her, but her response was shallow. Again he thought: the baby.

He even cut back on his fishing, despite the fact that he was now seeing more and bigger trout in the brook than he had in the spring. Nor did he practice anymore with the shotgun. He knew that disturbed her. (But the lack of practice didn't really matter, he knew. He was indeed a quick study: now he could pick a starling from the air with a simple swing and slap on the trigger: a starling—Shakespeare's bird—pelting along like a mini-duck, turned to a blown dandelion of shot-ripped feathers just . . . like . . . that.)

Yet she remained remote.

Perhaps it had been an error to move from the city. She missed her pals, that he knew, her job and her posing, her makeup, the restaurants, the boutiques, the watching herself on television—just by chance, that night, and the night after—and she missed making the money. Yes, the money.

But where did you draw the line?

She wanted the baby. At least as much as he. More than he, if the truth be told. Oh, sure, he wanted to be a daddy, but he couldn't for a moment visualize—if he was honest with himself—what it would feel like. Yet *she* had a feeling about it. A preconceptual feeling. (He hated himself for the pun.)

For him childbearing occurred each day, with his painting. Now he knew it was what he should have been doing all his life: taking the world onto his palette, its viridians and its burnt umber, cobalt and cerulean as the sky, okay, give it some terre verde to take the skylark down: the cadmiums gaud, the ivory black as cold death, alizarin crimson, crimson: poor Polly's blood boiling in the dark that night when he wanted to rush into the flames . . . had he felt it even then? The love of the two women, not really denying his for his wife, but in some odd way contradicting it? Could any man ever know a woman, apart from sexually, better than even her meanest, dimmest girl friend knew her?

Thalo green—the willow in spring.

But Jim Boggs's blood, unboiled, rolling out on the ground up there in the woods (like my blood rolled that day when Billy cut the meadow: thick blood, slow, and the poor forker just flat laid down there on the ground an' twitched!).

Yes, those colors (Mark Avery thought)—I put them on the palette and from them I create shapes, images, emotions. That's my meaning and my life. "Those images that yet"—how did Yeats put it?—"fresh images beget . . .

"That dolphin-torn

"That gong-tormented sea . . ."

So it must be the baby, he thought.

As they stood in the fading dusk watching the deer feed at the top of the meadow, he placed his hand on her warm belly.

"It doesn't *feel* any different," he said.

"Don't be a nerd," she laughed, turning to him. "At this stage of development it's so small you could cup it in your hands."

"I cain't see it," whispered Gillie Brunette.

"It?" said Billy Munro. "It? There's only six of 'em—no, I'm wrong, eight. On'y eight of 'em up there altogether. Three big does, two button bucks, and the rest yearling does. All along the top edge there. Here, look through the scope. It gathers the light the way your maw sucks aigs." He handed Gillie the scope-sighted .308 caliber Remington 700.

"Oh, yeah!" The scope swallowed the thickening dusk and thinned it to grainy midday. The deer were feeding not an arm's length away, it seemed. Gillie laid the cross hairs on the neck of the nearest doe. "You want I should take her?"

"You ain't quick enough yet, Gillie," said Munro.

"I don't mean to put you down, but you gotta get off two killing shots real quick-like. Hand that piece over to me and get your gutting knife ready." His voice sounded kindly and Gillie felt thrilled.

They had left Bill Munro's truck on an old logging road a quarter of a mile downhill, already turned around for the mandatory quick getaway, and with the tailgate open to receive the dead deer. The back of the truck was loaded with hay bales. The hay would cover the deer carcasses and anyone seeing the truck on the ride out would reckon it for just another couple of farm boys bringing in bedding straw for their paw's livestock. Billy Munro always figgers ahead. That's why he ain't never been caught. That's why he's a livin' legend.

An' by Gawd, thought Gillie Brunette, I'm his protogay!

Ker-pow!

One of the does dropped dead in her tracks, a half-chewed sludge of hay paste spilling from her mouth. The echo of the shot rang around the hollow.

Before she hit the ground, Gillie saw the bright spin of brass out of the corner of his eye and heard the rifle bolt slam home. The other deer, tails up and wagging, bounded toward the safety of the oaks. Wham! The second doe lurched forward in mid-leap, twisting as she fell, and ploughed face forward into the darkness. The rest of them were gone.

"The Big White Bye-Bye," Billy Munro said softly. "Okay, let's be quick about it. You take the first one."

Gillie ran forward pulling the knife as he ran. The doe lay on her side, one eye bulging amazed in the last light.

"My God," Laura gasped, "someone's shooting the deer!"

Mark took the binoculars and refocused them as the shot echoes faded down the hollow. Two dark blurs on the meadow grass; two thin, quick shapes bending over them, the glint of knives. He reached for the telephone.

"I can't make them out, but there's two of the bastards," he said. "Quick, look up Chub Markham's number."

"Chub?"

"He's the deputy game warden. We'll report the fuckers."

Chub's phone rang half a dozen times before a recording came on: Sorry, the deputy warden was out on patrol, would you care to leave a message?

"Gawddamnit!" Mark slammed down the phone and ran upstairs. A few moments later he was back with the shotgun in his hand, fumbling shells into the magazine.

"Mark! You're not going up there?"

"Damn right I am. They're not getting away with this."

"But they have guns! They'll kill you."

"Not if I nail them first." He slammed out of the house, with Laura right behind him.

When Gillie Brunette finished gutting his deer, he wiped his bloody hands on the grass and looked up. Billy Munro stood over him, long since finished with his own animal. It lay beside him in the near-total dark, jaw agape, the tongue lolling from one side of its long, crooked mouth.

"Well," said Billy, "you're learning. Let's make tracks on out of here." Then, as he turned to pick up his own deer, "Wait a sec. You're not gonna leave the heart and liver, are you? That's the best-eatin' part of these mangy critters." He fumbled a plastic garbage bag out of his game pocket. "Stick 'em in this." Gillie stuffed the heart, heavy and hard and still warm, and the wobbly liver into the bag. As he rose to his feet with the deer's front hooves in his hand, ready to drag it down to the truck, he felt Billy's hand hard on his shoulder.

"Shhh!" The older man was staring intently downhill, in the direction they had come from.

"What is it?" Gillie hissed, fear now suddenly hot in his bladder.

For a long, loud minute they stood crouched in the darkness. Gillie could hear nothing. Then he heard something moving in the wood edge below.

"There—you see them?"

"Where? Where?"

"Down there, at the edge of the woods. A man. Two men."

Gillie peered hard into the darkness. Then he saw it too: A darker darkness, upright, hard to make out the size, but surely a human being. Or . . . This was Drooker's Woods and anything was possible.

Christ but he had to pee! All those goddamn beers down at the Beech Seal. Never again, not on a night he was working.

"We gotta split back into the woods and slide uphill around them," Billy whispered.

Into Drooker's Woods? Oh shit oh dear.

"Why don't you take the deer and head in, Bill? Leave the rifle with me and I'll hold 'em off." Anything was better than going into Drooker's.

"Don't be a asshole. It's Warden Markham likely as not, along with a pal. He's carryin a twelve-gauge loaded with double-oh buck. He'd be glad to blow you to rags. Come on! There's a old hollow tree in there with its top held open by a blowdown. We'll stuff these carcasses into the hollow and then just mosey on back to the truck. If Markham stops us, we'll say we was huntin' coyotes. They're fair game year round. Then tomorrow we'll just sneak back up here and fetch our meat."

The moon was beginning to peak over the crooked shoulder of Widdershins, filling the tops of the oak grove with a steely webwork of light. The twisted branches looked like skinny fingers, waiting to grab the unwary trespasser. A thin, cold wind began to hiss through the upper branches, rattling them against the pale sky. Far across the valley a great horned owl called: "Huhu-huh-*hoooo*!"

They headed into Drooker's Woods.

FIVE

When Mark and Laura reached the top of the meadow the poachers were gone: they found only the gut piles, steaming lightly in the icy autumn night. Laura realized it was the twenty-second of September—the fall equinox. She also realized, during the fast, hard climb up the meadow, that her young tomcat, Bone, was missing. She hadn't seen him since the late afternoon. Now her fears were doubled: not only for Mark but, also and intensely, for the cat. If poachers could kill deer so gleefully, what was to keep them from doing the same to Bone?

"You better go on back down, honey," Mark said. "Try the warden again."

"What are you going to do?"

"I'm going in there. The moon gives plenty of light to follow them by. I want at least to see who they are."

"I'm coming with you. Bone is missing, and I'm damned if I'm going to sit down there in that kitchen worrying and waiting for the phone to ring."

"Look—there's the baby . . ."

"If you get killed I don't want to be a widow with a newborn. Let's go."

They pushed into the woods.

"Billy? Where are you?"

Gillie Brunette had stopped to relieve his aching bladder and now a cloud had skittered over the three-quarter moon. He felt as if someone had suddenly slipped a heavy-duty Hefty trash bag over his head and twisted the wire. The deer he was dragging weighed less than eighty pounds but he was sure that his arm had already stretched three inches longer than normal. Gillie groped in front of him like a blind man—then yanked his hand back in panic. He'd touched something —something rough and hard. Something with *teeth* in it!

Then the moonlight flushed through again and he found himself nose to bark with the trunk of a giant oak tree. Wha'fuck? It hadn't been there when the moon went under and he'd taken no more than three or four steps. The freakin' woods was movin!

"Goddamn you, asshole!"

Gillie nearly jumped over the oak tree—all eighty-five feet of it. The voice was right in his hear. But it was only Billy. He grabbed Brunette's shoulder and spun him around.

"What you been doin', jackin' off? We got to get a move on before Markham nabs us. Move!"

With Munro leading the way, they pushed deeper into the moonlit grove. Gillie's back crawled under the cold, sweaty touch of his work shirt. The oaks seemed to glower down on him, the knots where old branches had grown before they were snapped off by wind and ice storms looked like hollow eyes following his every step. Billy grunting ahead of him, dragging the deer as if it were filled with feathers, was some reassurance, as was the black, thin barrel of the rifle that swung like a metronome across Billy's shoulders. But what good was a rifle against a ha'nt? What could mere lead do to dense, time-cured heart of oak?

As the moon rose and increased in luminosity, each cloud that crossed its face cast a darker, more ominous shadow. And the wind was quickening with his heartbeat. Small twigs, larger dead branches, scales of oak bark began to clatter down through the trees and the very leaves they landed on seemed to jump up to receive them. The trees themselves—Gillie Brunette was sure of it—were moving.

He could feel the scream coiling just beneath his diaphragm: a mottled, swollen snake, pus yellow, puke green, cocking for the strike.

"Here it is."

The two trees stood just as Billy had said they would. A young beech, an interloper among the lordly oaks, had blown down in the winter winds and hit a snag protruding from the top of a truncated oak, itself long dead of whatever it was that killed oaks—time? The beech's weight had prized open the hollow top of the oak bole, exposing a hole that measured a good yard across.

"You skinny on up the blowdown," Billy said, "and I'll tie this rope to the deer. Then I'll toss the bitter end of the rope up to you and you hoist the fuckers up there and stuff 'em in. Got it?"

"Uh . . ."

"Listen, you all right, kid? You look kind of strung out."

"I'm okay." Like hell I am—shakin' like a popple leaf!

"Good. Now get on up there."

Gillie began his climb up the angled blowdown with

rubbery knees. The clouds crossing the moon's face were moving at such a rate now that they created a kind of strobe effect, like he'd seen in the disco over to Rutland that time. He wished he was there right now, boogying with Babs ("the Slut") Hunnicutt. Hell, he wished he was back home in the trailer in Tinmouth watching *The Dukes of Hazzard*—anyplace but here in the goddamn Gore. The Gore was chilly to strangers, and Drooker's Woods was downright fatal if the old yarns could be credited. . . .

"Here it comes." The coiled clothesline unfolded as it rose and Gillie snagged it with a numb hand. He began to haul. As the deer's weight came into play, the beech tree began to rock. A groan like that of a dying hog rose from its trunk.

"Is it going to hold?" Gillie asked in a hoarse whisper.

"Damn well better," said Munro.

Gillie untied the deer and eased it, head down, into the hollow trunk. Then he dropped the rope back down to Billy. Another couple of half hitches, another toss, another catch. An another groan from the blowdown. Like cold fingers up his spine. This time, though, the tree actually moved, slipping a few inches with a creak of wood tissue as it settled into a firmer grip on the dead oak's bark. Gillie teetered for a sick moment against the sky. Then he caught himself. The second deer began its slow ascent, its front legs raised as if in some grotesque pagan rite. A dead leaf stuck by dried blood to its lolling tongue flapped audibly in the wind. It was as if the deer were giving Gillie the raspberry. He giggled in girlish hysteria. Gillie had draped the deer into the hole and was just beginning to lower it when the sound came.

Footfalls in the dry leaves.

He froze and stared into the dark. Figures emerged

from the edge of the blackness to stand, silent, at the very edge of illumination. Black, bipedal, erect. Dead silent.

Gillie dropped the deer down the hole. At that moment the beech blowdown collapsed with a quick raucous screech. Before he fell, his arms waving wildly against the backdrop of cloud-torn, lopsided moon, Gillie Brunette saw that one of the figures carried a long, crook-topped stave. He raised it. . . .

The tree came alive: like the fanged head of some scaly dinosaur, its jaws wide open. Then the jaws, relieved of the pressure the beech had exerted, snapped closed with a raspy crunch. Gillie's body, falling, met the bite with perfect timing. The oak tree's splintered gums locked on his chest.

The scream, so long suppressed, came shrilling out for one quick instant. Then Gillie Brunette's lungs came rushing up his throat and out of his mouth.

"Did you hear it?"

"Who couldn't?" Mark answered. The scream had come from somewhere close by, but with the wind whipping and swirling so, it was hard to tell the direction. "Probably just two tree trunks rubbing together in the storm, or maybe even a bobcat. That's the sound they make, I read somewhere. Like a woman scared to death."

Like me, Laura thought. But she could see that for all his offhand bravado, Mark now clenched his hands on the shotgun more tightly, and he proceeded deeper into the dark woods much more slowly.

Lightning began to snap on the ridge across the hollow and the first few heavy splats of rain zapped the leaves overhead.

"I don't like that lightning," Laura said. "We're on high ground, under high trees. It's damned dangerous."

"Just a little ways more," he said. "Another twenty yards or so, then we'll head for the barn. The clearing with the big oak can't be far off now."

Lightning was turning the night to day and the rain hit in earnest when they entered the clearing. Laura caught her breath. At a far corner, clearly illuminated by a flash of lightning, she saw the figure of a man caught in the vise-jaw of a dead tree's top. The man's face was gaping, agog, his eyes bulging like autumn puffballs from his head. A great dangling mass of blood-red pulp hung from his mouth. His arms dangled limp down the barkless bole of the dead tree. She grabbed Mark's arm and pointed, but then it was dark again. He turned to her, and in the next flash she could see he was as frightened as she. And over his shoulder, in the far shadowed edge of the clearing, she thought she saw scurrying figures—figures of people ducking into hiding.

They fled down the mountain toward home.

Later that night, when the storm had passed, she saw the flickering red and yellow glow in the oak grove again. This time she knew it couldn't be the moon, since that orb was already angled well on its downslide to the west. Mark said it was probably a tree set on fire by the lightning storm. Perhaps that same dead tree in which she had imagined she saw the mangled dead man, who obviously had just been a strange burl or perhaps the stub of a broken branch, transformed into a horror by her tension and the rapidly changing light.

And sure enough, in the sunny, sparkling morning when they climbed back up there, they found the charred, still-warm trunk of the lightning-struck tree smoking in the dripping sunlight. There was no sign of a body, nor of anything but nature up to its usual mysterious tricks.

SIX

Trooper Kane rested his right hind on the grip of the .44 Magnum Ruger Blackhawk and immediately felt better. Not that a pistol could help him, but it was a talisman of sorts. God but it was uncomfortable here in the oak grove. Cold rain dripped from his curling hat brim and soaked his uniform; his boots were wet clean through. He'd have to get his Smoky hat reblocked after this outing. But more than the physical discomfort of an icy drenching, the very spookiness of the place was getting to him. In the course of his fifty-two years, all of them lived in Vermont, Tom Kane had heard enough weird stories about Hubley's Gore to keep his neck hairs on edge even on the finest day the town ever saw. Still, duty was duty, and Tom Kane was a good state cop.

He had come to the Gore seeking information about Gillie Brunette. A no-goodnik if ever there was one. Two arrests already on the books for burglary—B and E of nonresident summer places—and three for possession. Now the word was out that he was into deer poaching. The boy's mother, herself a round-heeled lush and whiner, had reported him missing three days ago. Kane drew the assignment because he'd been with Fish and Game before switching to the Highway Patrol ten years ago. The past catches up with you, he thought ruefully, like it or not.

At the town saloon he'd learned Brunette had been seen there in company with Billy Munro, long a suspected deer poacher. That was the night Gillie disappeared. Kane had caught up with Munro at the town barn, where the lanky countryman was changing the oil in his pickup truck—illegally, at that, using facilities and oil paid for by town taxes. Nothing Kane could do about that, though; it was town business, and besides the Gore's road supervisor, Nate Trumpey, was right there helping Gillie.

Munro admitted having a drink with Brunette that night, but claimed the younger man had gone his own way afterward. Where, Munro had no idea.

Yet in the course of their conversation, Trooper Kane had noted oak leaves stuck in the tread of Munro's left rear snow tire. Leaves of white oak. There were "scrub" oak growing all over the township, but the only white oaks left in any numbers grew on Widdershins Mountain. Kane got back in his cruiser and headed out of town, pretending he'd drawn a blank in the Gore. But later he circled back around Widdershins from the east and approached the oak grove from above. Parking his car up a logging road, away from the eyes of nosy townsfolk, he'd hiked up into the oak grove. The rain began as soon as he was too far from his cruiser to make a return for his raincoat practicable. Wouldn't you know it?

Sure enough, he'd found two gut piles near the edge of the grove, already well picked over by crows but still clearly recognizable as deer innards. The drag marks led him into the grove itself—his eye, despite ten years out of wildlife enforcement, was still that of an

Indian tracker. Not too far into the grove he found a charred oak stump, and leading from it another faint track, highlighted just enough to be visible out of the corner of the eye, by the glittering drops of rain that sharpened the surrounding, undisturbed ground litter. It looked like a whole group of people had gathered at the burnt (or still-burning?) oak stump, then traipsed on back into the woods together. He followed their track to the center of the grove. There stood the hugest, ugliest oak tree he'd ever seen, a true monster of a tree, scarred and weathered and older, it seemed, than the very hills. Fresh ashes were spread in a circle around the tree.

In a perfect circle. Obviously man-made.

Now, as the rain pelted down and lightning muttered from the west, Trooper Kane was poking through the ashes, looking for something—anything—to link them to Gillie Brunette. He was just about to give up and head for the nearest coffeepot when he found it: a broken white object protruding from the leaf litter. It was partially buried in the soft mold, and when he extracted it, he saw it was the fragment of a jawbone. A piece of bone about three inches long and maybe two wide at its broadest. A pair of brown, half-rotted molars still wobbled loosely in their sockets. But were they deer? Could be human, he thought. He wasn't forensic expert enough to tell. But there was a lab in Rutland that sure could.

He placed the bit of bone carefully in an evidence bag and headed back down to his cruiser. The lightning was snapping all around him now and he ran the last few hundred yards, wheezing heavily with his half-century-old lungs. The final crash of thunder sounded so close it nearly knocked him down.

He took the dirt road back up over the southwest shoulder of Widdershins, the way he'd come, so that he wouldn't be seen down in town. No sense tipping his hand to Billy Munro that he'd been poking around on Billy's illegal hunting turf. The bastard might skip town. And he would definitely like to talk to that scrawny outlaw again, at length, under a white light if possible and with a hunk of rubber hose in his fist. . . .

From where Kane had parked, the road snaked wet and twitchy up a steep rise, hemmed in on both sides by heavy brush and second-growth woods. He drove light-footed but steady, his rear wheels hardly spinning at all as he kept a steady speed of twenty-five miles an hour up the grade. That was the trick of driving these snot-slick gravel roads in the rain: steady as you go. Then, as he rounded a curve, he saw a logging truck lugging uphill dead ahead of him. Where had that sumbitch come from? He cursed, slowing to a crawl behind the muck-spray of the truck's double drive-wheels. WIDDERSHINS LUMBER said the chipped paint on the mud guards. The truck was piled high with saw logs, some of them three feet across the butt. Judging by the bark they were oak. White oak. That frigging town co-operative down in the Gore, Kane cussed to himself. Richest business in the region. How could you figure it? You'd think they'd have done like the rest of these hill-folk—cut their valuable wood long since and blown the money on new tractor motors or TV sets or whatever.

The logging truck grunted and whined to the top of the grade, with Kane cursing and fretting behind it. He always felt uneasy driving behind a logging truck. What if the straps didn't hold? What if one of those huge goddamn logs suddenly skidded loose and came bouncing back toward you, end over end, like some huge battering ram gone berserk? You wouldn't stand a Chinaman's chance. Kane had once investigated a fatal, upstate somewhere, in which a young married couple had been driving behind a truck loaded with big boulders. The gate had come undone on an upgrade and the rocks, some as big as a car engine, came caroming back at them. One of the boulders, which later proved to weigh 922 pounds, landed square on the windshield of the brand-new Ford Granada. The newlyweds were mashed like bugs. They had to be removed piece by piece, from their shattered luggage. Kane himself had extracted the young man's pelvis, by its natural handle, from a blood-soaked tangle of his virgin wife's frilled nighties.

You see strange things working the highways of America.

As the road neared the summit, it climbed especially steeply. Here the natural drainage had created its own water bars in the form of deep "corduroy" corrugations. Kane saw the truck hit them and begin to bounce. Like an elephant in a disco, he flashed. But the giggle that rose with the image suddenly caught in his throat.

The top logs of the load were coming loose!

There was play in them, under the clamp, under the wire-rope cinches!

Kane hit his brakes, skewed to his right, gunned himself straight again and stopped. The log load was jumping higher now, he could hear the heavy thump of oak on oak, giant tom-toms beating not fifty yards ahead of him. Then one of the logs began to skid. He watched it, helpless, as it squirted out of the stack, its bark mud-slick from being dragged out of the woods. As if in slow motion it fell butt-first onto the roadway, stood upright, teetered for a moment, then spun slowly, toppling, downhill. End for end; end for end.

Kane cowered low in his seat, watching the great club skip toward him. He could see the very corrugations of the bark.

His last image was of a strange and leering face,

glowering at him from the bark itself, grinning as it hammered down on the cruiser's roof.

The troopers who removed Tom Kane's mangled body from the wreck spent two hours at the job, even with the aid of a Hurst Jaws of Life cutter. Two of them got sick at the side of the road while they worked. They did not find the evidence bag with its bit of jawbone tucked neatly inside. And Chub Markham, the Gore's town constable and the first lawman to the scene of the regrettable accident, shook his head in the negative when asked if anything had been removed from the crushed car.

BOOK THREE

Autumn

ONE

The change began slowly, almost secretly. A few hectic spots at first, blood red, appeared in the fat green leaves of scattered sugar maples, then spread as the nights cooled and the days shortened. Yellows and oranges added themselves to the pallette. Sumacs flashed red along roadsides and meadow edges. Beech leaves paled to a warm, rich tan and the tiny, spiked beech mast rattled to the leaves below. The ash trees, slower to start, moved swiftly once the change got under way: within a few days they had gone almost totally yellow, and their long, narrow, spear-point leaves began spinning earthward to brighten the forest floor.

The oaks were the last to change, sullen and reluctant, it seemed, to don the stiff, brick-red hues of autumn. There were no acorns this fall—none, or at best very few. Only near the Bull Oak were they abundant. It was as if the oaks were marshaling their strength for something grave. A long, harsh winter?

At the same time, as the woods changed colors and the weather chilled, another activity was adding excitement to the lives of the Hubleyites. Old men and boys alike hauled rusty tangles of chain and steel from the barn lofts and set to work boiling, waxing, and refurbishing them: their traps. For trapping season was at hand and muskrats, raccoons, mink, coyotes, foxes and otters of the Gore would soon be in peril with every step they took, night or day. And when trapping was near, even better was the proximity of hunting season. The hollows and hillsides rang, occasionally, to the loud quick roar of a deer rifle as its owner sighted it in, ensuring that that one quick shot at a racing buck (which was all he could honestly hope for) would not go astray.

Now Mark gave up his painting entirely for the balance of the fall. Billy Munro took him into the Cauldron to show him where to set the newly purchased steel traps Mark had picked up cheap from Ike Minter. He also showed him the best covers for partridge, woodcock, cottontails, and snowshoe rabbits. And when opening day of the small-game season—birds and rabbits mainly—rolled around at the end of September, Mark was ready. He had resumed practice with his shotgun and knew he could hit whatever he flushed within twenty-five yards' range. Late that afternoon, while Laura waited in the kitchen, distraught every time she heard the hollow thump of a gun from somewhere in the hollow, she saw him sauntering loose-hipped down the meadow from the oaks, his face flushed near as red as the game vest she had sewed for him. He was striving mightily not to break into a boyish grin of triumph. From the game pocket at the back he produced first one, then two, and then finally four plump brown-feathered big birds: his day's limit of ruffed grouse (or partridge, as the locals called them).

"Oh, they look so . . . dead," she mourned. Indeed the poor creatures' plumage was matted in places with dried blood, their iridescent dark blue ruffs all stiff and ruffled, and their once-bright eyes cloudy as opals, glazed with death. Yet Mark cheerfully plucked and drew them, and when she tasted her first apple-stuffed Vermont partridge, all brown and crispy from the Dutch oven, she felt some of her regret fading. And even more so, a month later, when Mark lugged into the kitchen a huge black bird with a naked blue head, bigger than anything she had seen since the ostrich at the Bronx Zoo. It was a wild turkey. Billy Munro had called it in while he and Mark sat squatting in cover high on Widdershins, clad in camouflage suits with their faces painted black and green with greasepaint. The bird, a gobbler or male, weighed nearly twenty pounds when plucked and drawn. It would be their Thanksgiving dinner.

Still, the sight of Mark in camouflage gear, with his face painted like something out of a nightmare and a gun in his hand, sent a sad chill through Laura. It reminded her of the television pictures during the Vietnam War of brave young Americans—Marines or Green Berets, whatever—grinning proudly as they prepared to die. Or worse: to kill innocent little Asian children. She wished Mark did not feel this absurd need to show off his machismo—how childish in the late twentieth century!—yet she knew that to argue with him about it would only make him set his jaw and stick with it regardless of how his feelings might change. She could only hope that it was just a phase he was passing through and soon he would come to his senses. In the meantime she was glad enough to eat the wild meat. At least it did not have any preservatives or vicious steroids in it. And thanks again to Huldy's country culinary hints, she was able to prepare it deliciously. What the hell, as Mark liked to say, they eat game in Europe, and they're civilized over there, aren't they?

Meanwhile her pregnancy was proceeding nicely, thank you. She had not felt a single tinge of morning sickness, for which she was enormously grateful (poor Judy Monkhouse had whoopsed her ears off for her first two months). And her weight was well within the limits Doc Peggs set for her, thanks mainly to the work she'd been doing all summer in the garden and the long walks down the hollow she took each day, rain or shine. Doc insisted on seeing her every week, but only charged her for one visit a month. "I'm lonely down here with no one but Dad Sweet to talk to most of the time," he said with his wry, gentle smile. "I need a beautiful woman in my life."

And it was indeed pleasant to drive down to the village each week, shop and listen to town gossip in Minter's, then spend an educational hour over tea and biscuits with Doc. Sometimes after his few medical questions were out of the way, he played for her on the spinet: old ballads and archaic stately chansons, the courtly music of a bewigged and powdered world long dead and gone. He sang, too, in a rich yet delicate baritone, smiling at her and rolling his eyes in mockery at the sillier phrases of the love songs. She joined him in some of the easier choruses, her sweet contralto counterpointing him prettily.

Mainly though they talked about town history, Doc's favorite subject. He was eloquent as Emerson on the matter of Yankee independence and individualism, arguing that the Gore itself was a pure, communal expression of these qualities—one of the few townships, sadly, that still practiced what old New England preached. As to Yankee inventiveness, most people equated it with nineteenth-century mechanical genius, but it applied even in the "softer" areas of social institutions. Where else in the world could you find a political structure so open and democratic as the town meeting? Why, even in the realm of religion, the Gore was unique, independent, and inventive: it had created its own lovely creed, one most appropriate to these woodsy hills and peaceful valleys—the Church in the Wildwood. Laura asked him more about Ahaz Ashburn and his mother, who together had founded the church, but Doç merely waxed poetic and nostalgic, playing church hymns on the spinet for her and explaining the meter, rhyme scheme, and imagery of the lyrics. He was better—or at least more informative—when he talked about things like local economy: glorious sheep farming days; the old marble quarry (now the town swimming hole), which had flourished briefly after the Civil War to provide material for new statehouses, federal buildings and memorials to the Union dead; about the old cheese factories that had thrived in the days before "agribusiness" and the slow death of the family farm.

"To some it may seem we are nothing more than a senile anachronism," he said one afternoon. Wasps buzzed at the window screens and from the brilliant hillsides came the occasional thump of a hunter's shotgun. "Warriors in a lost cause of clannish nineteenth-century xenophobia. And it's true that we are shy of outsiders, for we have seen what they can do to our way of life with their ski resorts, their fast-food chains and adult bookstores and Radio Shacks and discount outlets and Medusa-eyed multitheaters. But we built this town out of raw howling wilderness, taming both it and ourselves in the process. We showed an ecological consciousness before the phrase had been conceived, much less devalued by sentiment. We have never overcut our oak forests and thus the sawmill can maintain, forever if need be, its high level of quality lumber, and the sawmill's prosperity is the prospertiy of the town."

"The Gore lives!" laughed Laura. Doc did not smile, but gazed thoughtfully into her eyes for a long buzzing moment.

"Yes," he said at last, breaking into his incandescent

smile. "And all good men within it! Now then, to practical matters. It's time for us to do the amniocentesis right quick now. You're well into your fourth month, the fetus is well developed and easily palpable so there is no danger of mishap with the needle. Yet still small enough that, if something is amiss with it genetically or otherwise, we can still . . . take action. What do you say to next week, Laura? Shall we make it on Thursday afternoon? Threeish?"

Laura hesitated. But she had always been a girl to take doctor's advice, and her New York friends, when she had mentioned the prospect of the amniocentesis to them recently, had all been enthusiastic, urging her to go ahead with it. Midge Bunyan told a horror story about a girl she knew, younger than Laura, who had recently given birth to a deformed infant despite the fact she had never used drugs, smoked, drank, or taken any medication stronger than chicken soup. She had, however, lived a long time in Chicago and New York. Just as Laura had done.

They set the date for the following Thursday.

Mark was bucking up firewood that day and she was too proud to ask for his company during the procedure. She would have welcomed it, despite her ever-growing confidence in Doc (not just as a physician but as a friend, almost an uncle), but Mark had been working so hard at his hunting, trapping, and now his woodcutting that she would have felt like a sissy. He had purchased a slightly used Stihl chainsaw from Pastor Thorpe's second cousin, Obie Ashburn, who had found it too heavy for his aging arms. The saw had all the modern safety devices one could find, and thus he hoped to allay Laura's fear and distrust of the machine. Yet though she said nothing, her frown told him that all his words about safety tips, hand guards, automatic chain brakes, etc., made no impression: Laura was deathly afraid, he told himself, of things that were loud (guns and chainsaws particularly), dangerous, and work-saving. A city girl, doggone it.

But Mark was determined to burn no oil that winter. The firewood left in the barn by the Eldridges would take them, he figured (and Billy Munro confirmed), through the New Year. But he would have to make enough wood this fall—another four or five cords—for the balance of the heating season, which in these parts ran well into April. The sooner he cut it, the sooner it would air-cure and the less creosote buildup they would have in their chimneys. This argument at least made sense to Laura, who recalled it was creosote that had killed Polly Boggs by triggering the fatal chimney fire. So far Mark had cut in the second-growth woods close to the house. Billy Munro helped him out the first few days, showing him how to drop a tree precisely where he wanted it; how to work it into stove lengths, and how to stack it in such a way that wind and sun worked through the wood to cure it. They had borrowed a hydraulic splitter from Ike Minter to presplit the wood before stacking, thus expediting the drying process.

In the old days Laura would have bemoaned the felling of these trees, although as both Billy and Mark pointed out to her, they were all sickly or ill-formed specimens, or else trees of little value either as timber or to wildlife, and were at the same time shading their more valuable neighbors and inhibiting their healthy growth. Yet now she felt no great, knee-jerk sympathy for trees. She much preferred sunny, open meadow, and welcomed this cutting, which enlarged their own fields. Still, she hated the ugly yowl and growl of the saw, the fearsome, bonebreaking crackle when the tree finally surrendered and fell, with a whooshing roar, to thud on the resilient earth.

So this fine fall afternoon she was delighted to get

away from the house and head down into the drowsy village. She was even more delighted when she reached the store and Ike, in his capacity as postmaster, handed her a package with Bill McGregor's return address. The note inside was short: "Dear Laura, Too busy right now with midterms and grading papers to write at any length, or even to do more than skim the enclosed, which should have quite a bearing on the matters we discussed during your recent visit. Still hope to make it up your way for Thanksgiving. Best to Marco Macho! Love & Kisses, Billy Befuddled." The enclosed was a leather-bound, gilt-edged volume on vellum titled *The Book of Ahaz*. As she began to flip through it, she noticed Ike Minter peering intently over her shoulder. So she went out onto the store's front porch.

Chub Markham was sitting on the bench, his feet up on the rail, sipping an Orange Nehi. When Chub wasn't being the town constable or deputy game warden, he drove the school bus, and his vehicle was parked nearby waiting for school to let out. "Whatcha readin' there, Miz Avery?" he asked. "Looks like one of them old-timey boo-uks, like Doc Peggs's always got his nose stuck into of."

Why all this sudden curiosity? Laura wondered. Neither Ike nor Chub seemed the bookish sort. "Oh, nothing much." She laughed weakly. "Just some ancient history a friend sent me from New York." She took the book down to the far end of the bench from Chub and sat down to leaf through it.

It was a handsomely printed work, with steel engravings that she recognized from the town rising around her: there's the church, there's Minter's store; look here—the Eldridge place, *our* house! The frontispiece showed a stern-faced, biblical-looking man with a goatee beard. He carried a tall shepherd's crook with a strange, winged device at the point where the staff bent backward: all through the book, as she flipped it, she saw that the illustrator had ended his chapters with what she had come to think of as "Cassie's Symbol." And she suddenly realized with an inexplicable thrill that the symbol was merely a two-dimensional, simplified rendering of the crook on that shepherd's staff.

"Hey," Chub said, leaning over her to her surprise, "ain't that the church there?" He pointed an orange-stained finger at the plate. She slapped the book closed.

"I gotta laugh," Chub continued, sinking down on the bench beside her. "That durn Pastor Thorpe was over again yestiddy. 'Ain't seen you much around church lately, Chub. Air you gonna stop by an' worship with us?' I says to him, I says, 'Say, Padre, I don't have to go to church of a Sunday to worship. No, sir. Ever' day when I come home from drivin' that school bus, I just park her in the barnyard, I go into the house, I mix myself a martini and turn on the cartoons on TV, and I flop on back in that big easy chair and say: 'Thank *Gawd*!' " His beefy face split into a wide, happy chuckle.

"Well, I've got to be getting over to Doc's," Laura said, rising. "Good talking with you, Constable Markham."

Snoops! she grumbled to herself as she drove up the street the short distance to Doc's. Then she caught herself again: Why be so urban and snotty about it? These people were her neighbors, her fellow townsmen. Of course they were curious—who isn't, even in a huge, anonymous metropolis like New York? How else did people get to know each other than by studying each other? It was just that here in the Gore, with its tiny population, that scrutiny became much more obvious. And thus more readily resented by a "private person" such as herself. You'd better get used to it, girl, she told herself. There are no secrets in small-town America. No room of one's own—not even a private library.

She looked at the book once more when she was parked in Doc's driveway. It appeared to be a wordy, overwritten study of Druidism and other forms of tree-worship in Asia, Africa, even among the Indians of North America. There were individual chapters on famous sacred groves and special trees, such as the one in the Punjab where villagers still (as of 1873, when the book was printed) sacrificed a maiden each year beneath the Sacred Cedar. There were plates that showed huge wicker cages full of human victims, to which dancing worshipers were setting fire—a Druidic rite, she read in the caption. The author, that very Ahaz Ashburn whom she had been discussing with Doc just a week or two ago, had included a very emphatic disclaimer saying that "no contemporary European or American tree-worshipers still practice the vicious, pagan rite of sacrifice, human or inhuman."

She was just beginning to skim a chapter called "The Tragedy of Obed" when the church bell began to toll the hour of three. Doc would be waiting. She decided she would rather read the book thoroughly before quizzing Doc more closely on the subject of the Church in the Wildwood, so she placed it in the glove compartment and went in. Doc was on the phone. He waved her inside.

Not until she was naked on the examining couch, and Doc was readying the longest needle she had ever seen, did Laura remember that she had left her purse and her keys in the truck.

TWO

"This won't hurt a bit," Doc Peggs whispered soothingly.

He stood above her, his white hair haloed by the glaring overhead light. His face was in shadow but Laura's eyes caught the luminous glow of his false teeth, her nostrils the clean, dry, not-unpleasant old man scent of him. She felt helpless in her nakedness on the padded couch: woman as victim, she thought bitterly. His strong fingers probed her abdomen.

Then she felt the icy touch of alcohol-soaked cotton on her belly, the pressure of the needle's tip beside her navel. Doc Peggs grunted with concentration. She felt her skin give, then pucker around the needle, watched its gleaming length disappear deep within her. Perhaps it was just her overwrought imagination but it seemed she could feel every millimeter of its cold, hard slide down into her womb.

"The idea," Doc said, "is to remove a little of the amniotic fluid that surrounds the fetus. The trick is to do so without touching the fetus itself. Try to relax now, no movement at all if you can help it. This is the sly part. . . ."

At that moment she heard an auto engine start up close by.

The truck!

My God, some one was stealing the truck! The keys in the ignition. My purse! She would recognize that throaty roar anywhere. Her eyes widened, and Doc, mistaking the look no doubt for fear of the needle, clucked and murmured comforting *there, theres* as he withdrew the plunger of the hypodermic. She started to speak. . . .

"Hush, hush—not a move!" he chided. "Not a word or we don't know what will happen!"

Helpless with frustration and fury, she listened to the truck back out of Doc's driveway, then grumble through its gear changes and out of her range of hearing. The hypo barrel filled slowly.

"There," Doc said at last, withdrawing the needle. He held it triumphantly up to the light. "Eureka! That's Greek for—"

"Goddamnit!" Laura screamed. "Somebody just stole my truck! Didn't you hear it? They just backed right out of your driveway and drove away in it. My purse! My truck! Ooooooooooh—*shit*!"

Doc staggered back, his long face shocked, eyes blinking rapidly.

"What? What?" As she pulled on her clothes, he dashed to the side window, then returned shaking his head sorrowfully.

"Quick!" she yelled. "Call the store. Chub Markham was there just a few minutes ago. Maybe he can catch him."

For twenty minutes she fretted while Doc muttered savagely about "these rowdy kids nowadays—too much TV, that's what it is." Then she heard the truck pull back into the driveway. Chub Markham stepped out with a triumphant grin on his face.

"Found 'er parked just off the main road, a mile outta town," he reported. " 'Fraid whoever done it got away with your purse, though, Miz Avery. I searched the weeds for it but found not a trace."

"What about . . ." Laura looked inside the glove compartment. *The Book of Ahaz* was, of course, also missing.

"What's that, dear?" asked Doc.

"Nothing," she said. "Damn—my driver's license, my credit cards, and fifty dollars in cash. Not to mention my favorite compact and comb."

Doc wrapped an arm around her shoulder.

"Chub will get the word out for hunters to watch for your purse, out there in the woods. Usually a thief like that doesn't keep the main part of the evidence. It'll turn up, I'm sure."

That evening, as she lay sleepless listening to Mark's throaty snore, Laura suddenly recalled where she had seen that shepherd's staff before:

In her dream . . .

Up in the oak grove . . .

Doc Peggs was carrying it.

The purse turned up before the week was out. One morning while Mark was hunting, Laura heard a hesitant knock on the back door. Dolph Rooney stood there, scuffing his knee-length moccasins on the slate stoop and smiling shyly, like an ancient pet monkey caught in a bad deed. From behind his back he produced the purse.

"Found it up by the oak grove," he explained, "while I was out hunting for 'crazy wood.' It was just lying there under that great big oak tree there. Open. I closed it but I ain't looked in it."

"How did you know it was my purse?"

"Heard the word from Ike, down at the store."

She opened the purse. Everything was there but the money. Then she remembered her manners and invited Dolph in for coffee. He came in warily, she thought, like a cat into a dark barn loft. But he relaxed as she showed him around the house, admiring the way she had decorated the old place and the handiwork of Mark's improvements. He was particularly fascinated with the portrait of Cassie Eldridge Ashburn.

"Strange woman," he mused.

"What do you know about her?"

"Oh, just the usual. How she opened the sawmill and saved the town. How she and her son started the Church. But I never seen a portrait of her before." His eyes were hooded in that booze-ravaged face. "That *look*."

"Yes," Laura said. "So distant and dedicated, it's eerie."

"I knew a woman with that look once," Dolph said slowly. "Back before Repeal, it was. I had me a little shack on the Traticook River over there in Rhode Island and I used to run out in my boat at night to bring in hooch from the big freighters operating out of Canada. My partner was a 'legger named Leary, a mean old boot he was, but he had the decentest wife in Christendom. Name of Meg. A lovely lady, churchgoing, God-fearing, never cussed nor smoked nor tasted so much as a drop of dandelion wine. But Leary got too big for his own good, began flashing his money around town and lording it over the other folks. Well, they turned him in to the feds, and Leary got croaked in a gunfight one night down in the marshes. That's when The Look began.

"After Repeal, Meg opened the swankiest gin mill north of New Haven. A proper watering spot for the swells who used to come up in the summer back then. Of course all the local businessmen, the very ones who had blown the whistle on old Leary, they were customers too. They hobnobbed with the summer people and carried on like butter wouldn't melt, you know. They didn't notice *The Look*. Then one Labor Day weekend, when all the town nabobs were partying there with their wives and hoity-toity city pals, Meg Leary locked all the doors, barred the fire exits, and torched the place. Killed the lot of them."

"How dreadful!"

"She stayed in there with 'em. That's The Look for you."

He got up to leave, retrieving his knapsack from the hook near the door where he had hung it. He unbuckled the top flap and reached inside.

"Remember I promised you a carving?" he said. "Here it is." From the pack he withdrew a long object wrapped crudely in newspaper and tied in butcher's string. "If you don't mind, ma'am, I won't wait around to see your reaction." Once again he was nervous, shy, almost guilty, Laura thought. "I know what I feel about it, and what the tree that grew it was feeling." He laughed embarrassedly. "Crazy wood, I call it. Maybe it's the woodcarver who's crazy?"

He left as silently as he had arrived.

The phone rang before Laura could open the package—just Ike Minter saying that he'd like Mark to call when he got back—and then she had to attend to her bread dough, which had been rising, and put it in the oven. By the time she remembered the package it was late afternoon, with autumnal darkness turning the windows steely blue. She made herself a cup of tea and sat in the gloom as she undid the string.

Then she sat back with a start.

The package contained a severed human forearm, muscular, knotted with veins. The long-nailed hand was cupped around a cracked skull. The skull of a baby!

Her stomach muscles clenched and for an instant she thought her very womb was convulsing. Then reason asserted itself and she saw that the forearm was wood. Yet she could not bring herself to touch it for a long time.

Yes, wood—the hand and skull carved from a creviced oak burl, the arm itself just a branch that had grown immediately beneath the burl. But so cleverly, so realistically carved that in the evening half-light it had seemed the real thing. She shuddered but could not tear her eyes from it. Graved on the brow of the baby's skull was Cassie's symbol.

From outside came Mark's halloo—the hunter home from the hill. For some reason she could not let him see the carving. It was too horrible, too dreadful, and of course he would admire it as he admired everything these benighted people did up here. He would insist on putting it atop the living-room mantel, on counting it among his "trophies"—like those spread grouse tail feathers he nailed up when they had mummified on the paneled walls, and the dried foot of his first wild turkey, and those smelly rabbit hides she had insisted he keep in the barn. The wild trophies perhaps she could live with—but this . . . abomination!

Fortunately she had built a fire in the kitchen wood stove. She opened the door and stuffed in Dolph's offering.

Later that evening, while Mark snoozed in front of the television set, she put more wood into the stove. As she did so, she could see the forearm and its gruesome burden glowing softly among the coals. The face of the baby's skull seemed to open its mouth as she watched, then change shape slowly into a man's bearded face, into a woman's, finally into a flaking, sparking wraith of all shapes and no shape at one and the same time. Then the air ignited the wood and the apparition vanished. She fired in enough wood to bury it, slammed the door, and hurried back into the living room.

They were the faces she had seen on the Bull Oak, up there in the grove, that dreadful afternoon in June.

A few days later Doc Peggs called to say the results of the amniocentesis had arrived. "Everything's just fine," he told her jubilantly. "It's a perfect specimen, healthy as its mommy and daddy."

She thanked him warmly and they chatted for a few minutes.

"Of course," he said mock-slyly, "now I know what sex it is, I'm going to have to be especially careful when I talk to you for fear of giving away the secret. What names have you picked out? Maybe we could work up a composite and skirt the problem."

"I've always like alliterative names," Laura said. "If it's a girl, I'd hoped to call her Adele after a favorite aunt of mine. If it's a boy, well . . . I haven't really settled on anything yet. Mark says he doesn't want a junior, but he doesn't like names like Andrew or Aaron or Abner. Asah is rather nice—biblical and resonant—and we could call him Ace for short, Mark says." She sniffed disapprovingly and Doc laughed. "My son, Ace Avery. The all-star shortstop running-back forward fighter-pilot. I just don't know."

"How about Ahaz, after our illustrious founding father?"

"Why don't we just call it Baby X for now," Laura said. "You'll just have to be extra careful when I come for my visits. And don't you go letting on to anyone in town. The word would be back to me in flash."

"My lips are sealed," he promised. "The secret of Baby X is safe with me." She could hear him chuckling and humming to himself as he hung up.

THREE

Bill McGregor arrived the weekend before Thanksgiving. He chugged into the barnyard late one afternoon in a "Blue Funk." (The battered '72 Maverick was actually red in color; its nick-name derived from the perpetual cloud of exhaust fumes that followed wherever it went.) Deer season had begun and Mark—still buckless—was out hunting. It was one of those steely November days with a cold wind and quick-scudding skies that changed hue every minute from blindingly bright to icy blue-black. Laura greeted her old friend fondly and they quickly scooted inside to the warmth of the fire.

"You're positively radiant," Bill said as she poured him a Scotch. "Impending mommy-dom obviously agrees with you."

"I've never felt better," she laughed, "and look, I'm beginning to show!" She turned sideways, in profile, and demonstrated her tiny bulge.

For an instant the nightmare descended on her again—the picnic horror on the mountain.

Doc Peggs.

Rape.

She shivered.

Bill laughed in turn. "You sound like a little girl who just got her first bra."

"Oh, right now I'm proud of it," she said, shrugging off the nightmare mood. "But a few months from now, when I'm out to here, I'm sure I'll be sniveling and cussing just like all the other pregnant ladies I've known. Judy Monkhouse used to complain something fierce. The abdomen—she said—is the most uncomfortable, ill-engineered part of the anatomy for carrying a heavy load. Why couldn't women carry their babies on their backs, both before birth and after?"

"Good old Judy," said Bill. "She sends her love. Freddie thought for a while that maybe she could come up with me for Thanksgiving, but she got tied into a quick-closing job for Underalls, or something. She sends her best too. So listen, how've you been, really? You seem to have kicked that monkey of gloom and doom who was riding you last summer. Did that book I sent you help any?"

"It might have," Laura said, "but it was stolen." While she showed him around the house, she told him about the incident. Unfortunately Bill had not had time to read the book himself. He had found it only after the most intensive search of Lower Manhattan used-book shops, then mailed it off posthaste after only skimming it.

"If the thief didn't burn it," Laura said, "it's probably lying up in the woods somewhere, moldering in the fall rains. Mark and I looked for it one afternoon in the grove where Dolph Rooney found my purse, but nothing. Probably ripped up for squirrels' nests by now."

"Damned high-priced housing," said Bill. "The old goniff I bought it from wanted fifty bucks."

"Oh, Bill," Laura said, embarrassed. "I hadn't thought . . . Let me give you a check."

"No, no." Now Bill was embarrassed. "I didn't mean that. I . . ."

But she insisted, and wrote out a check for fifty dollars. Bill accepted it, then tore it to shreds and fed it into the kitchen stove. "Call it part of my housewarming gift," he said. "I was going to wait until Mark got back, but what the hell."

From his day pack he pulled a tastefully wrapped flat package. When Laura opened it, she was gazing at the portrait from which the frontispiece of *The Book of Ahaz* had been copied: the bearded, biblical man with the odd shepherd's crook. In style and color, even down to the frame, it was the mate of Cassie's portrait.

"My God," she whispered. "Who is he? Where did you find this?"

"I'll answer your second question first," Bill said, "and you'll see why it's absurd of you to pay me for the book. The painting was my mother's. She grew up in the Gore, you'll remember, and for years this old geezer used to hang in the hallway outside my bedroom when I was a kid. Gave me nightmares, he did. Finally my mother took it down and it disappeared, but after she died I found it in the attic, where I was weeding through stuff when I sold the house. For some reason—maybe to lay the old ghosts—I kept it. Then when I found the book for you and saw the print of it in the front, I remembered it. And what you told me about the portrait you'd found in the attic. I thought they'd make a nice matching set. This is Obediah Magrute, the mystery man in Cassie Eldridge's life."

" 'The Tragedy of Obed,' " Laura said. "I was just going to read that chapter when the truck—and the book—got stolen."

"Did you read about 'The Druid's Curse'?"

"What's that?"

"When the lynch mob came to finish off Obed, he laid this heavy curse on them. . . ."

"Lynch mob?" Laura said. "Doc Peggs told me Obed committed suicide—burned himself to death in his cabin up in the oak grove when Cassie spurned his proposal."

"That's not the way Ahaz tells it. Nor my mom, when she told me the story. I guess it was that that gave me the nightmares."

As they sat in the living room, a fire blazing in the open stove and darkness dropping blue gauze over the hills outside, Bill told her the story of Obed Magrute's death at the hands of Colonel Thorpe and his cohorts.

"As the fire blazed up around him," Bill said, "old Obed's voice came booming out of the smoke and flame. Anyone who cut in the woods thereafter, no matter what the purpose, would die for his sin." He stopped, got up, poured himself another two fingers of Johnnie Black, then turned to Laura. "And what's more, old Obed said, just as these men were taking his wife and unborn child from him, so too would the Bull Oak take their wives and children of those who sinned. Full-circle revenge. The Druid's Curse. And by God—or Obed—it worked, didn't it? Nobody cuts in the oak grove nowadays, and damn near every man, woman, and child in the Gore is a card-carrying member of the Church in the Wildwood, which is nothing more than a watered-down congregation of latter-day Druids. Tree-worshipers to the last lowly sapling."

"Wait a minute," said Laura. "They call the grove 'Drooker's Woods.' Is that a corruption of 'Druid's Curse'? Drooker's, I mean."

"Could be," said Bill. "I didn't see anything about that in the book, but it makes sense."

"Well," said Laura almost brightly, "that lays a lot of ghosts for me as well. It's a very pretty little piece of local legend, and it explains why these people are so nutsy about that stand of timber up there. I guess Mark and I are lucky to own a historical landmark of that magnitude. Ancient American history right on our own back forty."

"There *have* been accidents up there in the grove," Bill said. "Even when I was a kid, summering in the Gore, you'd hear tell about some would-be lumberjack—usually an outsider: the locals were too smart to try it—getting scragged by a freak windfall or a tree dropping the wrong way or splitting while it was being cut and kicking back on the sawyers."

"Maybe psyched by the legend," Laura said. "It would figure. The self-fulfilling prophecy: a subconscious mistake in a very dangerous job, set up by the very legend itself."

"You don't have to look to Freud for answers," said Bill. "I learned enough about logging from helping my uncles around the farm to know there are pieces of ground that, by their very shape and the wind patterns that work them, are much more dangerous to cut than others. Sidehill logging, for instance, is a hundred times more dangerous than cutting on a flat. Vectors of gravity and all that. A tree can split a hell of a lot easier on a sidehill."

"At any rate," said Laura, "it's nothing supernatural. Now I've got to start getting supper ready. The Wandering Boy will be back any minute and he'll be hungry as a bear after pounding the woods all day."

"And probably grouchy as one, too." Bill laughed. "I've been listening while we talked and I haven't heard any rifle shots."

"Skunked again," Laura giggled. "It's mean of me, I know, but I feel a little thrill of triumph for the deer every day he comes back empty-handed. Am I a naughty wife?"

He leered at her, in a playful way. "I wish you were," he said.

For a guilty moment, Laura wished so too.

Apart from the wine and coffee, everything on Laura's supper menu had been baked, grown, caught, or killed by the Averys themselves: cold poached brook trout vinaigrette on a bed of watercress from Cauldron Brook; a stew of partridge, rabbit, what proved to be raccoon (but tasted delicious), carrots, peas, and potatoes from the garden; home-baked bread to mop up the plates; a salad of leaf lettuce, wintercress, Jerusalem artichoke, and fresh dill; baked apples in maple syrup for dessert. Laura had gathered the apples—ugly-looking, warped, rust-flecked things that nonetheless tasted crisper, tarter, and more flavorful than any store-bought fruit—from the trees that grew wild on the ridge of Abednego Mountain across the road. These trees, like the townspeople of the Gore, were so inbred that the fruit they produced bore no resemblance to any apples ever grown commercially. After eating himself out of his usual belt notch, Bill McGregor sat back in his chair, impressed.

Clearly, though, he was worried about the changes in his friend Mark. The close-cropped hair, the Hemingwayesque beard, the wind- and weather-darkened skin, the heavy bands of new muscle on shoulders and forearms, and especially the newfound swagger in both Mark's speech and his gait—all combined to make him appear a different man: not the sensitive, tentative, painterly Mark of yore, but rather some rude impostor. He didn't even sound the same. Laconic, almost taciturn, he might have passed for a native-born Vermonter, Bill thought.

Nor was Bill overly impressed with the paintings

Mark showed him after dinner. The work was heavy, dark, cruel, totally lacking in the wit and humor, the sense of humanity that had pervaded his earlier serious work. Bill McGregor was no art critic, but like most educated New Yorkers he knew good painting when he saw it. Yet he was reluctant to tell Mark that he thought the works unsalable. Mark planned to ship them off to his gallery the next morning. That night Mark got roaring drunk, regaling them (he thought) with hunting tales he had heard from his new buddy, Billy Munro. Bill laughed, but Laura could tell his heart wasn't in it. No more than was hers. Then Mark fell asleep, snoring, on the living-room couch while Bill helped Laura wash the supper dishes. They turned on the radio to drown out Mark's sound effects with a Brahms symphony.

The next day, after another fruitless morning hunt for Mark, the three of them drove down to town for the annual Fall Fire Festival. Toward the end of October strange stuffed figures had begun to crop up throughout the Gore. They were dummies made from old clothes, pillowcases, and stockings, man-sized figures stuffed with straw and wearing crudely painted human faces. You might come around a corner on the Cauldron road and find one swinging from a noose tied to an overhanging oak branch. Or see another perched witchlike on the roof-pole of a house in town. Or impaled on a stake, grotesque and flopping in the wind, in the center of the town square. The practice of making these dummies was widespread in the region—both Mark and Laura had seen them even as far west as the small towns of New York, just across the Vermont border—but usually they disappeared at Halloween, and were reused year after year. But in the Gore, in a tradition that dated back well into the nineteenth century, they were gathered at the time of the Fire Festival and ritually burned on a huge town bonfire.

"We're all supposed to bring a stone with our name on it," Laura told Bill. "Then, Doc says, after the fire is burned out and we've roasted all the weenies we can eat, they rake the coals into a big circle and we all put our stones inside the ring. The next day they check the stones and if any of them have moved outside the circle, it means that person is 'special.' I guess the kids love it, and it's a good way to relieve the arsonistic tendencies of the young. Or so says Doc, anyway."

"That's another Druidic holdover," Bill said. "The pre-Christian Celts used to build big ritual fires twice a year, in midsummer when they were driving the cattle out into the newly regenerated pastures, and again at the onset of winter when they welcomed the cattle back into the byres. I remember reading about it in Fraser—*The Golden Bough*—for a religious-history course I took as an undergraduate. What the hell, almost all the big quasireligious Christian holidays like Christmas, Easter, and even Halloween are just lightly glossed-over pagan fests."

A big crowd had already gathered at the town park when they arrived. It was a bright afternoon, windless and pleasantly warm in the sun, and a huge mountain of sticks, broken-up old furniture, rung-sprung ladders, dry-rotted railroad ties and telephone poles, had been stacked in the center of the town baseball diamond. Men, women, and children stood chugging from gallon jugs of what smelled, in passing them, suspiciously like hard cider. There was much laughter and jocularity. Beside the unlit bonfire lay a heap of straw-stuffed dummies, and for an instant Laura flashed on those gruesome postwar photographs from Auschwitz and Bergen-Belsen. She saw Doc Peggs, who waved cheerily to her, and Huldy, who offered them a slug of the cider.

It was hard indeed: Bill said it was probably spiked with pure grain alcohol, in the fine old country tradition of these parts. Little children stood around expectantly, many of them holding wieners already stuck on fresh-cut green-wood withes. There was no speechmaking. Doc Peggs lighted the bonfire with a guttering, oil-soaked torch and everyone stood back as the flames caught.

The fire roared upward with the voice of an angry dragon and the heat waves pounded outward; Laura was suddenly back at Polly Boggs's house. The night she died. She reached out blindly and found herself clutching Bill's arm. She looked at the faces of the crowd: red and dancing in the fire-flare, mouths agape, eyes wide, hungry—eyes that themselves were filled with flame. Despite the heat she felt chilled, frightened. Then with a shout the children ran to the pile of dummies. They began hurling them gleefully into the flames. Laura recognized Jermyn Boggs, Polly's oldest son, among the bigger boys. The dummy he took from the pile was that of a female figure. It wore a dress that Laura was sure was Polly's Sunday-go-to-Meetin' dress, the one she had worn to church that Sunday so long ago. The dummy wore a wig of yellow yarn that had slipped sideways, drunkenly, on the round, fat, pillowcase head. As Jermyn raised it to throw, Laura saw the face.

It was Polly's.

She felt sick, weak at the knees: the whole thing was a reenactment!

Mark was busily sketching away, his eyes riveted on the scene. Bill too looked captivated. But that would figure, with his interest in early American folkways.

"Fascinating." He grinned when she caught his attention. "I can use this in my graduate course on pre-Industrial Revolution culture."

"I don't feel very well," Laura said, trying not to whine. "Could we go?"

"Hell, honey," said Mark, "this is great stuff. Why doesn't Bill take you . . ."

"Bill's got as much right to watch it as you do," she said angrily. "He's going to use it in his graduate seminar. And I'm *your* wife, carrying *your* child."

"Okay, okay. I've got about all I need anyway." He smiled placatingly, but she could see he had just figured out that if they left right now, he could get out with his rifle for the dusk deer hunt. "Bill can put our namestones in the ring. But how's he gonna get home?"

"I'll walk, or else bum a ride with one of your neighbors—that Munro woman? Don't worry about me."

"I'll introduce you to Doc Peggs," Laura said, feeling better already but still determined to leave. "He knows everything there is to know about town history."

Up on the grassy hill that flanked the park to the west, distant figures had been moving. Now they suddenly saw flames fire near the top of the ridge. The figures moved busily and the flames grew into huge fiery circles, upright hoops of fire twice as tall as a man. Then the hoops began to roll, the men running beside them, guiding them with long poles. The crowd's attention turned from the bonfire—all the dummies had been consumed—and a great cheer went up. The speed of the rolling hoops now turned them into disks of fire as they bounced and careened down the steep slope, sparks flying like miniature sun dogs.

"Great balls of fire!" laughed Bill McGregor. "That's just plain beautiful. They're duplicating the decline of the sun toward the winter solstice. Homeopathic magic, right here in Hubley's Gore in the late twentieth century. I'm going to do a paper on this!"

"Ah," said Doc Peggs, who stood nearby, "a scholar in our midst. How delightful!"

When Laura introduced them, Doc studied Bill's face closely.

"Bill McGregor," he said slowly. Then his face brightened. "Ah, yes. Mavis Cowper's boy. Cornell, Class of '62. Doctorate in American history from . . . Princeton, was it? Nineteen and seventy as I recall." He shook Bill's hand warmly.

"Laura says you know everything about Hubley's Gore history," Bill laughed, "but she didn't say down to the last half-breed expatriate."

Doc said he'd be glad to drive Bill up the mountain when the festivities ended, his only charge being that Bill stop off at his place for a glass of sherry and a look-see at Doc's collection of town memorabilia. As Mark and Laura left, the two historians were talking excitedly about "Beltane fires" and the Celtic influence on American Scots-Irish yeomanry.

"Are all the stones in place?"

"Yes, every one."

"Ashes cool enough yet?"

"Just warm to the touch."

"The newcomers' stones?"

"Over there, in the upper right-hand quadrant of the ring. About two o'clock."

"It's so dark that these old eyes can't see anything but the pale glow."

"We're getting old, no denying it."

"Can you read the name on *his* stone? No mistakes now."

"Yes, I can read it."

"Remove it from the ring."

A pause. In the autumn darkness the ring of hot ashes glowed faintly red beneath its coat of flaking gray. Far off at the end of the village a dog barked, high hollow yaps that echoed back from the ridges and set the owls to answering.

"Done."

"Good. Now he is special. Now he is *fey.*"

"He will be dead within the year."

"Indeed."

"And the other? The scholarly one, whose mother was with us in the old days?"

"With us now. All the way: blood will tell, as they say. Provided we do not harm her, which of course we won't."

"You'd best be sure of him."

"In addition he gets full power, after I'm dead, until the boy reaches his majority. I made sure of him before coming here tonight to meet you. I think he knew all along what we were, how it all worked." A bitter laugh. "Two glasses of sherry and the promise of a woman, that was his price."

"And power."

"*Some* power, not all. That comes only with Cassie's blood, my blood—the blood that will flow in the boy, whose name will be Ahaz."

"Ahaz."

A wind lifted the gray ash into a small whirl. Ash glared red beneath.

"Ah, his father answers to the son's name!"

"Our ageless punishment." Then again the bitter laugh. "And our endless glory. How much longer must the Curse live with us?"

"Until the last Oak dies."

FOUR

The wild turkey Mark had killed was far too big for just the three of them, unless she and Mark planned on eating turkey hash for a month straight, so Laura invited Doc Peggs and the Munros to join them for Thanksgiving dinner. She was busy that whole week with her preparations: molding cranberries, prebaking sweet potatoes, boiling and peeling the chestnuts Bill had brought up from the city and preparing them to cook with the brussels sprouts she had grown in the garden. She baked three pies—pumpkin (from their corn patch), apple (from Abednego), and cherry (from Huldy Munro's tiny orchard). Bill helped her. He loved to work in the kitchen and had a quick, sure hand with the cutlery.

Meanwhile Mark hunted. And hunted. And hunted. To no avail. Each night he dragged in sullen, distant, more unresponsive than he ever had been when he ran into difficulty with a painting. What made it worse was the sight of other hunters, successful and jubilant, driving down the road with buck deer on the roofs of their cars. Even going to town was painful: killed deer had to be checked in at the town clerk's office, just up their road from the church and the general store. Swifty Baines, the jovial and elderly town clerk, had a big block and tackle in front of his barn where he hung and weighed the animals, and to massage the hunter's ego he made sure that everyone in town had a chance to see the successful nimrod and his kill. Whenever Mark bumped into Swifty at the store, the clerk grinned teasingly and asked when he would be coming by with his buck. He called Mark "Mork," and although it was a pronunciation consistent with the Vermont dialect, Mark himself suspected that Swifty meant it in reference to the silly little dork from Ork on the boob tube.

The irony was that twice Mark had tracked a big buck high up onto Widdershins, spending hours working out the trail, stalking carefully, testing the wind, pushing himself to his physical and mental limit; and twice he had had the buck in his sights. It was a splendid ten-pointer, thick-necked and scarred on the shoulders and flanks from many a mating battle. But both times Mark had found an excuse not to pull the trigger. First he convinced himself that the buck had only to take three more steps to open up the perfect shot. Instead the buck stepped behind a scruffy little beech tree, apparently unperturbed, and simply did not reappear. The second time Mark argued to himself that the wind was too strong right now for a sure shot at this range. He would wait until it abated a bit—after all, the buck was browsing, unaware of his presence two hundred yards away behind a spruce blowdown. But before the wind died, the buck exploded from his quiet, flagged his long white-lined tail, and bounced like Superman over the top of a nearby ridge. Two easy shots, untaken.

Bill tried to divert him with witty gossip about their New York friends and new developments on the art scene but Mark wasn't having any. Each evening he would slump in his chair, drinking Scotch-and-Genesee boilermakers, then slide into snoring sleep. Each morning he was gone before dawn, rarely even taking a lunch with him. He was honed down wire-fine: a hollow-eyed hunting machine with death on his mind.

Laura pretended it wasn't happening. She reveled in Bill's company, especially his gossip. He even had witty opinions about Hubley's Gore. He'd hit it off splendidly with Doc Peggs, as she could tell when he accompanied her that Wednesday for her weekly checkup. The two men gabbed constantly while they were there, all in that dusty-musty historical lingo that Laura had given up with college. Indeed she found herself feeling jealous at being left out of the conversation. Heretofore she had been the center of Doc's attention whenever they met. Jealous and—what?—*anxious* as well. For all his charm, Doc remained a dubious character in her book. The nightmare scene on the mountain last summer kept echoing back to her at odd moments. Dreams can seem more real than reality. But no. And when she realized the childishness of her reaction to Bill and Doc together, she laughed at herself. Incipient cabin fever, she thought. I'll have to look out for that when winter sets in for real.

As it seemed to do that night—Thanksgiving Eve. Snow ghosted in from the northwest, silent on a steady wind that sibilated through the chimney caps, and by the time they had finished supper, the meadow had gone dead white. Mark was jubilant.

"A tracking snow!" he whooped. "Just what I've been waiting for. Tomorrow morning at first light I'll pick up that goddamn ten-pointer's track and run him to the ground. He's dead meat for sure now! Tomorrow morning!"

So delighted was he with the snow that he didn't even drink that night. Instead he chatted happily with Bill and Laura, his eyes sparkling and his long-absent smile as winning as ever. Just like a little boy, Laura thought, who's waited too long for winter.

And in the morning, while Laura and Bill stuffed the turkey and finished up the last-minute menu chores, he did it. About noon they heard his whoop from far up the snowy meadow. When they went out the door, they saw him up there, capering and dancing with his rifle over his head around the fallen brown body of the buck. Bloody to the elbows from gutting it, sweat pouring down his joy-reddened face, stripped down to his long-john top despite the twenty-degree cold, he had dragged the deer down from the top of Widdershins where he'd shot it three hours earlier. Bill helped him drag it the rest of the way, leaving a pale red groove in the six-inch snow. It was indeed a handsome animal, heavy-shouldered and noble-necked, with a wide, thick-tined set of antlers polished like ivory at the points. Glad as she was at Mark's jubilation, Laura could not help feeling a pang of regret. What a shame that so peaceable, so handsome an animal as this had to die just to make a man-boy happy. Mark and Bill put the deer on the truck and drove it down to Swifty's for the ceremonial weigh-in, then cranked the deer up on a block and tackle under the hayloft door of the barn for all passersby to see. (Although Mark argued that you hung a deer outside merely to cool the meat properly, Laura was sure it was just another sign of male macho show-offiness.)

But she soon forgot her pique with the grand success of Thanksgiving dinner. While the menfolk sat in the front room watching pro football and sucking down hooch (as Huldy put it), Laura and Huldy administered the final touches: making the gravy, whipping cream for the pie tops, warming up the precooked dishes, basting the turkey to a crisp-skinned, golden brown turn, cooking the last-minute veggies and slicing others raw for hors d'oeuvres to be served with the mayonnaise Laura prepared in her Cuisinart. Huldy marveled at the machine, but when Laura told her what it had cost when Mark bought it for her three years ago, she humphed and allowed as how a aig-beater was good enough—and gave a person more control, to boot.

When dinner was served at five o'clock precisely, all hands fell to with a will. For half an hour no one uttered a word. All that could be heard was a steady, almost furtive sound of food being consumed, punctuated on occasion by a gasp as diners quickly caught their breath, then resumed eating. Billy Munro ate with his face nearly at plate level, clutching the cutlery fist-style, napkin tucked into his buttoned sport-shirt collar, and shoveling the food into his brown-fanged mouth as if he were filling a coal bin. Doc of course ate elegantly but nonetheless eagerly. Huldy, despite her paucity of front teeth, gamely held her own with the better-equipped youngsters, and Bill McGregor watched her with awe as she tackled a giant drumstick.

There was no gauge by which to compare wild turkey with domestic, unless it was the difference between real meat and sawdust. The wild gobbler was sweet, succulent, bubbling with juice, and amazingly tender despite its great size. "Now you see why men hunt," Mark said proudly when conversation resumed. Doc sat back with a groan, unbuckled his belt, and offered his sincerest compliments to both hunter and chef. Even Huldy the Kitchen-Wise praised Laura's cooking with actual awe in her voice.

"A real country Thanksgiving," said Bill McGregor, "is truly something to be thankful for. Tell me, Doc, how long can it last? I mean, a town like this, untouched by the worst poisons of the twentieth century—a place where a man can actually go out and hunt his own

Thanksgiving turkey. Aren't you afraid the Gore will go the way the rest of Vermont is going? Gobbled up and plasticized by developers and shopping malls and ski resorts and city folks looking for vacation homes? What's to keep it from happening?"

"Oh, we have our ways." Doc laughed. "We've seen what's happened to other towns around us. When a Vermonter is hard pressed for cash, he just sells off another five acres here, ten acres there. Pretty soon he's got no land left for farming, so he either moves away or takes a job in the nearest ski town. The problem is economic, and here in the Gore we've got a sound economic base with the sawmill and the town forest up there on Widdershins. Kids don't have to move away for work. Farmers don't have to sell their patrimony. There's always a job in the mill, at top wages I might add, with the price of lumber what it is today. Enough pay to tide a man through hard times. And folks here never bought that 'revolution of rising expectations' folderol of the fifties. Thanks to Pastor Thorpe and the Church, our youngsters don't have any yen for fancy cassette players and disco togs and racy cars. Nor do the grown-ups have to have a flashy new Thunderbug, or whatever they call 'em, every year or two. Take a look at that old crate of mine—sound as a preinflation dollar. We like it the way we've got it, thankee, sir."

"But what about television? I see plenty of antennas on all the roofs in town. Hasn't that influenced your young folks? I mean, violence and sex and all that."

"Funny thing about that," Doc said, bemused. "I was worried about that a while back, when the papers started to get full of it, and I made an informal survey of the youngsters in town. They said that the sex and violence on TV seemed unreal to them. Not like the real thing. I guess they meant the farm life, what with the breeding season, the hog killing, and the hunting and all. Didn't seem to have bothered them a whit."

"But what about the outsiders who move in here, bringing their alien ways and fancy life-styles? Doesn't that pervert the town's way of looking at things? No offense, Averys."

"Flatlanders either assimilate or get out," Doc answered. "Mark and Laura here have done a dandy job so far of assimilating. Mark hunts and fishes, does his own carpentry and mason work, cuts his own firewood, and next year, Laura tells me, he plans to run some livestock on the meadow. What's it going to be, Mark?"

"We were thinking sheep," said Mark.

"That'd be right appropriate." Doc smiled. "This used to be the most successful merino farm in the Gore, back in the nineteenth century."

"And I want to get into carding and spinning wool," Laura added, not to be left out. "There's a good income to be had from wool these days, and once the baby's here I want to pull my own weight again with the family economy. Maybe I'll even get back into knitting, or open a little wool and knitting shop in the barn. Something like that."

"Sounds like a fine environment," Bill said as Laura and Huldy served the pie. "Doc tells me that the school system still leaves something to be desired, though. We're going down there next time I visit to look at it. I may have some ideas for improvements in curriculum. I almost went into elementary and high school education myself, back in my Jesuit days, before I lost the faith and gained the Great Ambition." He laughed. "Once we get that fixed up, Laura, your . . . Baby X will have the ideal place to grow up in, won't it, Doc?"

"Almost slipped up there, William." Doc laughed. "Hope you don't mind, Laura, but your friend just weaseled it out of me t'other night, after too much sherry."

Laura was angered that Doc had told Bill the baby's sex, but the general warm mood of the dinner party was too strong for her to take true umbrage.

"Just so you don't say a word to the New York crowd about it, Bill," she warned. "If you do, I swear I'll send Mark and his deer rifle down there to take my revenge. You can just tell them that the baby will be a Vermonter."

Huldy laughed wryly. "There's an old saying about that, Laura dear. Us Vermonters is right jealous of the label, and you durn near have to have four sets of great-grandfolks in the burial ground to call yourself a Vermonter."

"What's the old saying, Huldy?" Mark asked.

"Jest 'cause the cat has her kittens in the oven," Huldy said, "that don't make 'em biscuits."

They all laughed. All, that is, but Billy, who belched and resumed picking his teeth with his finger.

"But don't worry, Laura dear," Huldy said. "Your Baby X may not be a true-to-blood Vermonter, but he/she'll shure be a prized and precious Hubleyite."

"Amen," said Doc.

FIVE

Next morning the mail brought disaster. A letter arrived from Mark's agent in New York saying that his gallery had rejected the new paintings. The wording was polite, vague, circuitous, but there was no mistaking the message: The new stuff stank. What's worse, the agent advised, the magazine from which Mark derived most of his commercial-art income was going under, a victim like so many others of the nation's current hard times. In one blow the Averys' economic base had been blasted out from beneath them.

Fortunately Bill was still there to cheer them up. "Come on," he said, "it's not the end of the world. You've still got plenty of money in the management fund, not to mention all those blue-chip stocks you were always buying. You'll muddle through, and if worse comes to worst, Laura can always go back to modeling once the baby's born."

"I'll be damned before I see my wife the sole support of my family," Mark said. He sat hunched at the kitchen table, sipping hot tea spiked with rum. More rum than tea, Bill thought, judging by the level of the bottle.

"Well, oink oink to you," Laura said, unsmiling. "I'll work if I goddamn please, Mr. Macho."

"Like hell . . ."

"Now listen, you two," Bill interjected. "This isn't the time to start a civil war. You've got to pull together now. I mean, you're not about to go on relief, or lose the house or anything like that. Remember, this is Hubley's Gore, home of the original backwoods communism, as Doc Peggs describes it. Neighbors help neighbors in these parts. If you have to, Mark, you can always take a job in the sawmill until you make new contacts in the magazine world, or get a new batch of paintings finished."

"The sawmill," Mark sneered. "I can just see myself brown-bagging it and borrowing a chaw of Red Man from the boys on the line. Sneaking a coupla beers with the gang down to the Beech Seal before bellying on home. Laura waiting at the door with a rolling pin behind her back. Fuck that. I wasn't cut out to be a mill worker."

"We could sell the place, if it came to that," Laura offered. "With all the work we've done on it, we could get sixty thousand easily, maybe seventy-five."

"I'm not a quitter either," Mark said. He poured a straight slug of rum into his cup and chugged it back. Then poured another.

"Yeah, but you're going to be a lush if you don't watch out," Bill said. "I don't see why you're so goddamn upset. You're acting like a couple of kids whose allowance was cut off for a week. Who never learned to spell the word *setback*. Remember, O ye of little faith, this too shall pass away. Or whatever."

"You're right," Mark said finally. He got up and poured his rum down the sink, though he watched it whirl away rather wistfully. "We'll work something out. But the first thing to do is help Laura clean up the

Thanksgiving crockery, and then set to work cleaning up the Thanksgiving turkey."

It was later that day that Mark conceived the plan he quickly dubbed "Operation Salvation."

"It's all here on the back forty," he said excitedly. "I've got the saw, I've got the truck, and right back there I've got the money. Unfortunately it's in the shape of trees. All I have to do is apply the saw, pile the result into the truck, drive it down to the New York suburbs and, *voilà,* I've got the money. Up to a hundred twenty-five dollars a cord for firewood down there, I read in the *Times* the other day. Doesn't even have to be cured. The suburban yokels can't tell green wood from dry to save their ass, and according to the paper, wood stoves are selling like food processors used to. Wood has surpassed nuclear power as an energy source in this country—it's the instant solution to the fuel-oil shortage."

"Yeah," Bill said, "I saw that piece. But can you do it? I mean, that's damned hard work, isn't it? Tricky, dangerous, not to mention back-breaking. Wouldn't you be better off working in the mill? At least you're in out of the weather, and according to all reports it's going to be a savage goddamn winter."

"I like it in the woods," Mark said. "And I know how to drop trees. Billy Munro says I'm a natural with a chainsaw—got an instinctive eye for which way a tree wants to fall. And Billy's Mr. Backwoods himself in all those things."

Laura held her peace in Bill McGregor's presence. Mark already knew her views on the dangers of logging. She would take it up with him in private.

"You'll see, pal o' mine." Mark grinned. "Tomorrow morning bright and early we're gonna don our Paul Bunyan togs and I'll show you what it's all about. Unless, of course, you suddenly remember an appointment in the city."

"No." Bill laughed. "I don't have to be back until Monday. Old Uncle Bill'll be glad to lend a hand."

That night, as he lay reading in bed in the guest bedroom, Bill McGregor could hear the Averys arguing. He heard the words *oak grove* and *Druid's Curse* over and over—Mark's low volcanic rumble and Laura's insistent contralto batting them back and forth like verbal tennis balls. But the argument petered out, before he turned off his light, into the rhythmic creak of bedsprings, as all marital arguments short of disaster end. Bill was thankful that they had resolved their difference. But the sound of the bedsprings soured his dreams.

He still loved Laura, intensely, to the exclusion of any woman he'd met before or since. Oh, it was all well and good to be civilized about these things. Mark was a good egg—hell, he was a decent chap. But in that lonely moment before sleep, when a single man feels most vulnerable, like a little boy without his Mommy, he hated Mark with a bitter passion.

Next morning they loaded the truck—chainsaw, gas can, chain oil, ax, half a dozen red plastic wedges, and a stubby-handled tool with a hinged hook mounted just above the steel point at the business end. A peavey, Mark called it, the "Woodsman's Best Friend." Then they drove through the snow up the meadow to a stand of white birches.

"Ike Minter says city folks love to buy birch logs," Mark explained. "Don't matter to them that it burns too fast to make a good fire—they love the look of it in their living-room woodbox. Well, we'll give 'em some."

After touching up the chain teeth to razor sharpness with a precalibrated file, Mark showed Bill how to fell a tree where you wanted it. He selected a big birch just inside the stand of trees. Its trunk measured a good foot and a half in diameter at the cutting level. "Just judging by the straightness of the trunk," he said, "you'd probably figure this tree would fall wherever you wanted it to. Not so. Take a look up topside and you'll see that there's more branches on the woods side than the meadow side of the tree. This guy could fall over backwards on us. Now watch." He yanked; the saw roared.

He made a wedge-shaped face cut swiftly, about a third of the way into the trunk, the chain teeth spewing clean chips that disappeared on the snow. Then he made two side cuts at a slight angle downward into the face cut, and deeper on the front side of the tree than toward the back. Bill could see that the "hinge" created would lie well forward on the meadow side—where Mark wanted the tree to fall. Then as Bill stood clear, Mark made his felling cut, his lower lip gripped under his teeth with concentration as he stared upward, waiting for the tree to begin its fall.

The tree groaned slightly, a sound audible even above the ferocious ripping howl of the saw, then began to teeter—toward the meadow. Its speed increased as it fell with a whooshing roar, underscored by the tearing sound of sundered hinge wood, to slam and bounce once on the meadow snow. Mark killed the saw.

"Don't you love it?" he yelled, grinning hugely. "Ain't it grand? What was it Joyce Kilmer wrote—'Only God can make a tree'? Well, only man can unmake 'em, and then make something better out of the leavin's. Oh, I do love it so. I love it so dearly!"

They limbed and sectioned the big birch, with Bill hauling the few unusable tops off to a heap he started in the meadow, then loaded the unsplit log lengths into the truck. All morning they worked felling more birches and rendering them into logs. The brush pile grew to twice a man's height in no time.

"I'll leave the brush in the meadow there over the

winter," Mark explained. "Makes a good hidey-hole for wild critters—cottontails and snowshoe rabbits, even field mice and voles—and the deer will come out at night and browse on the branch tips. Then next spring when all the suption's out of it, I'll burn the sumbitch on some nice drizzly day. That'll get the nutrients in the wood back into the soil quicker than rotting would. Nothing goes to waste."

"Are you going to leave any of these birches?"

"Not a stick. I'm going to clear-cut this stand—what is it, maybe an acre?"

"Clear-cut?" Bill said. "Isn't that a dirty word among the ecologists?"

"Among the armchair ecologists maybe." Mark laughed. "More goddamn posey-fucker propaganda. If these bleeding hearts had their way, the whole country would be one big, parklike climax forest. The way they imagine it, this park would be crawling with fat, happy Bambis and Thumpers, with song birds and lovely pheasants twittering in the treetrops. It don't work that way. Wildlife needs what the biologists call 'edge' to survive, edge being the juncture of forest and grasslands. It's there that the shrubs and small young trees grow. And it's only in shrubs and dense stands of tree suckers that wildlife—most of it anyway—finds food and shelter. A deer would have a hell of a time browsing the top of an eighty-foot oak, wouldn't it? Anyway, when you clear-cut, you let light into the forest, you make room for new plant life to succeed the old. And it's on those successional stages that most wild critters live, and in which they roost and breed and raise their young out of danger from predators. The best 'friend of animals' isn't Cleveland Amory and his merry he/shes. It's the logger with his chainsaw, if used in moderation, and believe it or not, wildfire."

"Smokey the Bear wouldn't like to hear that."

"Maybe not, but it's true. I've been doing a lot of reading on current thinking in forest and wildlife management since we moved up here, and it's been a real eye-opener. We've all been brought up to think of forest fires as nature's worst calamity. After all, they make Smokey Bear cry, right, so why shouldn't we? Actually, before the white man arrived, forest fires were part of the scheme of things over most of this continent. Every few years the weather turned dry, lightning started a fire in the woods duff—the dead branches and blowdowns—and the fire swept through, cleaning up all the litter and returning nutrients to the earth. It cleared the way for new growth to spring up, thus providing bonus food supplies for animals. Some trees actually are dependent on fire to reproduce. Take the northern yellow jackpine. Its cones can't germinate until they've been scorched by a hot, fast fire. They'll lie dormant for years, waiting for that blaze, protected from rot by their high pitch content. Yet it's that very pitch—easy to light but damned hard to extinguish—that fuels the fire the trees need to continue living. Goddamn clever, these trees."

"But now man's entered the picture," Bill said. "And whether wildlife likes it or not, he doesn't want forest fires and he's actually legislating against clear-cuts."

"Well, this is Vermont, pal o' mine." Mark grinned. "We don't believe in a whole lot of legislation, nor in Big Brother government that tells a man you can't do that 'cause you might hurt yourself. After you've lived up here awhile, you begin to see what Calvin Coolidge was all about—and you start to wonder if maybe he wasn't right. The best government is the least government. If I want to clear-cut, I'm gonna clear-cut. I *know* it's going to put more partridge in the coverts and more deer in the edges. There'll always be big woods—pole timber—for the turkeys. I'll only burn my brush when the weather's wet, and I'll be standing by all the while, you better bet, to see it doesn't get out of control. I sure don't want my house to burn down, do I? Common men have common sense, pally."

"Are you planning to cut up in the oak grove?" Bill asked suddenly.

"Well hell," Mark said, looking away. He was taken aback by the question. "I don't know. Laura doesn't want me to—she half-believes that bullshit about the Druid's Curse. Hell, she doesn't like me using a chainsaw at all, even to buck up already dropped trees. Wives are goosey. She doesn't like me hunting, either, but I notice she scoffs down the meat just as happily as everyone else. She's a government unto herself, as all wives are, I guess. She doesn't want me taking chances." He turned and looked Bill in the eye. "But, Bill, I can't help it, I'm a man."

"Yeah," Bill said wryly. "A *live* one. And that happens to be the way Laura prefers you."

"But I can't back off and live inside all my life, Willie. Cowering in corners for fear a beeping satellite will fall on my head if I so much as cross the street. I've found more inner satisfaction outdoors than I ever did in a studio. And I like the tingle I get from an element of risk. I'd be a traitor to myself to deny it."

"Maybe you're right," Bill mused. "I was reading that Ruskin you lent me last night, before I fell asleep, and I found an interesting passage that's pertinent. Here—I copied it into my daybook." He pulled a green-backed pocket journal from his jacket and flipped through it. "Ruskin spent a lot of time in the Alps, as you know, and he actually turned into quite a mountaineer. He's musing on the risk element in mountain climbing. 'That question of the moral effect of danger,' he said, 'is a very curious one, but this I know and find, practically, that if you come to a dangerous place, and turn back from it, though it may have been perfectly right and wise to do so, still your *character* has suffered some slight deterioration; you are to that extent weaker, more lifeless, more effeminate, more liable to passion and error in future; whereas if you go through with the danger though it may have been apparently wrong and foolish to encounter it, you come out of the encounter a stronger and better man, fitter for every sort of work and trial, and *nothing but danger* produces this effect.' "

"Amen," said Mark. He clapped his hands together. "In answer to your question, yes. I *am* going to cut in the oak grove."

Downhill they saw Laura making her way up to them, carrying a picnic hamper. She spotted them and waved.

"Just as soon," Mark said, "as I can persuade my old lady to let me."

They both laughed, but the next day before he left, Bill took Laura aside. "You know how to reach me," he said gravely as he kissed her good-bye.

SIX

The only problem with Operation Salvation was that it worked too well. Mark had no trouble unloading his first truckload of wood at the very first fuel dealer he visited in the New York suburbs. The man was eager for more wood, as soon as possible, but warned that suburbanites were wising up: a little birch in the mix was fine, but they now wanted hardwoods that held a fire longer—maple, ash, and most of all that king of firewoods, white oak. The hang-up was that the little Luv truck couldn't haul enough wood to take advantage of the market.

But Billy Munro knew an independent logger who was willing to rent his truck at a reasonable rate. Billy would come in with Mark as a quarter-partner. Together they should be able to work up twenty cords by the week before Christmas, then rent the truck and make a two-grand run to New York. And it would be almost pure profit.

By the week before Christmas they had fully fifteen cords cut and split, a great sprawl of wood that covered most of the barnyard. Very little of it, however, was oak. "On Monday," Mark told Billy, "we'll start cutting in the grove."

"Okay by me." Billy shrugged.

"You're not spooked by the big bad legend of Drooker's Woods?"

"Naw. It's a old wife's tale."

"Ole Billy. Ain't nothin' spooks you, does it?"

"Well," said Billy, deadpan, "I was a mite bit spooked the day the cow kicked over the shit-house. 'Course I was sittin' in there at the time."

"Haw haw haw!"

Then Doc Peggs put his oar in. He knocked at their door on Saturday morning, concern writ large on his patrician face. Laura smiled smugly as she ushered him in.

"Didn't know you made house calls, Doc," Mark said warily. "Hope it's nothin' serious, haw haw." He looked over at Laura, without smiling.

"I'm not here in my usual capacity," Doc said, equally serious. "I come under my other hat, that of town historian. It's been brought to my attention that you intend to cut wood in the oak grove."

"That's right, first thing Monday morning."

"Of course there's nothing I can do to prevent you from cutting whatever you wish on your own property, Mark, but the grove, as you well know, represents a piece of local history—a significant piece, I might add."

"I'm well aware of that. Pretty ugly history, *I* might add."

"History is neither beautiful nor ugly," said Doc. "It simply *is*. Yet as my Harvard classmate several decades removed, the esteemed George Santayana, so succinctly put it: 'Those who do not remember the past are condemned to relive it.' The grove represents just such a memory to us in the Gore. I ask you—no, I *beg* you—to reconsider your plan."

"Aw, Doc." Mark unbent. "Come on. You're not the begging kind. Hey, can I pour you a cup of java?" He went over to the stove and poured. "Look," he said, putting the mug in Doc's hand, "I know the place has sentimental value to you and the rest of the churchgoers in town. But we're living in a hard, realistic world. Those trees are just trees. They have value—very little on the lumber market because they're too old, they've been left too long and they're shot through with carpenter ants and dry rot. But they have enormous value today as firewood. *Today,* when the goddamn Arabs and Libyans and our greaser neighbors to the south have America over an oil barrel. I'm only doing my duty as an honorable American to ameliorate that blackmail."

"I understand you need money," Doc said, not unkindly. "The Historical Society is willing to buy the five acres that comprise the grove for twice the value of the timber that stands on it. I'll guarantee you twent" thousand dollars. We'll turn it into a town park."

Mark's reasonable mood evaporated as quickly as it had formed. He looked long and hard at Laura, who avoided his eyes, then he turned and stared coldly at Doc. His hands seemed to quiver as they clenched.

"I don't know who told you that I need money," he said at last, his voice low and grating, "though I can guess. But get this, Dr. Bluetooth. I don't want a goddamned park in my backyard with a bunch of goddamned churchy Holy Rollers groaning their goddamned hymns up there and praying for the Christ's sake to the goddamned trees. I don't want your goddamned charity and your goddamned condescending pitying tone of voice or any goddamned thing you've got to offer. Now as soon as you've—"

"Wait a minute, Mark," Doc said soothingly. He raised a hand, palm outward, smiling his luminous smile. "I didn't mean to offend you. I may be wrong about your, er, financial needs. Word gets garbled along the sugarbush grapevine." He avoided looking at Laura as he said this last. "And I can appreciate your not wanting a park abutting your property. After all, we cherish our privacy even as you do. But since you refuse my offer as town historian, I have no alternative but to don my third hat, that of senior selectman. I'll have to call an emergency town meeting and propose that Hubley's Gore proclaim the right of eminent domain over that acreage. I have no doubt but that the vote will be heavily in favor. Now, I don't mean to offend you further by talking money, I know how that challenges your sense of self-respect as a man. But I have a concern for your wife, in my capacity as her physician not to mention the strong friendship I feel for both of you, and I'll see to it that the price paid you by the town for taking over that land will be as fair, as generous as my earlier offer."

"When you gonna call this meeting?"

"With the holidays at hand, I doubt I can call it before Wednesday next," Doc said.

"What's that?" Mark said, looking at the calendar on the wall. "The twenty-fourth? And today's the twentieth." He turned and grinned at Doc. The grin was both challenging and triumphant in the same instant. "You'd better pray to Old Obed that the grove is still standing by that date."

"*You* told him!" Mark was white with fury. "You went down there while I was out working my ass off in the woods and you told him how I'd blown it with the paintings and how we were damn near flat bust. *You* told him and now the blue-toothed old bastard is going to do us a *favor*!"

Laura did not deny it. She stood with her back against the sink edge, watching him. Fascinated. Horrified. Too numb to talk. Male pride, she thought. It's a terrible thing. She had never seen him this way before. "Male pride . . ."

"Goddamn right male pride!" he yelled. "*Yes,* male pride! What the hell else do I have? The pussies in the gallery say my stuff is too strong, too cruel. Too *crew-ell.*" He minced the words, faglike. "The magazines are toppling right and left. The freakin' Ay-rabs are dictating to the White House at the same time they're buying up America. And a white-haired, blue-toothed old geezer with a Harvard degree and no more balls than a Christmas capon is wooing my wife and doing me favors." A crafty look came into his eyes. "Or is he paying me back?"

Even he was shocked by the implication. She saw his eyes go out of focus for an instant. But then they lit up again, angrier than ever.

"Is that it, Laura? Laura *my dear*?" He mimicked Doc's intonation. "Have I been pimping for you without my knowledge? Is that why you have to go down there every goddamn week even though you're stronger than an ox and most pregnant women only visit the doctor once a month? Maybe he likes it that way. Maybe he can get it up only when their bellies are a little pooched. Is he diddling you, Laura?"

"That's enough!" she yelled suddenly. "This is like watching a geek show. What's happening to you? Do you know what you're saying?"

"Yes, I know what I'm saying and it's *not* enough. You're trying to turn me into some pussy-whipped little fairy like those photographers who used to shoot you for the double-trucks. You get all mopey and moody whenever I go out hunting—for our meat, let me add, *our* meat, baby, which you gobble down without a single tear in your big bright eyes—or pick up my chainsaw to cut wood so *we'll* stay warm and now maybe bring a little bread into the house to pay the fucking electric bill. And why? Because you bleed in your heart for poor Bambi. Because only God can make a tree. We moved up here and I found out what I'd been missing all my life. I learned what it was to become a man. To take care of myself and my woman and my space. To work with other men, in the woods and on the water, and to work alone. And to come home at night tired and bone-cracking hungry and *content*. Because I did it on my own, babe. And what do you want to make of me? You want to turn me back into a *New Yorker*. You . . ." He searched for an epithet. "You *woman*!"

The word hung echoing on the air for a long, long time. He stared at her, triumphant, waiting.

"Because I don't want to lose you," she said simply.

"What's that supposed to mean?" His voice was quieter now.

"Because I didn't think you knew about guns and I was afraid you'd shoot yourself. Okay, I was wrong, you're a good hunter—I mean it. I know you're good. And because I'm afraid, myself, of guns and chainsaws, especially chainsaws. They're so loud and unforgiving. Because I love you more than any . . . Because I love you, see? And I don't want you to die." She was fighting the tears now—*damned* if I'll give him the satisfaction. "Like P— Like P-Polly's husband died." The tears broke through: triumphant as Mark's grin: and hating herself for crying only made them grin wetter. "I don't want to be Polly Boggs," she said.

It always works, she thought bitterly. His arms were

around her and he was holding her head against his sweat-rough flannel shirt and he was patting her on the back the way you'd comfort a child, or burp a baby. She choked on a sob and then said it:

"If you cut up in Drooker's, you'll die."

It was her last chance and she knew it.

They made love and once again reason prevailed. His reason. He convinced her once again the superstition was no basis for either action or inaction. As of course she had known all along. Once again. And once again they made the essential compromises that keep a marriage intact.

Next spring he would help her more around the house and in the garden.

Next spring she would come fishing with him, see what it was all about.

Next spring they would talk more openly with one another—especially about how they felt regarding the baby.

Next summer he would look after everything while she spent a month back at modeling.

Next summer she would find time to help him out in the woods while he made the winter's wood, and with luck erase her chainsaw phobia.

Next summer they would invite more friends to visit—Bill and Judy and the whole lot, even their dogs and cats. Because the baby needed exposure to real situations.

Next fall he would resume his painting full time, not shying from the commercial work, either, so that they didn't have to rely on the firewood trade.

Next fall she would learn to shoot and accompany him into the woods, and get over her fears of guns and hunting.

Next fall they would open a special savings account

so that Baby X could go to college when he/she was grown. They agreed that Baby X should not be encouraged—overly much—in either painting or professional narcissism.

Then they made love again. Once again.

The next morning Mark went out to begin cutting in Drooker's Woods.

SEVEN

Unfortunately Billy Munro couldn't help him. Billy had gotten drunk down at the Beech Seal on Saturday night, then fell out of his truck in the parking lot. He figured he'd "sprang" a couple of ribs but reckoned he'd be fit enough by Tuesday to at least work the splitter they'd borrowed from Ike Minter. So Mark was cutting alone.

The grove was guarded on its meadow-side flank by a dense stand of saplings and young oaks, outriders of the forest's slow advance into the open country. Before he could get to the valuable wood—the bigger oaks, each of which would yield up to a cord of salable logs—Mark had first to cut a pathway wide as the truck through this living shield. It would take him all day Sunday to accomplish this. Each tree, regardless of size, had to be dropped, limbed, sectioned, and loaded onto the truckbed. Then the branches must be dragged clear and the stumps sawed down to ground level.

Though he was visible from the kitchen window during this early going, Laura could not bear to watch. She busied herself around the house, cleaning and dusting in a fury of mindless activity, playing the FM radio at high volume to mask the snarl of the chainsaw rolling downhill from Widdershins. But then she realized that the sound of the saw meant Mark was still all right. Only if the saw stopped might it mean that he'd been . . . She shut off the radio.

But that was even worse. Every now and then, she knew, Mark would stop the saw to refuel or haul branches or sharpen the chain teeth. During these pauses her heart rose in her throat and she dashed to the window, staring up wide-eyed until she saw him moving. She thought of taking a walk into town—the weather was mild for late December, sunny and windless with only a few fluffy inches of snow on the ground. But then, if Mark did get hurt, who would be there to help him? To put on the life-saving tourniquet and drive him down to Doc's?

She thought of Jim Boggs bleeding to death up near the grove, unable to walk with his split foot, too weak even to crawl. He could have yelled his loudest and no one would have heard him. No one but the grouse and the deer. And the oaks.

So she hovered all day between helplessness and fury.

But the saw always started up again: that evil, whining snarl, that mindless taker of life.

From time to time Mark drove a truckload of logs down to the barnyard, coming in once for a quick sandwich and again for a beer: it was hot work despite the season. Then as the sun sloped over Abednego Mountain and darkness moved like a blue racer up Widdershins, he came in for the last time. He had completed the alleyway into the grove and in the morning would tackle the real trees.

"I'll only have to drop two or three of them to complete the twenty cords," he said, flopping heavily into a kitchen chair. "But I better drop more in case Doc gets that right of domain."

"Couldn't you just fill out this load with other wood?" Laura pleaded. "I mean, the grove really means too much to the town, and even if you had to take a little less money a cord for the wood, it would be a neighborly gesture."

"We've been through all that," Mark said wearily. "The fact is, those trees are on their last legs—most of them, anyway, especially that so-called 'Bull Oak'—and it's only sound silviculture to clear them the hell out of there to make room for new, healthy growth. Besides, if I chicken out now these townies will press harder on other fronts, just where I don't know. I've told them I'm going to do it and to back down would be a sign of weakness. They'd be on me like a pack of New York street kids."

He sat there hollow-eyed, sweaty, and dark with chain oil, with oak chips in his hair and beard and the sweet-sour reek of green oak pouring off him in the warm kitchen air. He grabbed a bottle of Scotch and poured himself a water-glass full, drank it silent and brooding. He was so wrong, but she loved him so: she couldn't sway him, not an inch.

Overnight the skies grew cloudy under the push of a northwest wind with ice in its teeth. The big clocklike thermometer on the barn read twenty degrees. As Mark drove up into the meadow at first light, heading for the grove, he waved at her jauntily from the truck cab, teeth bone-white against his dark beard. For a disjointed instant she could scarcely recognize him: so cocky, tough, so absurdly virile.

Again began the agonized vigil—the listening for the saw to stop, then start again. But now it was worse. Snow began to fly, just a light angling fall of it at first, then thickening toward noon. She saw the white haze shroud the top of Widdershins, then obscure the Cauldron, moving downward like a dirty white stage curtain until she could not see even the top of the meadow. Only the saw's voice reached her, whining and yowling, and then the crackling thud of falling timber that shivered the pots and pans hanging over the stove.

And then the saw would stop.

And start again.

To hell with it, she decided, I'm going up there. She had been making hot borscht that morning with beets from her root cellar, spicy blood-red soup with juicy chunks of corned beef in it—Mark's favorite cold-weather soup. She would bring a Thermos of it up to him for lunch, along with a couple of cold meat-loaf sandwiches and some pickles—her own kosher dills—and maybe even a beer. They would lunch *al fresco,* up there in the snowy woods, just like they had so often during the summer. Maybe even a little hanky-panky in the snow: they'd never done it in the snow, she thought with her cheeks flushing. She wondered . . .

With the lunch stowed snugly in her picnic hamper along with a spare Hudson's Bay four-point blanket (just in case), she pulled on her mukluks and green loden coat and went outside. The snow was coming heavily now, slanting down out of the northwest so thick at times that it obscured the barn. The woodpile in the barnyard looked twice as tall, ghostly, each log wearing a cockeyed cap of snow lipped at the leeward edge, like a badly made white beret. She plugged her way uphill, following the truck tracks, feeling the pull of the baby across her belly and hips. She was in her sixth month now—no, just entering her seventh. Yes, the twenty-second of December, that was the date. Only three months to go—the worst three, she thought. As if in response to the notion, the baby suddenly began to move: he (or she) was playing basketball in there, dribbling cagily—all the moves. She smiled.

And the saw stopped.

She hurried on through the snow, the basket pulling clumsily against her arm, the fresh snow clotting on her boot soles. Each foot seemed to gain five pounds with each step. She couldn't distinguish the thudding of her heart from the baby's pounding movements.

Then the saw's hideous yowl resumed—music to her ears. She saw the truck through the snow haze, its cab top wearing one of the absurd berets, its windscreen blank, droopy-eyed, the bed piled high with raw-butted logs. She could smell the sour green reek of cut oak. The pathway Mark had cut threaded raw and mucky into the heart of the grove. Now the wind increased in velocity and she could hear it moaning through the oak tops. Twigs and bark flew on it, slapping against her cheeks and forcing her to duck her head deeper into the parka cowl. The snow blew nearly horizontal now. Through it came the insistent mindless yammer of the chainsaw: banshee howl, the plaint of souls in a vegetable hell. And then again it stopped.

Mark stood before the Bull Oak, staring upward at its thick, twisted arms. The saw idled now in his hands, humming and muttering to itself like an idiot in a cobwebbed corner. He was measuring the tree, figuring where to lay his cuts and bring it low. His eyes, she saw, were full of hate.

"Mark!" she yelled over the groan of the wind.

He turned and looked at her: his eyes were pale, cold, almost contemptuous, and there was a defiant twist to his mouth under the snow-hoared beard. He waved her off with his gloved hand: rejection. Then he grabbed the pistol grip of the saw and triggered the throttle. The idling mutter rose to a shriek.

Right now you bastard, he thought. Your time is up. He had it figured: Half a dozen deep thrusting cuts around the trunk, then a sweeping sideways cut and the Bull Oak would fall, right into the middle of the clearing. If the upper branches made contact with trees at the edge of the clearing, the sheer weight of the Bull Oak would force them through. There was no way the tree could hang up. And its great size would mean a slow fall, plenty of time for him to skip out of the way. A tree this size simply could not split. There was too much of it.

Its limbs and carcass alone would contain five, maybe seven cords of wood. Nearly a thousand dollars' worth. Two months of mortgage payments. The cost of a new rifle—maybe a nifty small-bore, high-velocity varmint rifle complete with a variable power scope, so he could do some 'chuck hunting in the spring. A Sako perhaps, or an Anschutz—something well tooled and classy. Or maybe a motorcycle. A 250-cc Husqvarna like Steve McQueen used to ride, or an Ossa. A good quick dirt bike to carry him lofting and popping wheelies through these hills, right down along Cauldron Brook, racing with the water peeling away under the front tire in a muddy bow wave as he caromed down the runs and rapids. Or . . .

The wind picked up in the branches overhead. Snow sheeted across his eyes. He could hear the tree's voice rising, the groan of wind-stressed wood escalating to a guttural, a warning roar. The voice of the saw sounded puny in contrast.

He touched the spinning steel to the thick, gray bark.

And it happened.

A surge came up the saw bar, into his hands: a tingling, electric pulse of power, something dark and deep and dreadful, something old as the earth, made of rotten rock and leaf mold, of bones gone to dust, of roots wreathed with awakening worms. His eyes locked on the gray crenellations of the bark. He felt his mind jump sideways but his hands remained frozen on the saw. Snow in his eyes: sleep.

The bark began to shift and spin before him, and shapes emerged. Random geometry, absurd convolutions, smoke in a still place. And then, from the smoke, a face: the goat-bearded man with the crook, the woman with the strange eyes, other men, other women, old old old. And then Doc Peggs, smiling his eerie blue smile.

His finger tightened on the throttle trigger.

And Laura watched. She saw Mark's hand grip tighter on the throttle, saw the sudden spurt of oak chips fly from the chain, heard the Stihl's engine roar into full power. Then she saw Mark's left arm fall free of the grip, limp, lifeless. The saw bar was deep into the tree now, and yet it cut on. She saw, breathless, the teeth of the saw snag Mark's left coat sleeve. Saw his arm snap into the crotch between saw and tree trunk. Saw his right, his trigger hand still clenched on the throttle trigger: white-knuckled.

He slammed against the trunk, shoulder first, and she heard the saw struggle for a moment as its teeth contested with wool and meat and bone.

A pink roostertail of blood and flesh arched out to smear the dirty snow.

All this in an instant.

And he was sawing off his own arm!

She ran forward, screaming over the howl of wind and motor, grabbed him by the shoulders and yanked. Yanked. Yanked again. Finally he broke free of the saw and stumbled backward, falling over her. She felt the hot gush of his blood across her face. But before he broke free, she had felt it too: the surging pulse of the Bull Oak coursing through him.

* * *

And then, somehow, she was with Doc Peggs. How she had managed to drag Mark, bleeding and semi-conscious, muttering madnesses, down to the truck; how she had rolled him into the cab and driven to town; how she had found Doc waiting on the porch as if he knew she was coming—of these things she had only the most fragmentary of memories. She must have wrapped that tourniquet of manila rope around his nearly severed bicep, but she could not recall doing it.

She heard the clank of steel on enamel, Doc mumbling to himself, cursing as he worked. She felt her mind spreading, thinning, like a drop of blood in water. Mercifully, she lost consciousness.

Doc was standing over her when she swam back up from the depths: tall and solemn, his face in shadow, the glint of his steel-rimmed glasses. When he bent over her, she felt the cold touch of alcohol on her arm, the sting of the needle.

"You'll need this now," he said gently into her ear. "I'm sorry, Laura. I couldn't save him. You did your best, you were heroic. But he'd lost too much blood. The shock . . . I'm so terribly sorry."

She sloped back down into the blue deep, drifting and spinning as she sank into her loss. . . .

That night the "coyotes" howled again; the eerie flames danced in the darkness on Widdershins; the winter moon rose blear and cold: a pitted skull bleached white by time and emptiness. But Laura Avery heard nothing, saw nothing. She lay under heavy sedation in a deep, blank sleep. Billy Munro kept watch over her, reading a comic book and raiding the refrigerator from time to time. When he moved, he did so with his customary lithe agility: you would not mark him as a man with two mending ribs.

Only Bone, the cat, heard the "coyotes" and saw the red light show on the mountain. His guard hairs bristled and he yowled once, mournfully, until Billy hurled the comic book at him. But Laura slept on.

BOOK FOUR

Winter

ONE

Winter on Widdershins Mountain: The slugabed sun creaked over the horizon at midmorning, shrunken and wan, so low, so distant that it might have been shining on another world. There was no heat in it, only a weak white light that cast shadows the color of bruises on the deep-drifted snow. The woods were silent. A few brave chickadees perched in the upper branches, their feathers puffed against the cold. Now and then the quick, hard hammer of a hairy woodpecker, prizing frozen ants and larvae from the tree bark, broke the heavy stillness. Even the coyotes kept quiet, moving silent as the sifting snow as they made their rounds, hunting mice beneath the meadow drifts.

The few houses in the hollow squatted impassively under caps of snow, their windows shaded and shuttered to prevent heat loss, each chimney raising a pale blue-gray column of woodsmoke into the windless sky. The smoke columns rose ruler-edge straight into the ice-blue sky, and on days when the outdoor thermometers on the barns read thirty below, the smoke did not climb far before it cooled and collapsed of its own weight.

Farmers bundled Santa Claus–thick in their red-and-black-checked wool mackinaws, earflaps down and heavily mittened, trudged quickly from house to barn to do their chores. When they spat en route, the tobacco juice popped like firecrackers, so quickly did it freeze.

It was warm in the barns with the sweet-sour smell of silage and cow dung and the moist breath of livestock, and when you opened a barn door, a puff of sweet steam rolled out into the cold to condense instantly in clear-weather snow dust. Gigantic icicles the color of honey or pale amber grew from the barn eaves, thickening and lengthening every day until they fell finally of their own weight. When they hit the ground, it sounded like rowdies smashing a plate-glass window.

Christmas came and went, celebrated only perfunctorily in the Gore, and there were the customary New Year revels: applejack and dandelion wine fizzing syrup-thick from the recycled quart beer bottles favored by Hubleyites; and remorse and hangovers and resolutions the morning after—all very Rural American; Norman Rockwell would have loved it.

But those holidays were the only times of excitement in the north country winter—those and of course the storms. When the blizzards came howling down from the northwest, the whole town stirred as if stung by a cattle prod. The houses shuddered and creaked like ships in a gale and even the placid cattle grew restive, bellowing in the hollow barns in tones that matched the wind. It was then that a man prone to cabin fever might hone his ax of an evening and study the crooked part in his wife's hair. Sloppy, he'd be thinking. Messy. Such a little thing, but why can't she keep it straight? And then he might decide to straighten it for her. . . .

But mostly the days were brief and bright. The woodpiles shrunk and the icicles grew. By midafternoon the sun winked out. All creatures sought shelter and huddled inward on themselves. With the darkness came the true cold.

Laura Avery lived through it all in a daze. Doc Peggs kept her sedated, fearing for the baby's health and wishing he didn't have to resort to the needle so often. But whenever he allowed her to emerge from her semi-comatose state, a wild look came to her eye and she spoke frantically, in anguish. She wanted to leave the Gore, she told him, leave it right now, flee back to the city, escape this nightmare of death and despair. Doc or the townswomen who watched over her would try to comfort her, distract her with small talk or country gossip, but ultimately Doc would have to break out the needle again.

The women were always there, day and night—Huldy mainly, but also Liz Markham, or Tabitha Minter, or Swiftly Baines's fat wife Maud, or Pastor Thorne's faded frail lady. Sometimes Billy Munro would take the watch, and he came by at least once a day to haul in cartloads of wood from the barn, or handle other "men's work" about the place.

The women were kind and solicitous, always busy and bustling around in the kitchen, baking cookies and pies, tending to savory stews of deer meat (cut from Mark's prize buck, alas), sharpening knives or knitting sweaters or scrubbing walls and floors. Even a woman like Maud Baines, overweight and sixty years old if she were a day, had more energy than all of Laura's city girl friends rolled together. They smiled and chattered, sang church hymns or old folk songs, and worked, worked, worked. Laura couldn't stand it.

Nor could she remember much about the funeral except that it was cold and sunny, the snow too bright for her eyes. The mourners stood shifting from booted foot to booted foot, slapping their mittened arms stiffly against their bodies, and their breath puffed white against the sky when they sang their sweet silly hymns. The earth at the graveside was frozen so hard that upsidedown icicles grew from it, ice-flowers, actually, vegetation from the world of the dead. But Laura was too stunned to feel pain. She only felt the cold. And the ice lump of loss, deep down numb in her belly.

Had Bill McGregor been at the funeral? She couldn't remember. It seemed to her sometimes that he had been, that he held her close in his arms while she wept her heart out, but it had been a dream: when she awoke her pillow was sodden. Slowly the conviction grew that if she could only get in touch with Bill, everything would be all right. These people were holding her prisoner—Doc and Huldy and the lot of them: they only wanted her to live long enough to have the baby. Then they would kill it in some obscene tree-worshiping rite, sacrifice it to the Bull Oak up there on the mountain, at night under the full moon, bloody, and burn it in their awful fires. Like they did with Polly's baby.

And then they would kill her.

"They kill outsiders," Polly said, didn't she? And didn't they kill her? Wasn't Dolph Rooney there the night Polly's house burned? Hadn't he kept Mark from saving Polly? And then that ugly wooden arm, gripping the cracked skull, the skull of a baby. . . . her baby? He must be the high priest, she thought. Dolph Rooney and his "crazy wood." But no, there was something wrong with that notion. Something . . . Damn, she couldn't concentrate! That dope Doc was shooting her up with, it erased her intellect like a wet rag on a chalky blackboard, leaving only blurred smears and illegible letters.

But if only she could reach Bill McGregor. They were keeping him away, she was sure of it now, keeping even the fact of Mark's death from him. She needed

Bill now. And she wanted him—always had, down deep. Who loved her—yes, she knew it, he still loved her and wanted her. And he would come up here, the valiant knight riding his steed, the "Blue Funk," and (giggling) rescue her from her dark tower. I'm silly with that stuff from the needle.

And, giggling, she began to cry.

One afternoon when only Billy Munro was looking after her, Laura finally felt strong and coherent enough to try something. She waited until Billy went out to the barn and then headed for the telephone. She couldn't remember Bill McGregor's phone number in New York, nor could she find her Rolodex—they must have hidden it, the bastards—but she dialed New York City information. And waited. And waited. The telephone system in the Gore was still 1960s primitive: you could not dial anywhere direct. First you must dial 1, then the number you wanted. With luck, an operator would come on the line and ask for your own number. Then you waited some more until the call went through.

So she waited. She could see Billy moving around in the barn, loading firewood into the cart, pausing occasionally to split a piece that was too big by itself for the stoves. Finally, though, the Gore operator came on and she gave her number. Clicks and whizzings, electronic woodpeckers in the wires, then a distant, hollow ring, ring, ring.

"New York City information, what borough?" The voice was thick as sugarcane: Puerto Rican.

"Manhattan."

Long pause. Heavy breathing. Then: "Yowss?"

"William McGregor, on Macdougal Street in the Village."

"Billage Maduga?"

"Macdougal, yes, the Village. Greenwich Village."

"*No hay* Grench on Magrega Street."

"No no. I want Will-yum Muck Gregor. Muck Gregor. On Muck *Dougall* Street."

"Muck . . ."

"I'll spell it. *M-C-G-R-E-G* . . ."

"Spell please."

"I *am* spelling. M . . ."

She saw Billy emerge from the barn with a cartload of wood. She hung up.

The next chance she had alone, she began searching through the drawers in Mark's studio desk. She knew he had a memo book with the numbers of his city contacts in it, and she was certain he'd have Billy's number in there as well. But the drawers were a mess—Mark had never gone in much for neatness. (She felt a painful stab of guilt at even thinking this posthumous remonstrance.) She found postcards, old letters, snapshots from their vacation in Greece two—no, three summers ago. She even found an old porn magazine he'd bought years ago in a sex shop in Amsterdam when he was over there on assignment for one of the magazines. He'd bought it because it had an angelic-looking brunette—her lookalike—doing something absolutely unspeakable in the centerfold, and they'd gotten quite a giggle from it when he came home. (Oh, Mark!) But she could not find the memo book.

She did, however, find a scrap of envelope with the name "Sarah Eldridge—widow" scrawled on it in Mark's handwriting. Under the name was a number with an upstate New York area code. She remembered that Mark had taken the Widow Eldridge's name and number from the realtor when they closed on the house, just in case he had to get advice on any of the plumbing or wiring. But then she heard Huldy clumping up the stairs, calling for her, and she stuffed the slip of paper down into her bra.

A few days later she had another chance at the telephone. If the Widow Eldridge had gone through this ordeal—and she must have, the way her husband died—perhaps she would help Laura. At least tell her what was happening, maybe even get in touch with Bill for her. And again, when she dialed, she had an unusually long wait before the call rang through. While she waited, it seemed she could hear the operator talking to someone in the switchboard office. A man, it sounded like. Doc? Dolph? Then the phone was ringing.

"Hullo," a man's voice, gruff, country.

"Hi, I'm trying to reach Mrs. Eldridge," Laura said brightly. (I mustn't sound nutsy, she warned herself. Try to sound like a long-lost friend.) "Mrs. Sarah Eldridge, who used to live in Hubley's Gore, Vermont?"

Long pause. Then: "Uh-huh." She could hear the man breathing. It sounded as if he could use an allergy pill.

"Well, I'd like to speak with her," Laura said a bit snappishly. "Is she there?"

"Just a minnit." The man put the phone down and stomped away. Country people never asked who was calling. Anyone who would spend actual cash money just to talk to someone must be serious. That "Whom shall I say is calling?" snottiness was a city affectation.

She could hear the man bellowing something at a distance. Then she heard him stomping back.

"Who's calling?" he demanded.

"Laura Avery," she said. "I'm the party who bought Mrs. Eldridge's house in the Gore, and I have a couple of very minor housekeeping questions I'd hoped she could help me with."

"Just a minnit." Thump. *Stomp stomp stomp*. More bellowing. Then the light tap-tap of a woman's shoes.

"Miz Avery?" It was a woman's voice—a young woman, a bit breathless. "I'm Wanda Chafee, Mrs. Eldridge's granddaughter. My grandmother's, well, not feeling so perky right now and I don't want to disturb her. Is it something I could help you with?"

Oh, Christ! Suddenly Laura's self-confidence collapsed, and with it her sense of decision. How could she explain to this chirpy middle-aged woman all the things that had happened? How could she even begin without sounding like a freaked-out paranoid schizophrenic? Like Polly Boggs sounded to Laura herself a few decades ago, last summer? And if she asked Wanda Chafee to call Bill McGregor for her in New York City . . . Impossible.

"No," Laura said at last, "it's nothing all that important, actually. But do you think Miz Eldridge might be able to talk sometime later this week, or even next week would do?"

"I . . . don't . . . know," said Wondering Wanda. "You see, Miz Avery, my grandmother's been, uh, not quite right lately. I mean, in the head, you know? She's quite old, the dear, and then with Grandpa's death . . . She never quite got over it."

Tell me about it, Laura thought. Then she felt tears welling in her eyes.

"It's okay," she choked. "Maybe I'll call again later anyway. Thanks for your time, Miz Chafee." She waited until Wanda Chafee hung up and stayed listening on her own receiver. She heard another, more distant click. Then she hung up. The operator had been listening in. The operator, or someone else?

And the winter slept on.

TWO

Downstairs, Huldy and two other women were doing the dishes, singing sad ballads as they washed and dried. Laura waited, her teeth grating: she knew they would sing it finally, they always did. The saddest song in their doleful repertoire, a Civil War tearjerker that no doubt dated to those grim days, more than a century ago, when apple-cheeked lads from these hills marched bravely south to get blown away by the cannons of Dixie.

Yes, here it came. They always saved it for the last:

Oh the shot and shell wuz screaming . . .
(Huldy's quavering alto.)
Out on the battlefield.
The boys in blue were fighting
Their noble flag to shield. . . .

Came a cry from their brave captain—
"Look boys, the flag is down!
"Who'll volunteer to save it from disgrace?"

"I will!" a young voice shouted
  (Liz Markham squeaked off key.)
"I'll bring it back or die!"
And he dashed into the thickest of the fray. . . .

Saved the flag but gave his young life
All for his country's sake.
They brought him back and softly heard him say:

"Just break the news to mother,
"She knows how much I love her.
"And kiss her dear sweet lips for me . . ."
  (A gulp from dippy Meg Hardesty.)
"For I'm not coming home.

"Just say there is no other
"Can take the place of mother,
"And tell her not to wait for me . . .".
  (Even Huldy was sobbing now.)
"For I'm not coming . . . home."

They had a good, long, sweet-sorry cry when they were done, all in the worthy cause (Laura thought) of momism. How Philip Wylie would cackle if he could hear them. Then they got to remembering: Chumley Watkins, dead of the yellow jack on his way home from Cuba ("Cuber," Meg called it); Fred Harpster in the Belleau Wood; Amory Ashburn and Ikey Watson on Tarawa where the monkey-men had a machine gun under the pier there out in the lagoon that took them in defilade as they waded ashore. (Where did these women learn such words—*defilade*? It sounded like a new, spring-scented douche.) Caleb Markham, Chub's brother, somewhere in France after the St. Lo break-out. And Chris Peggs, Doc's nephew, at Saint-Vith, part of the big butcher's bill from Bastogne. Eddie

Minter up near the Yalu, Mike Thorpe on the way back from Changjin. Pretty little Ivar Jones at Hué, pretty little Ivar, the Marine, at the tail end of the Tet Offensive. "Veet-nam."

"Oh," wailed Huldy, "it's a sorry business these menfolks get us into. Dead they are, those boys, those lovely boys. Dead and go-un."

The ladies agreed in a clink of drawer-bound cutlery.

So how can they be so cruel? Laura thought. They weep as I do over war, they regret the waste of life. Oh, sure, their songs are so silly, so soppy, so out of touch, but yet they weep. They knew these boys, dandled them on their knees, saw them come back proud from basic or boot camp with their peeled-egg haircuts and their spruce new dress greens. Consoled their mothers when the man came from DOD. How can they be so murderous?

For a moment she actually considered getting out of bed and going down there, hitting them with it: a plea, a woman-to-woman request for freedom, for sympathy, for—yes—love. How could they refuse her? She too shed fat, salty tears when people she loved died. "Sisterhood is powerful."

But then she remembered something even more potent. Mark's deer rifle. It was up there, right over her head. Up there in the attic. Where he'd put it, at her ardent request, after he'd bagged his buck. Both the rifle and the ammunition ("ammo," he called it), those ugly long-nosed, sucker-mouth bullets she hated so. The needles of death, she called them to herself. Yet now . . . Now they might well be the keys to life. If she could get to the rifle, load it, *then* go downstairs . . .

She eased out of bed, keeping her hands pressed hard on the mattress as her body weight shifted to her feet on the floor, then letting the springs open gradually, quietly. So far so good. She felt for her robe and slippers, slipped into them, found the flashlight on the bottom shelf of the night table where Mark had insisted they keep it in the event of a blackout, then crept mousestill to the bedroom door.

Downstairs she could hear the rustle of fabric and the sibilant snip of scissors. The women were sewing again, around the kitchen table. They had been doing a lot of sewing lately, of what she had not a clue since they put their work away whenever they heard her coming downstairs. And as usual they were gabbing gleefully as they worked, talking about old times and recent peccadilloes. Laura waited until Tabby Minter was well launched into a scurrilous anecdote dealing with Ike's cousin Nobbie from Rutland, who it seemed had found himself a "conquerbine" in the hippie quarter of that sinful city. Then she slid out of the bedroom and padded softly toward the attic door.

The attic. She had been up there only once since the day she found Cassie's portrait and got chased by the bat. And that time she had been escorted by Mark, who was stowing his deer rifle for the winter. He had hung it from its sling on a wooden peg protruding from one of the hand-hewn posts that supported the ridgepole. The box of ammo lay on the crossbeam directly above the rifle. But . . . the Attic.

For a moment, quailing, she almost gave up the plan. Maybe even captivity was preferable to going up there in the dark. After all, she could bide her time, act cooperative, then make a dash for freedom someday when her kindly captors were relaxed and unsuspecting. But a dash to where, and how? She didn't have her truck keys any longer: they had taken them, along with her phone book. And for all she knew, they had drained the truck's gas tank or bollixed the battery—something simple and commonplace, unprovable as sabotage in a court of law. Without the truck she would have to flee on foot, over the mountains, through four feet of snow. In the eighth month of her pregnancy, when climbing stairs was already a problem.

No, she had to go up in the attic. After all, hadn't Mark said that the bats would be hibernating during the winter—and thanks to Bone, whom she suddenly felt wreathing himself around her ankles, the mouse population was at an all-time low. She leaned down and scratched the young tom behind the ears and he stared up at her with his wide, weird yellow eyes, purring like a tiny outboard motor. With a surge of love she picked the cat up and hugged him to her breast, warm and solid under his silky fur, feeling his rough vibrations pour into her like a fresh shot of courage. She opened the attic door.

The stairway led up to the left. About halfway to the top, she knew, there was a board that creaked despite Mark's having replaced it and shored it with wooden shims. She would have to keep her feet to the outside edges of the stairs to prevent alarming the women downstairs. She put down the cat and flicked on the flashlight. Outside the wind was moaning and the big hollow attic acted as a kind of sounding board. The light beam picked out cobwebs that fluttered like ghostly flags in the perennial drafts of the attic. She started up the stairs.

Bone remained on the bottom landing, watching her wide-eyed as she went.

It was fearsome cold up there: her breath puffed in the flashlight beam and the draft swirled up the skirt of her nightie: she could feel the goosebumps starting on her legs. Spraddle-legged she climbed, and the stairs maintained their silence. The post where Mark's rifle hung was about twenty feet to the left of the stair top, at the far end of the attic from the hulking pile of stored furniture. In the side-loom of her light she could see the old sofas, tables, sideboard, and chairs as a dark, irregular shape. She shone the beam to the left and was rewarded with the wink of well-oiled steel and wood—the rifle. They hadn't removed it! She saw the green square of the ammo box as well, just where it should be, above the rifle. She shuffled flatfooted over the splintery floorboards toward them: no sense risking a squeaky board now, when she'd come so far undetected.

Outside the wind was gusting harder—or did it just seem so now that she was up in the hollow attic? She could feel the house shivering to its blows. The ancient posts and beams, wood-socketed, sang a high-pitched dirge as they flexed. The wind was coming in pulsating waves, strong, then easing off, then hurling itself even more powerfully against the house. She unhooked the rifle by its sling—its weight surprised her: solid and heavy, and suddenly reassuring now that it was her ally—and slung the strap over her shoulder the way she had seen Mark do. Then she reached for the ammunition box.

And something creaked . . .

At the far end of the attic. . . .

Something that wasn't the wind or the beams, and that wasn't Bone either for now she felt him rubbing against the side of her leg.

She froze, the weight of the rifle pulling her shoulder downward, her hand just touching the waxed cardboard carton of bullets. The creaking was slow and rhythmic, steady, unlike the random wind. She remembered the old rocking chair that stood among the discarded furniture at that end of the attic. The sound was just the sort of sound a rocker would make if the wind had set it in motion.

But then the wind died. And the rocker kept on creaking.

She unslung the rifle and with shaking hands, slid open the bolt. She fumbled a few slippery cold cartridges from the ammo carton. Mark had simply pressed them, point forward, down into the top of the open bolt. Then when he closed the bolt, the rifle was loaded. She pressed a bullet downward and heard it click home, then pressed in the rest of the cartridges. She grasped the knurled bolt handle, rotated it forward, then down, and felt it lock in position with a wicked snick. She felt with her thumb for the safety catch. When it was forward, Mark said, the rifle was ready to shoot. It was forward.

With the rifle stock held by the pressure of her elbow against the top of her right hip, she could just hold and point it steadily, her finger on the trigger. With her left hand she retrieved the flashlight from the cross-beam and readied her thumb on the switch. She pointed the rifle barrel in the direction of the sound, took a deep breath, and flicked on the light. . . .

A man was sitting in the rocker, grinning madly at her. Leering and rocking, his eyes fixed on hers. She fired. . . .

Even down in the kitchen, the roar of the rifle was ear shattering. The women dropped their jaws and their sewing in the same instant. Then they bolted for the stairway, with Huldy, despite her years, leading the way. Two steps at a time she pounded upward, her white hair flying. The attic door gaped wide and as they approached it, running, a black and white fuzz-ball shot past them, ears laid back, tail straight up: Bone pelting for safety.

Huldy groped blindly for the attic light switch as she

hit the stairs. The lights flashed on, cold bright against the cobwebbed beams.

Laura was on her knees at the far end of the attic, head down, the rifle lying beside her. The sharp reek of cordite filled the cold air. She was sobbing in great, lung-tearing gasps.

In the splintered rocking chair at the other end of the attic sat a grinning, bearded figure with a huge hole in its head.

Mark Avery.

Bits of shredded straw and chaff skittered in the breeze from a gaping hole in the siding of the house where the rifle bullet had exited.

Huldy was the first to reach her.

"Mark!" Laura sobbed. "Oh, I shot him! I shot him!"

"Honey, honey, honey," said Huldy, folding her arms around Laura. "No you didn't, dear, you didn't shoot him. It's just a dummy. Just a straw man, Laura darling. See over there? All the straw? And the other dummies over in that corner? We been sewing on them all week, and last week too, for the fire festival, like you seen last fall down to the park."

Laura looked up and stared. In the bright attic lights, which she had not dared to turn on earlier for fear the reflection on the snow outside would alert the sewing circle, she could see plainly that the figure she'd shot was indeed a dummy. Apart from the beard, it didn't even look much like Mark. Just a crude, shrunken simulacrum.

She vomited on the attic floor.

Half an hour later Doc arrived. With the needle.

THREE

Days in a daze. Days in a craze. Laura lies dying for days in a maze. Lorelei lying amazed in the haze. . . .

The nonsense verse kept spinning through her head, ringing all the changes. Outside the storms howled, the weather cleared, the icicles dripped tiny comets from the eaves. A blue fang grew outside her window. At first just the tip of it showed beneath the rolled-up shade. But each day it extended its bite downward and she watched the light play through it as the sun rolled westward: blues and mauves, pinks and instant scarlets. Toward dusk it dripped blood. Then one day it was gone. But soon another began growing in its place.

Now and then she was allowed to skim close enough to the surface for them to feed her—soups and gruels, stews and puddings—and to go, with company, to the bathroom. She was aware of Doc's presence from time to time, his icicle smile and eyes the color of winter skies. He spoke comforting words and rubbed her breasts and swollen belly with sweet-smelling oils. Something about stretch marks. One day she realized he was not sitting on the edge of the bed, but rather was under the covers with her. In a red flannel nightshirt, with matching cap. What was he doing to her? She knew what it was but couldn't remember the name for it. Something she used to do a lot with Mark? No matter.

Then Doc disappeared and was replaced by Pastor Thorpe, sitting in a chair beside the bed, reading to her. He was reading from the Bible. But again her ear and her memory played tricks. It didn't sound like the Bible she remembered from her girlhood. "And the trees shall inherit the earth, and the lamb lie down before the oak to feed its roots with blood. . . ." Yet the book itself looked familiar. The leather binding, the flaked gold lettering. Gradually, the words began to make sense, to connect with her returning memory. "Obed." "Ahaz." "Cassie." "The godless shall not dwell long in the Gore." It was *The Book of Ahaz*. She recalled the old wives' tale, the Lamarckian fallacy: prenatal influence. They were making a believer of the baby even before birth. You want your kid to be a musician? Play a lotta Chopin while you're pregnant. Oh, sweet Jesus!

She had to get out of here. Okay. The phone ploy didn't work, and by now they'd have the operators alerted and ready to pull the plug the minute they heard her voice on the line. She doubted the rifle was still in the attic—that had been a grave error on their part: doubting she had the nerve to use it—but now, after that dreadful night, she knew they were right. She could never shoot a gun again. If she did, whatever she was aiming at would turn into Mark, slouched in that rocking chair, grinning boyishly through his Hemingway beard. Even now she felt the double hammer blow: the bowel-chilling panic as she squeezed off; then in the awful bright roar of the rifle, the delayed recognition—her husband back from the dead! And the smack of the bullet as it blew his head apart.

Oh, God, Doc, give me the Needle—quick!

No! Don't get that way! Don't be weak now, not now when there's so little time left. What month was it? End of January? Early February? She couldn't tell by looking out the window. The whole world was hip-deep in snow out there, the sun an alien star. But they were allowing her to come back into the world now. Doc must be afraid that too much sedation will be bad for the baby. They wouldn't want to sacrifice a stillbirth. They had to have live blood, newly dead flesh, to feed the Bull Oak.

But how much time do I have?

The next time Huldy brought her dinner, she asked if she could have something to read. Anything—a magazine or even a newspaper? Preferably *The New York Times*. Sorry honey, we don't get furrin papers down t' the store. But I got a fresh copy of the *Ver-mont Guide*.

The last thing she wanted to read was local want ads and social notes, but the regional throwaway would at least tell her the date. She waited impatiently until Huldy brought the paper, then while the old woman sat beside the bed watching her, she leafed through it with sham delight, commenting wryly on the high real-estate prices and with enthusiasm on the sighting of a bald eagle near the Dorset Swamp as reported by the paper's avid "bird lady."

My God, she thought to herself, February 24. Only a month to my due date.

Later she pretended to nod off and Huldy left her.

All right: What are the options? The phone is no good. I can't shoot my way out. I can't run away—not with my belly out to here, and having to stop to take a pee every five minutes. A letter? She remembered

Bill's address now, even down to the zip code. But how could she get it into the post? Well, she'd just have to wait for the opportunity to open up. The first thing was to write it. Write it and hide it and wait. (Her triple-play combo: she chuckled darkly.)

They were letting her go to the bathroom by herself now, having carefully removed all sharp instruments—scissors and razor blades and even a rat-tail file—from the medicine cabinet. But at least she had some privacy in there. When her "guards" were busy in the kitchen, she rifled the dresser drawers, searching for writing materials. Eventually she had them: a pencil stub from Mark's messy handkerchief, small-change, and junk drawer; a used envelope in her purse on which the address had been written in pencil and could be erased; a piece of blank paper ripped (quietly: it took her ten minutes) from a piece of shelf lining, and the most marvelous find of all—a half-used book of stamps tucked away in a compartment in Mark's wallet.

She pondered long and hard over the wording of the letter. At first she considered writing it cryptically, almost in code, so that if it were intercepted they wouldn't come down hard on her again with the Needle; maybe they'd even let it go through if someone as illiterate as Billy Munro happened to read it. But then she realized that she hadn't the time for such games. It was a one-shot deal: either it went through and Bill came racing up here, or she was finished. So she wrote it plain and crisp: "Bill—Mark is dead. Please come! Laura."

She wrote it in the early-morning hours, at first light, while someone—Huldy? Meg?—snored on the cot in the hallway outside her door. She addressed it with great care, put double the normal postage on it, then hid it under the lining in the drawer where Mark kept his socks.

Now to get it in the mail.

She began to complain of claustrophobia, to feign shortness of breath whenever Doc came to check on her. She had to get outside, get some fresh air, move around, see something more than snow on the meadow, snow on the mountain, snow on the barn roof. She summoned up all her acting ability, hard won through years of television commercial work, to make herself seem resigned to her reliance on them, and yet to need, quite simply, a little outing now and then. Never had she been required to sustain a role for more than a few minutes as a model. Now she had to keep it up for hours at a time.

They began to take her out for walks. Fortunately the weather was fine—the January thaw had arrived a bit late and temperatures were in the low forties—and they walked her nearly down to Dolph Rooney's, twice a day. It was easy to act delighted with the outings, because they truly delighted her: the warm reflections of sunlight off the snow, the chickadees "dee-dee-dee-ing" from the roadside shrubbery, the melting snow gurgling happily over the clear blue-green anchor ice of Cauldron Brook. And the delicious air, brisk and sweet: cool, clear water for her dessicated soul. She gave her escorts no trouble, chatting merrily with them about town happenings, the weather, the latest episode of *Laverne and Shirley* or *That's Incredible*—things that counted in their simple lives. They began to relax, to look the other way—to trust her. The goddamned fools!

Now for Phase Two.

Why couldn't she go to town? She wanted to visit the store, do some minor-league shopping, see people doing people-things. See the school kids shooting baskets in the school yard. See scruffy dogs snoozing in the sun on the south sides of cozy houses. Wave to the neighbors as she passed, talk to a few of them in the store. Maybe even go to church this Sunday.

They snapped up that one. Of course they would. To them it seemed that Pastor Thorpe's readings from *The Book of Ahaz* were paying off. She was ripening toward conversion. Ayup—church it would be!

That Sunday morning she dressed carefully (feeling her stomach churn with fearful excitement) in a schlumpy pink-and-purple maternity dress Huldy had dredged up somewhere, then when Huldy was out of the room, retrieved the letter from the sock drawer. She slid it down inside her gigantic bra (a loaner from Mighty Maud Baines) and quickly wrapped a scarf around her throat and upper chest to hide any possible bulge. Doc drove them down in his Plywoodie.

She tried not to fret and fidget too much during the service—Pastor inveighing stentoriously against the unchecked clear-cutting of the Amazonas rain forest, ho hum. The parishioners were all smiles when they turned to look at her, those gooey, keep-your-chin-up smiles people reserve for the recently widowed or terminally ill. When, at the end of the sermon, Pastor Thorpe called their attention to "the presence in our midst this happy day of our brave Sister Laura Avery," they actually applauded. Laura saw tears in the eyes of some women, and even old Swifty Baines pulled out a rancid blue bandanna to honk his hooter. Quite moving. Oh, yes, quite moving, indeed.

Then she noticed Dolph Rooney watching her from two aisles over. The look on his face was somehow different from that of the others. Not a welcome-to-the-fold kind of look, but rather a look of . . . concern? Yes, perhaps. A sympathetic look, as if he understood her true condition. But no, she thought, it couldn't be. Dolph was one of them all right. Even though he was nominally an "outsider," a "flatlander," he had lived here so long, unharmed, that he must be one of them. A convert—fanatical—the worst kind. And yet. And yet . . . how his eyes seemed to talk to her. To say: "I understand."

When the service broke up, she tried to act cheery and gracious as first one, then another town couple greeted her. Again the chitchat was weather and town doin's, and she brought it off very well, if she did say so herself. Doc himself seemed to buy it—he was all smiles, proud as he watched her "cope." Then, when he turned to talk with Pastor Thorpe, Huldy at his elbow, she slipped away.

She made it across the road and almost into the store before, looking back over her shoulder, she saw Doc spot her. He came legging it, storklike, after her. She let the door slam behind her and walked briskly toward the big blue-and-white U.S. Postal Service mailbox, at the end of the regular post-office counter. Ike Minter appeared from among the back shelves, his face flashing worry and puzzlement as he saw her. If I can get it into the blue box, Laura was thinking, Ike won't be able to get to it. It will be picked up by a proper postal-service driver when he comes to open the box tomorrow morning. She fumbled at her dress front, trying to reach the letter.

Damn! The scarf was in the way, enwrapping her hand in its mock-silk webbing. Ike was almost running up the aisle now. She got her fingers on the envelope just as she heard the door slam open behind her. She reached toward the mail slot.

"Wait a sec, Miz Avery!" Ike's own hand shot out and grabbed the envelope from her. He grinned, wide and false, flustered. "I'm drivin' over t' Rutland this aft and I kin mail this for you there. Get wherever it's goin' a hull lot quicker."

She heard Doc's footsteps pounding up close behind her.

Oh, shit—if he sees it! The Needle!

Smiling disarmingly, she snatched the letter back from Ike's hand. She tore it into quarters and took two quick steps sideways to the coal stove, opened the door, and fired in the late, lamented letter.

"That's kind of you, Ike," she said as sweetly as she could muster. "But I thought better of it. It was a prepayment to the IRS that I've been meaning to mail, but to heck with it. Let the gov'mint wait a bit."

Doc was hovering over her shoulder, worried. Ike's lower lip hung loose, half-flabbered. She smiled again, then began moseying down the aisles as if all she had planned to do in the store, anyway, was a little shopping.

But as she looked back, she saw Dolph Rooney a few yards away from Doc. From the look on his face, he had seen the whole incident. And he still looked sympathetic.

The following afternoon Dolph Rooney stopped by the house to pay his respects. Meg Hardesty had "the duty" that day, and when she ushered Dolph into the living room, Laura could have kissed his wizened, woods-monkey's face. She had just read a little item in the *Rutland Herald,* datelined Mingo Falls, New York.

"Mrs. Sarah Eldridge, 76, a longtime resident of Hubley's Gore, Vt., died yesterday of heart failure at the home of her granddaughter, Mrs. Wanda Chafee of Mingo Falls. She had been in ill health since her husband's accidental death two years ago. Funeral services . . ."

The letter had failed yesterday. And now, she learned, so too had the heart of her only nearby hope.

Heart failure! Everyone dies of heart failure, even prisoners who are executed. . . . But now Dolph. Maybe just. Maybe he's safe. Oh, God, please let him be safe!

"Just dropped by to say hello," he mumbled uneasily as Meg hovered around them. "I wuz glad to see you in church yesterday, glad you're up and about again is all." He looked sideways under his eyebrows at Meg and winced slightly. "Uh."

"Oh, please, Dolph," she said, "sit down, sit down. Would you like a cup of coffee? I was just going to ask Meg to make me a cup of instant."

"Why sure."

Dim Meg smiled happily and bustled out of the room.

"Look," Dolph began. "It maybe ain't no business of mine, but I saw that thing with the letter yestiddy. Is there . . ."

"Oh, Dolph, yes," she whispered. "Could you? They're . . ."

"I know," he husked, looking fearfully over his shoulder. "They're keepin' you here and you want to get word to someone. Right?" She nodded. He pulled out a dirty notebook and a carpenter's pencil. "Write down the name and number."

"Don't try to call from anywhere in town," she whispered as she scribbled. "Go over to Rutland. Or into New York. But don't call from the Gore, or . . . I don't know what will happen."

She could hear Meg stirring coffee in the cups. She handed Dolph the pad. "I can't thank you enough."

"Don't try," Dolph said, embarrassed. "I been playin' along with 'em for years, never helpin' no one. But I can't stay out of it no more." He looked at her mournfully. "You're a beautiful lady," he said.

Meg came bouncing in with three cups of coffee steaming on a tray.

"Maxwell House," she burbled gaily. "Good to the last drop!"

"The message got through?"

"Certainly."

"When will he be here?"

"Soon. Probably tomorrow."

"We must prepare a welcome for him."

Laughter.

"All in due time. In due time."

FOUR

Bill McGregor arrived the following evening.

Laura was sitting at the kitchen table—her hair ratty, no makeup, a crusty bleb at one corner of her mouth—sipping a cup of herbal tea. Huldy was doing the dinner dishes. They heard the loud rap of the brass door knocker and both of them started.

"Now who's that?" Huldy wondered. "I didn't hear no car, did you, honey?"

She went to the door and peered out. Then the door slammed open, pushing her back, and Bill was standing there, frost in his wind-blown hair and a stern look on his wind-reddened face.

"What's going on here?" he demanded.

"Why . . ." Huldy was nonplussed. She staggered back, clutching her dress front. "I do declare!"

Laura just gaped for a moment. Then she sprang from her chair and ran to him, waddling slightly with her ninth-month load. "Bill!"

He grabbed her and held her tight, glowering over her head at Huldy. Laura leaned against his chest, her head spinning: too good to be true! Then Huldy regained her composure and smiled sweetly at him.

"Why, it's Mr. McGregor from Noo Yor-uk! And look, you're all wet, pore man! You'll ketch yore death-a-cold!" She bustled around the kitchen, taking Bill's snow-sodden loden coat from him and hanging it above the stove, setting his boots to dry, heating up a pot of black bean soup. Laura looked warnings at Bill and he began to act less hostile.

"My car's in the ditch down below," he told them. "Poor old Blue Funk. I guess she's about had it. I heard about Mark only yesterday, Laura, and I raced right up as soon as I could get someone to take my classes. God, I'm sorry. Now tell me about it, if you can." He looked suspiciously at Huldy's back as she clanked and stirred at the stove.

How Huldy got to the phone, Laura never knew. But she must have, for within fifteen minutes Doc Peggs was pulling up in the driveway. He looked very worried. By then Laura had explained, as euphemistically as possible, about Mark's accident and her subsequent shock.

"She's been a sick girl, William," Doc said when she was finished. "Can't blame her, of course. It was a dreadful shock, though she acted bravely in the crisis. I've been trying to keep her quiet, her mind at ease, so as not to trigger something, well, *untoward* with the baby, you know. Sometimes Laura gets the feeling that we're keeping her here against her will."

"Aren't you?" Laura asked, glowering.

"Laura my dear," he answered disarmingly, "your feelings are entirely consistent with the medication I've been giving you. Unfortunately, a side effect of this sedative is a slight feelng of, er, paranoia. Entirely expectable. But really now, have you *asked* to leave? Where would you go? At this advanced stage of your pregnancy I'd deem it dangerous for you to return, say, to New York City. The travel alone would be hazardous. It could provoke a premature labor. And your mental state right after the accident . . . Well, it would have been criminal of me to let you wander off by yourself."

"We've only been trying to help you, honey," said Huldy. "Me and the other ladies, we love you, Laura. You're one of us now." A big fat tear of self-abnegation shimmered on Huldy's plump cheek.

What could she say? Bill was studying her gravely now, his eyes masked by doubt. She sobbed once, laid her head on her arms and began to cry softly. "There, there," said Doc, coming over to her.

"No!" she yelled. "Not the Needle! Not again! Never!" She pulled herself together and smiled cheerily (or so she hoped). "See? I'm fine now, really I am. It's just—I'm so glad to see Bill." She choked on her tears for a moment. Then Bill escorted her upstairs to her bedroom.

Later, as she sloped off toward sleep, she could hear Bill and Doc talking long and earnestly well into the night.

"It's true, though," Laura said flatly. "No matter what he says, it's true as we sit here."

Outside, the snow of the previous evening had turned to rain. The top of the Cauldron was aswirl with dark gray-blue clouds, like something out of Hokusai. Bill had persuaded the townsfolk to leave Laura in his charge for the day.

"I don't know," Bill said. "What Doc says makes a lot of sense. The shock and all. The side effects of the sedative. I mean, have they actually done anything to constrain you physically?"

"The Needle."

"Well, that's to keep you from . . . okay, miscarrying.

Doc told me he's been very reluctant to use it at all. But it's a no-win situation, honey. If he does, it just makes you nutsier. If he doesn't, you could hurt yourself—and the baby. You *do* want the baby, don't you, Laura?"

"Of course," she said angrily. "More than anything in the world, now that Mark's . . . More than anything. How can you even ask?"

"Look," Bill said firmly. "According to Doc, the baby's not due for another five days. Maybe longer. After all, it's a first pregnancy, and he told me that first pregnancies are almost always overterm. In many cases the obstetrician even has to induce labor with a first child. If you're really that worried about these people, what we'll do is this—wait a day or two while your system purges itself of those sedatives, then I'll drive you over to Rutland until the baby comes. I'll make some calls and find a good OB over there, set up a hospital room for you, the works. I'm sure Doc won't object—in fact, he suggested it himself last night while we were talking."

"Five days, he said?" Laura checked the calendar and shook her head. "Like hell. See? I've got it marked right here. Today's the twentieth, right? I'm due on the twenty-second or twenty-third."

"I know, he told me about that. But a pregnancy isn't something you can run on a time clock. No doctor can tell you to the day, you know that. But again, it's your first time, and the first baby is always a slowpoke."

"I'd much rather go over to Rutland now," she said obstinately. "Today. This afternoon."

Bill got up and looked out the kitchen window. The rain was sheeting down so densely now that the whole of Widdershins was obscured. The snow on the meadow slope had already shrunk by a foot, maybe two. Even through the closed windows and the double-glazed storms, Cauldron Brook roared like a runaway freight train. The barnyard was a sea of mud.

"Not today," Bill said. "The frost is out of the ground and the road is a mudslide. Even the potholes are moving. That's what put me off the road last night—I came through a corner a bit too fast, just touched the brakes lightly and, whoops, I was looping into the ditch."

"The truck has four-wheel drive."

"Yeah, but you haven't seen those potholes." Bill looked at her with that no-nonsense, get-serious look of his. "I'm afraid for the baby, Laura. Hell, I'm a history prof, not a New York cabdriver. If you went into labor, I wouldn't know what to do." She laughed. "Tell you what, though. Doc's amenable to your going over to Rutland for the delivery, so I'll just call him and ask him, as senior selectman, to have the town road crew grade the road tonight when the rain stops, fill in the worst potholes. Then we'll head over there tomorrow about lunchtime—how's that?"

"We'd better," Laura said slowly. "Because if we don't, they'll take my baby for a sacrifice. Just like they did Polly's. And then it'll be my turn. And your turn, too."

"Laura." He shook his head sadly, then reached for the phone.

They sat on the couch near the open stove, listening to the rain. His arm was warm around her shoulders and her feet were propped up on a pillow to ease the unceasing pain in her lower back. He talked to her in a low, steady voice, kind and sensible, strong, a man who knew the world and could not be rattled by it. He said he would be with her always now, no matter what; he had grown inside his head over these past few years without her, had found himself at last—too late, he'd thought. But nothing was too late when it was really love. He'd stay with her and protect her and the baby. No one would get past him. Then when the baby had come and she was strong enough, they would leave this place and go back where they belonged. He had called the university and been granted an emergency leave. His bank was sending him a certified check that would cover whatever expenses might crop up between now and then. Everything was fine now. Everything.

But the rain did not let up. The road outside the window ran hub-deep in swift-moving brown water so thick it could pass for mud. The brook was over its banks, and from down the road they heard, from time to time, the crash of uprooted trees. The power was off but Bill had lighted the Coleman lamps and stoked the fires in both stoves. A venison stew stood bubbling on the stove top in the kitchen. But they heard no sound of graders nor of dump trucks. Too much rain. Any fill the road crew put down would be washed away before they could level it. They listened to the radio, hoping to hear that the rain would end that night, but there was too much static to make out what the weatherman said. Only the words ". . . severe flooding in mountain valleys . . ."

They waited.

Toward dark, restless, Laura decided to pack for the hospital. She took a Coleman lamp up to the bedroom and Bill fetched a small suitcase from the attic. He said nothing about the straw men and she did not ask him. Perhaps the ladies had taken them away. Then Bill went downstairs to check on the stew and make some dumplings. When she had finished packing—nighties and undies, robe and slippers, shower cap, bathroom kit—Laura remembered she'd better bring along a set of normal-sized clothing for when she left the Rutland hospital. Only a few more days, she thought happily. God, is it possible? It's almost over now—the whole dreadful nightmare!

She selected a pair of light wool slacks, fine herringbone gray, and a green flannel shirt—spring-green, as the earth would soon be now the snow was going. She was recalling her first visit to the house with Mark when she noticed, at the back of the closet, a long roll of bound canvas. One of Mark's paintings, she thought. The cemetery painting he'd been so proud of—the painting whose rejection by the gallery had changed his poor mind, his poor damned life. She was about to close the closet door but then thought better of it. She had never seen the finished painting—Mark was very secretive about his work, preferring that her first view come in a proper gallery setting. Well, if she didn't look at it now, she would never look at it. There would be something incomplete about that. She was leaving Mark with this house, this town. She unrolled the canvas and weighted its corners with four books, then lifted the Coleman lamp high in her hand to study it.

The painting grabbed her by the throat. She wanted to scream, or whimper, to turn and run. The gallery was right: it was stark, cruel, the giggle of a madman-torturer. As if Norman Rockwell had suddenly gone insane and begun to imitate Hieronymus Bosch. The top third of the canvas was sweet and nice, down-home, too cute for words: the town seen in profile, the spire of the church, the general store, kids on bicycles with trout poles over their handlebars, riding one-handed in striped polo shirts and baseball caps, heading for the ole fishing hole. Then came a row of weathered headstones, their rounded tops echoing the green, feathery, Grandma Moses trees that lined the town's streets.

Below the headstones, grim and canted, the horror began. It was the Underworld in cross section: each grave a private hell. The roots of trees writhed through the cold earth. Gobbets of worms marched and regrouped around fresh corpses. Bodies writhed in synchrony with roots and worms: the tortures of the damned. She saw what could only be Jim Boggs, impaled on a splintery spear, twisting and cursing in agony. And Polly, awful, engulfed in flame, going black at the edges, fireheaded, her mouth wide and twisted in a silent earth-stopped scream. And the baby . . . Other people, faceless with rot, but yet alive and suffering, pointing upward, accusing. Dozens of corpses, hundreds of graves, marching off in unearthly perspective to infinity: an earth full of victims. Her eyes flashed up, unwillingly, to the headstones again. And then she saw it clearly for the first time:

Each headstone bore Cassie's Symbol, sketched in blood.

Each bore the words: "Taken to the Woods."

Each wore the date of a turn of season. March, June, September, December. The twenty-first or twenty-second of each of those months. The great hinges of the year, on which the weathers swing.

It was true! Here was the proof of it. These people—all those people in the fenced-off section of the graveyard where Mark and Jim and Polly and the little girl were buried—all were sacrificial victims. Mark's paints did not lie. The underground scenes of course were metaphor, but everything from the ground level up was hard-edge realism: Mark had told her that himself, it was his style. And it was in the contrast of that style and the Boschian that he felt the painting worked —and of that he was so proud.

She screamed for Bill in her epiphany, and he came running.

"Look at it!" she said, holding up the lamp. "Now do you see? I'm not imagining all of this. It's the truth, the God-awful God's truth. They kill people at every change of season, sacrifice them to their awful Tree God, the Bull Oak. Up there, on the mountain. See? 'Taken to the Woods.' And the symbol—the winged disk of Assur. The sin of Ahaz. And they're waiting for me right now. Waiting for the baby."

Bill stood there stunned. He started to say something but the words died on his lips. He too knew that his friend had not invented this date sequence, this gruesome metaphor. Mark had simply not had the imagination.

"All right," Bill McGregor said at last. "We leave in the morning, whether the rain has stopped or not."

"Tomorrow," she said, her eyes wide, almost crazy. "March twenty-first. The vernal equinox."

FIVE

In the morning the truck would not start.

"Dead battery," Bill said disgustedly. "Look, someone left the parking lights on and it drained the battery flat." He slammed the truck door and kicked viciously at the front tire.

The rain had stopped but the sky still lay low and churning overhead. A strong wind rasped high on the ridges and the barometer still crept downward. The temperature was falling as well.

"I've got jumper cables," Laura offered hopefully.

"But we need a live battery to attach them to," said Bill.

"Dolph Rooney," Laura said. "He's got that old flivver down there. If we could get it up here, we could get a start."

"Is he safe?"

"Of course. He called you, didn't he? I was skeptical but he came through."

"Ah," Bill said, "it was Dolph who called, was it? He didn't say his name, and in fact it sounded like he was talking through a mouthful of oatmeal. Just gave me your message and hung up. Okay, I'll go down there and borrow his electrics. Hell, maybe we could use his flivver, as you call it, to drive on out of here."

"Wouldn't make it," Laura said. "That truck of his is older than Ronald Reagan. But at least we can jump his battery."

"Be back in a flash," Bill said. He ran down the driveway toward the road, looking up apprehensively at the lowering sky. As he disappeared, Laura felt the sting of snow on the wind.

The first half hour of waiting felt like a week. Maybe he's having trouble getting up the road, Laura thought. Maybe there are trees down—we heard them falling yesterday—and he and Dolph are having to cut them up before he can get through. But she could hear no chainsaw over the howl of the wind. Maybe Dolph doesn't have a chainsaw. He's an old-time woodsman—maybe he uses a crosscut saw, or one of those Swedish bow saws. That's it: They must be cutting the trees with an unpowered saw of some kind. They'll be here any minute. She tried Dolph's phone number but as she suspected, the phone lines were down along with the power lines. They're coming, she told herself. They're on their way.

An hour. She got up from the kitchen table and rechecked the cat's food bowl. It was still virtually full, but she poured more kibble on the pile anyway. Bone circled between her ankles, staring up at her in what passed for puzzlement. She must remember to put the food dish out in the barn, along with Bone, when Bill showed up. If they were gone a long time, he could survive on mice, and there was plenty of water in Cauldron Brook. She could hear it racing along like a flattened Niagara.

Why am I worrying about the cat? He's better equipped to handle himself in this God-awful country than I am. He'd better be: she did not intend to return.

Her eye kept coming back to the calendar. March twenty-first. In small letters under the number: vernal equinox. Each time she saw it, her stomach surged.

An hour and a half now. She went out into the thinly slashing snow and listened. No sound but the wind. And the snow rattling against her parka hood. Another storm was on its way, no doubt about it now. The puddles at the edge of the road had ice around their rims. A proper spring blizzard. March was going out like a lion.

Face it: They've got him. When she finally said it to herself, she somehow felt easier. Her fate was her own now. She had to save herself. But how?

The truck was parked outside the barn, on a slight grade that led to the road. Vaguely she remembered something about starting a car with a dead battery. Mark had taught her. It was called a "roll start." If you could get the car rolling in neutral with the ignition on, then put it in gear and pop the clutch out, it would somehow—magically—start. Sometimes.

But it was her only chance.

Just climbing up behind the wheel left her breathless. Damn it, stop hyperventilating. All you need now is to pass out. She adjusted the seat to make room for her belly and put her hands on the wheel. She took some deep breaths. The snow was coming so thick now that she could scarcely see the end of the driveway. If I could pray, she thought, now would be the time to do it. She switched on the ignition, put the gearshift in neutral, depressed the clutch, and then, her jaw tight, released the emergency brake.

The truck didn't move.

Damn! I'll have to push it a bit to get it rolling.

Clumsily, cursing her bulk, she climbed back out of the cab. Leaving the door open, she leaned her hands on the forward door post and pushed. Nothing. She felt her belly muscles flutter with the strain. One more time. She heaved again—and felt the truck begin to move. She got her hand on the steering wheel to guide it straight down the driveway gradient and pushed some more to help the truck along. It was rolling faster now. Almost too fast. Better get in—now—before it rolls away from you. With all the strength left her, she heaved herself up into the cab.

The truck was rolling swiftly—so swiftly that she saw she would soon run out of driveway. She pulled the gearshift into low and heard it grate horribly—the clutch! Quickly her foot stabbed and found the clutch pedal. Pushed it to the floor. Her hand dragged again on the shift lever and she felt it slip into place. Almost at the end of the driveway. She popped the clutch.

Pow! Cuck-cuck-chuff—vroom!

The motor roared as she hit the clutch and the gas at the same time, a good ignition. She stopped at the end of the driveway and raced the engine, warming it up. If it choked out now, she was finished. Then, when the cylinders were firing smoothly, she turned and headed down the road.

She did not see Bill along the road, though she drove slowly, carefully skirting the deeper potholes. A few small trees were down on the stretch of straightaway just below the house but she was able to creep around them by riding wide on the shoulder. The rain had washed away all the snow. Two days ago there was no shoulder, only dirty banks of snow twice as tall as a man. She kept the truck in four-wheel drive. Then the storm hit in its full fury.

Lightning rolled down from Widdershins, accompanied by sizzling, near-simultaneous cracks of thunder. Snow swirled like wraiths along the road, dancing with rage. It was as if the elements themselves were outraged at her attempted escape.

Ahead of her Cauldron Brook swept under the road through a culvert. She could see the water kicking dirty-brown at the bridge abutments and the wide, scum-swirled expanse of backed-up water on either side. As she neared the bridge, a bolt of lightning so bright it hurt her eyes snapped down not fifty yards ahead. It split a tree just behind the bridge as neatly as an ax—the ax of Odin. The tree toppled slowly across the road, blocking the far end of the bridge.

Trapped!

From around the bend below the bridge she heard the rumble of a heavy truck. As she backed and turned the Luv, she saw it come around the corner: a big orange town truck with a 'dozer blade on the front bumper. Beside the driver sat Doc Peggs. She spun her wheels, completing the turn, and headed up-mountain at speed regardless of the potholes.

There was another way off the mountain. If she continued on up past the house, the road—though steep and badly rutted even in good weather—eventually linked up with another lane that wound on over the pass between Widdershins and Abednego. If there weren't any major blowdowns, she could make it. Even with the 'dozer blade it would take time for Doc and the road crew to clear the big tree at the bridge. She crossed over the smaller downed trees without slowing, the little Luv truck crunching and bouncing across them like a baby tank. Good little truck, she mumbled to herself. You got guts.

Above the Eldridge place the woods pinched in on the road from both sides—"bear country," Mark had called it—dark, dense second growth rapidly approaching climax size. Lightning smashed all around her as she twisted up the bumpy road. She could smell ozone, and up to her right she saw a whole tree on fire, blazing like a smoky sword in the green subaqueous gloom. But the very density of the forest seemed to aid her: the lightning smacked the tops of the tallest trees, up on the ridges to either side. A few big branches were down on the road, but the Luv vaulted them like a running deer. I love you Luv!

Then as she rounded a steeply rising curve, she saw it. The road was buried under a mudslide. Even as she braked to a slithering sideways halt, she saw more mud break loose and ooze like a giant brown amoeba down onto the road. No way she could get through. Nor was there room to turn the truck around.

I'll have to run for it, she thought. But the air outside the warm truck cab was opaque with snow and freezing rain. How far could she get? Maybe the best thing would be to stay right here in the truck and hope that Bill had gotten away, that Bill would turn up and . . . And what? Bill, the college prof, against a gang of husky road-crew apes half his age?

The first contraction gripped her low in the abdomen. She grunted with the pain.

Her foot slipped off the clutch and the motor died in a sudden jerk. Frantically she turned the key for a restart. The starting motor merely whined once and died. The heater died with it. Almost immediately she began to feel the cold infiltrate the truck cab. No, she couldn't stay here. Not now, with the contractions starting. But maybe it wasn't really a contraction? Just gas? She crossed her fingers.

Ten minutes later the second wave rolled over her.

No use kidding yourself. This is it. It's coming . . . soon. Now!

The thunder and lightning had moved off to the southeast and the snow seemed to be abating. She made her decision: she would go back to the house.

Even if Doc was there, at least she would be under cover, in the warmth. And he would deliver the baby. She would not let herself think beyond that. He would deliver the baby.

She made her way back down the road in a daze, her mind tightly focused on nothing more than the next step, the next pothole to skirt, the next downed branch to step over. Twice she fell when the pains hit her, fell on her back in the mud and screamed, her hands clutching the ooze and squeezing it through her fingers. It seemed she could hear voices calling her name through the blowing snow, but maybe it was just the wind in the trees. She got up and marched on, fighting now for her own and the baby's life.

The house loomed through the midday darkness. There were lights on inside, the yellow auras of kerosene lamps behind the curtains. Wet and exhausted, she slogged the last few yards and opened the door.

They were waiting for her: Doc and Huldy, Pastor Thorpe and Billy Munro, Meg and Tabby and Maud and Swifty—half the town, it seemed. Their faces, creased with worry, suddenly turned to smiles. They were genuinely delighted at her safe return.

Another contraction wrung her, the strongest so far, and she fell to the kitchen floor, screaming.

The baby was born that night to the sound of chanting. Laura scarcely heard it through her exhaustion. Doc had used the Needle again at the last, and she felt herself spinning down into nepenthe. Then Bill McGregor was there at her bedside, smiling and kissing her forehead, proud as if he himself were the father.

"It's a boy," he told her.

But . . . how could Bill be there?

"Where were you?" she asked in a whisper. "What . . ."

"Hush," he said softly. "You're safe now. The baby's safe. I'm with them."

"With . . ."

"Especially the baby, Laura. He is the heir, the inheritor. The new Arch-Druid."

She faded into sleep.

SIX

"You're with them?" she said. "*With* them? With *them*? What the hell does that mean?" Laura sat at the kitchen table, nursing the baby. Bill, avoiding her eyes, walked over to the stove and poked a few logs. He would not answer, would not even look at her.

"Look at me, you son of a bitch!" Laura yelled. "Didn't you tell me you were with them now?"

He turned and looked at her, and in his eyes she saw the true horror of it: He *was* with them, the ones who had killed Mark, killed Polly, killed God knows how many others for how many years. It was all true—all her fears, her anguish. Yet inside those haunted eyes she could also see his love for her, that old priestly aching and self-denial gone, now that he had taken the turn.

"Yes," he said quite simply. "For you. That's why I'm with them. They are powerful, a cult of tree-worshiping murderers, and I joined them to save you."

"Save me?" She laughed bitterly. "I'm still here, you bastard."

"But you might otherwise be dead." He gazed at

her, quite unashamed now. "This is how it was. The whole town is victim of Obed's Curse. When that lynch mob killed him back in 1816, he said just before he died that no man would cut those oaks who was not a worshiper of them, and that the worshipers would come from the bloodline of his assassins. It was Cassie who saw that, by appeasing the Bull Oak with blood four times a year, the oak forest itself would prosper, and that the town could prosper with it by cutting and selling the wood. She established the sawmill, and with it the Gore's independence from the outside world. But the blood and burned flesh had to be human now—now that Obed himself, the prophet and Arch-Druid, had been burned to death beneath the Bull Oak—yet the townspeople could not very well kill a true believer, could they? Painful to sacrifice people you love. So they sacrificed outsiders, wanderers who happened through, and those among them who had strayed from the believer's course. Ahaz perfected the system, along with the Church. He was the first Arch-Druid, after Obed. All the succeeding Arch-Druids have been of Obed's line."

"And who is today's Arch-Druid?" Laura asked. "Doc?"

"Of course. He is the great-great-grandson of Ahaz, who of course was Obed's son."

"But he's childless, isn't he? Didn't his wife die years ago, before they could have a child?"

"Yes," he said. "Since then Doc has sired many children, but none of them were Arch-Druid material. Little Jamie Boggs, for instance, was his child—but she was a girl, and the law of the Church does not permit of female Arch-Druids. Another problem was that the town has grown so inbred over the century and a half since Obed's death that many children are born deformed, demented, half-witted. The Church needed new blood, yet the Oak demanded blood of its own and in different form."

Laura looked at the baby nursing at her breast. He was wrinkled still, his skin rough and red from the birth trauma, and the wispy black hair on his soft head was certainly not Mark's. She pulled him from her nipple and looked closely at him—she had not yet decided on a name. Though the features were babyishly crude—flat nose, blank mouth still puckered and dribbling pale blue milk—she saw it instantly: his eyes, his great, grave wide eyes! They were the same piercing green as those of Doc Peggs!

She jerked to her feet, her bare breast aching.

"You mean . . . You mean that this is Doc's child? *This?*" Her eyes caromed wildly around the room. For a moment they locked on the wood stove, roaring with fatal heat. But then the baby cried—a long, ululating, hungry wail. And she felt the milk start again in her breasts.

"Yes," Bill said. Almost sadly. "That was not a dream you had, that day up under the Bull Oak. Huldy had drugged you with the strawberry dessert. Doc circled back on down and around, and knowing just when you would be ovulating, got his seed into you before Mark could impregnate you."

"So that's why Doc was so concerned about determining the baby's sex," Laura said, almost to herself.

"Of course. If it had been another girl, he would have had to look elsewhere."

"But why did Jamie Lynn have to die? And Polly?"

"Jamie Lynn was useless to the cult," Bill said. "She went as sacrifice for the summer solstice, as her father had gone for the vernal equinox. Polly was meant to die in the fall, but she had become too troublesome—she was frightening you, and Doc feared you might run away, taking his unborn heir and successor with you. So they killed her out of sequence, by placing magical oak logs in her stove—logs that never stop getting hotter as they burn. They burned the house down."

"Then who went for the fall sacrifice?"

"A kid named Gillie Brunette—a no-good from a town nearby. Billy Munro suckered him up into the grove on the pretext of poaching deer. Then told him to climb a dead, hollow oak to hide the deer they'd killed. The tree, though dead, was still under the command of the Bull Oak. It grabbed him and crushed him to death."

"I saw that, right afterward, but I couldn't believe my eyes," Laura said.

"Just as well," said Bill. "You might have fled, and if you had, they would have killed you before you left town. The way they killed the state trooper who was checking on Gillie's disappearance."

She could well believe it.

"And Mark?" she asked. "The winter sacrifice, no doubt."

"Of course. And more than that. He was growing too tough for them, too capable and competent. If he had come to suspect that the baby wasn't his, he would have figured it all out. In fact that graveyard painting of his, a voice from the subconscious, was nearly the whole story. The only thing wrong with it was that there are no bodies in those special graves. The bodies were burned, with most of the victims still alive, to feed the Bull Oak with their blood and ashes."

Laura put the baby back to her breast. Somehow, now that the truth was out, she felt an even stronger love for him.

"But you," she said contemptuously. "You sell-out bastard, you! How do you figure in this?"

"Doc approached me back in the fall, during the fire-wheel festival—remember? He knew my work and my interest in early American religious developments. He told me quite frankly that Mark would soon be dead. At first I thought he meant that Mark had some terminal disease—cancer or something. But that didn't seem possible—he was so strong, so vigorous. Then, slowly, he revealed the true nature of the cult to me. I was shocked, horrified, of course. But he knew that I still loved you. He convinced me of the power of the Bull Oak, that day he and I were supposedly looking at the school we were up in the grove, and the Bull Oak actually spoke to me. I have Gore blood in me, you know, from my mother's side, and the language came clear to me. What you don't know is that Billy Munro wanted you, once Mark was dead, for his own wife. And he would have made a fair-to-middling stepfather for the new Arch-Druid. But Doc saw that I was better suited. So he offered me what in effect amounted to a regency—I, as stepfather to the heir apparent, will be Druid-Regent after Doc's death, and until the boy reaches maturity. And you . . ."

"What *about* me?" Suddenly she was shivering despite the waves of heat pounding from the stove.

"You were to die if you refused Billy Munro's offer of marriage. Which of course you would have. They couldn't let you leave the town with the baby, of course. You would have been the spring sacrifice."

"Let's leave, Bill. Leave right now!" She looked wildly around the room for weapons. "We could do it, get out of here, report them to the authorities or whatever. End this whole bloody business for good and all."

He laughed, softly, cynically.

"We wouldn't get a hundred yards down the road. The Bull Oak is watching."

As if in confirmation of that statement, the wind began to howl around the eaves. A rumble of thunder shook the windows. Out of a clear sky. Up at the top of the meadow, she saw the oak branches waving, crooked, against a gunmetal sky.

"And after all, Laura," Bill continued, "what's so awful about it, anyway? These people have independence from the outside world. They aren't being pounded constantly—tenderized, if you will, like a flabby beefsteak—by the mauls and chemicals of the outside world with its TV and advertising and fast-food chains. They're thrifty, hardworking, clean, decent, God-fearing folks. The best kind of Americans. And they do not ask help from anyone, thank-you-ma'am. Except from their God—and this is, after all, the Land of the Free. For myself, I'm fed up with academia, with the bullshit publish-or-perish way of life. Of the vacuous idiots they call college students. Of the chi-chi New York life. I'll never be a macho man like Mark, I promise you that. And you know how much I love you. I'll take care of you and the baby with every ounce of love and care that's in me."

Now his eyes were blazing, and Laura was moved. He stood and came to her, placed his hands on her face, then her breasts. There were tears in his eyes. He had broken the bond.

"Laura, how I love you! If this is the price, then I pay it gladly."

"And who is the spring sacrifice now," she found herself saying numbly. "Now that it's not me anymore."

The baby bit savagely at her nipple, and she cuffed him lovingly.

"Stop that, you wicked little rascal!" she yelped.

"The spring sacrifice?" Bill said. "That's tomorrow." He walked over to the stove and pitched another log into the fire. "You'll see it then, and you'll see it isn't all that dreadful."

He peered out the window at the sky.

"Let's hope the weather clears," he said.

The stove's voice rose to a rumbling roar.

SEVEN

The procession wound its way joyously up the mountain. The storm of the previous week had been the last of the winter, and the weather had broken toward spring. Warm and clear with only a few puffy clouds in the dust-blue sky. The sun, as if in a single leap, had cleared the low hurdle of the mountains and already its warm weight felt doubled. The first red-winged blackbirds bounced on the brookside, singing their upward trills. Overhead a skein of geese barked high and hollow, heading north.

The Arch-Druid led the way, tall and sprightly for his many years, his white hair blowing in the spring breeze. His eyes sparked bluer than the sky behind his steel-rimmed glasses. The breeze caught his cape, rust-red as oak leaves, and whirled it behind him, revealing his antique knee-britches and forest-green coat. The brass buckles on his shoes winked bright in the sunlight. In his right hand he bore the Sacred Crozier, the winged crook of Obediah.

Behind trailed the worshipers, the women in their long dresses and lace caps chattering even as they climbed, the men stalking stern in their buckskins and linsey-woolseys, some with tricorne hats cocked defiantly on their brows: Huldy and Billy, Chub and Liz Markham, the Thorpes and the Ashburns, Ike and Tabby Minter—all the good churchgoers of the Gore. Around and through them scampered the children, laughing and playing tricks. None seemed happier with this church outing than the orphaned Boggs children. They were well loved by all the townsfolk.

Beside the Arch-Druid, Laura walked with the baby in her arms. Her dark hair flowed long and smooth behind her, catching the sunlight with faint red waves. Around her neck was a golden chain, and from it, on her breast, depended a winged circle hammered from gold. Her face was composed and smooth: the baby slept peacefully.

They stopped beneath the Bull Oak. Bill McGregor, tall and slender in his own rust-red cape, waited calmly as befitted the Druid-Regent. Beside him stood Dolph Rooney, glassy-eyed, his arms bound at the wrists behind his back.

While the men began to chant in an alien tongue, the women surrounded Laura, cooing and chucking at the baby, and smoothing Laura's long hair as they beamed at her. Occasionally through a break in the shifting crowd, Laura could see Dolph Rooney being bound to the Bull Oak. Someone was holding a knife. The crowd closed, and when it opened again for a moment, she saw that it was Bill McGregor. He was gesturing with the knife in front of Dolph, who stared at him with blank eyes. The women closed in again, cutting off Laura's view, but in a moment they broke into song, loud and joyous. Through the singing she heard a gasp and then a slow gurgle.

The women stepped aside and the Arch-Druid walked forward to Laura and the baby. He smiled his glowing blue smile. The Druid-Regent walked up beside him, carrying a brass bowl engraved with the winged disk of Assur. The Arch-Druid dipped his forefinger in the bowl and brought it dripping into the light. He carefully marked the baby's forehead with the winged disk symbol.

"And what shall this child be called?" asked the Arch-Druid.

"Ahaz," replied Bill McGregor.

"Let the mother name him," the Arch-Druid said severely. He smiled again at Laura, his bright eyes sparking. She noticed that the baby's eyes were exactly the same color. For just a moment she remembered her dream here beneath the Bull Oak. Her dream?

Dolph Rooney hung slumped in his bonds against the Bull Oak. From the chin down his chest was soaked in blood. Around his legs the men were piling great heaps of sacred oak-wood.

The baby looked up from beneath its blood-marked brow. Two rivulets ran down across his temples, staining them with red wings. The baby raised his right arm, plump and weak, toward the Bull Oak, and clenched his tiny fist.

"Let it be Ahaz," said Laura.

The pyre beneath Dolph Rooney's feet crackled and smoldered for a moment, sending an acrid puff of smoke through the crowd. Then the flames shot up high into the sky, their brightness rivaling even the sun. The congregation broke into song:

> Oh come to the Church in the Wildwood,
> No lovelier place in the dale. . . .

Spring on Widdershins Mountain.